# SOPIE

## Book Two of the Twin Flames Trilogy

## SPENCER MICHAELS

Evatopia Editions

Publisher's Cataloging-In-Publication Data
(Prepared by The Donohue Group, Inc.)

Names: Michaels, Spencer.
Title: Sopie / by Spencer Michaels.
Description: Beverly Hills, CA : Evatopia Editions, an imprint of Evatopia, Inc., [2017] | Series: Twin flames trilogy ; book 2
Identifiers: ISBN 978-1-63099-120-3 (paperback) | ISBN 978-1-63099-119-7 (mobi) | ISBN 978-1-63099-118-0 (ePub)
Subjects: LCSH: Clairvoyants--Fiction. | Families--Fiction. | Country life--Saskatchewan--Fiction. | Animals, Mythical--Fiction. | Moving, Household--Fiction. | Good and evil--Fiction. | Saskatchewan--Fiction. | LCGFT: Fantasy fiction.
Classification: LCC PS3613.I34 S66 2017 (print) | LCC PS3613.I34 (ebook) | DDC 813/.6--dc23

## Prologue

———————

The skies had blackened that Monday, the morning of August 29th in 2005. Initially, a voluntary evacuation had been called, but now everyone in New Orleans was ordered to leave immediately. It seemed inevitable that Hurricane Katrina was headed right for the city. All anyone could do was sit and wait. Thankfully, Marty had driven Vinnie to the safety of Crossett in Arkansas on Saturday. It looked especially bad for those in and around the area that Anna lived. Anna didn't care if she lost everything. She didn't have any real possessions of value other than Mark and Vinnie. Of course, she just had to stay. There were children at Charity Hospital that couldn't be moved. So she volunteered to stay and help, as was her custom. Mark also volunteered to stay and help her...well, of course he did.

When the hurricane had reached the Mississippi coastline it was a category 3 and nothing to play with. Years ago, Mark remembered going to "*Last Day on Earth Parties,*" as they called them, during the big storms back at the beach in Carolina. The foolishness of youth. Mark was old enough now to see the signs —this was NOT going to be a party.

As they approached the hospital Mark said, "Anna I love you. Please don't go anywhere without me."

"I will be by your side, tonight, forever and always," she said with tender sincerity. Mark could hear a trust in her voice like he was hearing himself say the words. It didn't take the effort to discern meaning from Anna's words that it did from anyone else's because, well, because it's like he understood her before she ever spoke. It's like every idea or emotion one had the other felt intuitively.

She put a hand on his arm. "Let's get busy and see what we can do to protect the children."

Inside, they monitored the radio closely to check on the quickly advancing storm. Earlier in the morning the east side of the Industrial Canal failed. The Lower 9th Ward was a rushing torrent moving houses from their foundations.

*6:10 a.m. Katrina makes landfall at Buros. A wall of water 21 ft. high crossed the Mississippi River and its levees into most of Plaquesmines Parrish.*

"Mark, this doesn't look good," Anna said. She looked at the children all confined to their beds. "If these levees don't hold, this hospital will flood and we will have no place to go."

"I agree, but for right now with the children being in the shape they are in, our only option is to sit tight and ride it out."

*7:00 a.m. Levee wall panels on the west side of Industrial Canal breach. Desire area and the neighborhoods of St. Claude, St. Roch and the 7th Ward wash away.*

As the hurricane hit, the winds were ferocious 100-140 mile an hour gusts. No one dared to venture outside. Mark and Anna huddled with the children inside, providing comfort as they could. Mark sang songs with them to keep their fears to a minimum, but it was a very scary time. Water was coming in from the basement and flooded up to the first floor. They decided that they had to move the children higher to the second floor.

"Alright everyone," Anna said, "Follow the leader up the stairs." The ones that could walk did as they were instructed, and the loving couple did their best to help those that couldn't. Much of the hospital staff were still there, but many had left to protect and secure their own families. New Orleans was already becoming a wild frontier.

They then heard the news. Another set of panel walls on a nearby levee had failed and water was flooding the parish. They had no choice but to move the children from the hospital.

*8:14 a.m. The National Weather service issues a flash flood warning for Orleans Parrish and St. Bernard's Parrish citing a breach on both sides of the Industrial Canal. Water is expected to rise 3-8 ft. and you are advised to move to higher ground immediately.*

"Anna, we have got to somehow get these children to the Super Dome where an emergency last option shelter has been set up. No matter what condition they are in."

"But how, Mark? How?"

"I noticed that they keep the transport vans on the second level of the parking garage. Maybe we can use those. We can take a look and come back and get the other volunteers to help evacuate the children."

Anna and Mark made their way outside to the garage to get the vans ready while there was still a road to drive on. As they rushed through the pouring rain toward the first transport, Mark saw someone in a security guard's uniform on the parking deck above them.

*CRACK!*

Mark heard the sickening sound of a gunshot as the would be assassin's bullet whizzed by his head. "Anna, get down!" Mark screamed as he looked up again to see a familiar face chambering another bullet in his rifle readying to take aim for another shot.

It was his chess playing companion *Pete…*

"Pete!" he yelled, "What the fuck?" A red flame seared through every vessel in his body. An angry horde of yellow jackets came swarming from his eyes and circumnavigated the hitman's head and torso. Pete flapped wildly at the bees to no avail. Mark's spirit separated from his body without a second thought and flew at Pete. Mark's ghastly form shot through him like a bolt of lightning. The instantaneous contact was something faster than the human mind could comprehend—the rush of energy made light-speed look like a snail's pace. Pete's corporeal form exploded into one gigantic fireball and disintegrated.

*"Checkmate...Coonass."*

As Mark's spirit emerged from the bloody mess, Pete was no more, or so he thought. Then he heard the voice of his mentor, Master Bennie, "Be careful not to kill him for his spirit will fight you to keep you from returning to your body."

Suddenly, Pete's spirit was holding onto Mark in a grip that was impossible to break.

He struggled to free himself, panicking, "No, stop it you psycho," he screamed, "I have to get back to Anna and the children!" Mark used all his might and fought relentlessly.

Pete's grip tightened as he pulled Mark farther toward the dark abode. Mark fought valiantly, but as he did Pete's grip just kept tightening. Mark heard the voice of Master Bennie again, "Water is formless, put it in a vase, it becomes the vase; heat it and it evaporates into the air. Be like water and evaporate and become air. You no be there." Mark relaxed and envisioned himself an inferno and as he did, he could feel himself becoming smaller and Pete's grip loosening. As Mark began to disappear, he suddenly heard the howling of what he thought was the hound of the Baskervilles. Chivas, his long dead and beloved golden retriever, appeared from out of nowhere, ripping and tearing at his attacker. Then Mark felt this strong but gentle force around his waist, the same eerie force that took control of his car years earlier. Suddenly, he was jolted back into his body, shaken but still alive.

As Mark reentered his body, he quickly turned to find Anna lying motionless on the ground...

Chapter One

___________

*L*ight always shines greyest when you can't seem to make sense of the world, when what you're seeing just can't be true. Like when you see the one person who was always so full of life, so brimming with love and light, lying still on the ground.

"Anna…" Mark whispered. But he couldn't hear his voice. The words were sucked into the blackness swirling around him, trapped by the black hole Katrina was tearing into the atmosphere. He stared at the woman he felt so whole with, watched as she faded into the dirt like a shadow at dusk.

"Anna," he said again. He wasn't speaking to her, but to the spirit of her that lived inside himself. Still unable to hear his own words, still unable to sense any kind of reply, he screamed. The fear paralyzing him now jolted him into a frenzy. "No, no, no!" He lifted Anna's lifeless body in the air, cradling her limp frame tightly against his chest. Looking up toward the heavens for some kind of answer, he again shouted. "No! Why?" Wailing and sobbing, he spun in a circle with Anna in his arms almost as if he were searching for a way out, some kind of escape.

In that moment, he remembered picking her up and spinning her around just like this so long ago. He waited ten eternities for her to speak. Waited for her to say, "Stop you bully, let me down!" But there was no response this time. How could this be happening? What now? What now?

"Someone! Please, anyone, help!"

The plea echoed through the parking deck, reverberated into the bowels of the Earth, and disappeared into oblivion. Rain was still pouring down—ripping through the air in all directions now—and Mark continued to spiral through storm. Then, the rain stopped. Time stopped. No sound, no motion, no existence. It was as if everything turned to ice, including the two of them. Every atom in the universe came to a full… and complete…STOP.

But, as quickly as it had stopped, everything started once again. One by one the molecules of air buzzed around him, the sound of the grass began to whisper, and, where there were none before, suddenly the song of birds filled the world.

Mark opened his eyes to find himself with Anna in his arms in a very different place. The sun peered around the clouds and he noticed he stood in a meadow near a rural two lane road. Dumbfounded, Mark kneeled down, resting Anna on the soft, warm grass. He looked around and couldn't find a sign of any impending storm. Not a single raindrop or cloud, no sounds of freight trains or rushing torrents in the distance, no sensations of panic. But, despite the miraculous change of scenery, one thing remained the same—Anna.

Mark sat next to her body. While most of his rain soaked body was frigid, the water streaming down his face was warm and fresh. Even though they had to either be dead or miles north of the city, he could only still think one word…*how?*

Finally, he could speak. "How, Sopie? How did this happen?" Mark wiped his eyes and took a deep breath. "How could you be…" he couldn't say the word. "Please," he mustered, "please, just wake up."

The world was quiet. And where the sky was once black and full of violence, it was now bright and gentle. Holding Anna's hand tightly, Mark shut his eyes tight and prayed. To God, to the universe, to Master Bennie and his dead dog and to any spirit or deity, living or dead, who would hear him. Just then, he felt movement that was not his own. Looking down he saw, or thought he saw Anna move.

"Surely not," he muttered. The twitch in her hand (or was it his hand?) could have been any number of things. Not least of which was a vision of grief. But despite the likelihood of it being rigor mortis or a trick of the mind, Mark spoke softly to her. "Anna?" There was a little more movement and she whispered, "Good morning, Sweetheart."

"Anna, Oh my God! I thought I had lost you! Are you alright?"

Anna still groggy said, "Yes, I think so." Smiling a wry little grin she added, "And don't call me Shirley."

Mark couldn't believe his eyes. Or his ears for that matter. He reached down and squeezed Anna so tight it hurt. Partly because she was alive and partly because she was still making bad jokes.

"Ow," Anna said from under his body. Then she uttered muffled words he couldn't quite make out.

"What's that?"

When he sat up, Anna took a deep breath. "You're crushing me, I said!" They both laughed a little, but not with ease. An uncertainty was settling over them both, and an exhaustion. "Where are we?"

Still bewildered, Mark said, "I'm not quite sure. But I can tell you, we're not in Kansas anymore, Dorothy." He tried to add a little levity to their situation, but again he broke down and sobbed.

"It's okay, Sweetheart, I'm Ok," said Anna tenderly.

Mark composed himself and kissed her cheek saying, "I just…for a minute there I really thought I lost you."

Anna smiled at him like he was the stupidest, sweetest man in the world. Reaching up to lift his chin, she said, "You will never lose me. Not ever."

Mark took a calming breath and smiled because he knew what she said was true. Helping her sit up, he said, "It appears that we are just outside of that city up ahead. Where we are or how we got here, I don't know. We just need to get you to the hospital."

"I think I am fine, just tired...very tired," said Anna.

Mark propped Anna up against him and brushed the hair away from her face. Tangled on her neck was the familiar gold chain. He pulled the necklace from its twisted spot and noticed the peculiar crease on the coin.

"It looks like this may have saved your life," showing the necklace to Anna. "But I still think you need to go to the hospital and at least get checked out. You could still have bruising or a cracked rib or two from the force."

Lifting her shirt Anna said, "See, I am no worse for the wear...no bruising. I think I remember what happened, but before we talk about that, the first thing I have to do is call someone to help us."

"Who might that be? We don't even know where we are."

"You have not met him yet. His name is Agent Kroner. He's the one that placed me in witness protection. He will know what to do."

"Well, he's done a bang up job so far."

"Now Mark...be fair. I got a little careless is all. He has really been my only advocate through this whole ordeal. Let me make the call."

Using Mark's cell phone, Anna called Agent Kroner's private, emergency line.

"Kroner here."

"Thank God. This is Anna Sopoulos. I...we need your help."

"Are you still in New Orleans? No? Where are you?" asked Kroner.

"I'm not sure...somewhere just outside of New Orleans, I think," Anna responded.

"Are you alright. What is happening?

"A little shook up is all. One of the mob's hitmen tried to kill us in the parking garage at Charity Hospital."

"How in the world did you get away?"

"That's not important right now. I will tell you everything later. Right now I need to know where I am and how I am going to get my son who is staying with a friend in Crossett, Arkansas."

"Let me track your cell phone on the GPS and see if I can get a location," said Kroner. "Stay on the line." There were some fiddling sounds and then the call seemed to go on hold.

"What's he saying?" Mark asked. He leaned in to try to share the earpiece of the tiny phone.

Anna brushed him back. "He's trying to figure out where we are—would you give me some space here?"

"Sorry, sorry, I guess I'm just a little excited to find out that the woman I love is a secret agent."

She pushed him away with a slight laugh.

"Fine, fine." Mark stood up as if to try and get his bearings. His knees felt a little wobbly and his head started to spin a bit. He shook it off. Taking a few steps in each direction he peered through his hands like they were binoculars muttering bits and pieces about the FBI and CIA this-and-that…

Anna ignored him and listened for Agent Kroner.

The line clicked back over and he came in loud in clear. "Holy Moses...you are a little more than just outside of New Orleans. In fact, you are 285 miles north, almost in Monroe!"

Anna's eyes widened. "Really? But how in the…"

"What?" Mark said excitedly. "What's he saying?"

Anna gave him her serious eyes and placed her finger over her lips to shush him.

"The good news is," Kroner continued," you are only 50 miles or so from Crossett. I still don't understand how you got to

Monroe. The roads heading north out of NOLA are closed due to the storm."

"Oh, well, we didn't take a car."

"What?"

Look, I will explain what I know later, but right now we are on foot and very tired. I will get Mark to call Marty, the friend keeping Vinnie, to pick us up. Where should we go from here?"

"You two go to St. Francis Medical Center in Monroe and get checked out. I will have a Dr. Dunleavy meet you there and I will be there shortly thereafter. We will talk then. Make sure your son, Vinnie, is with you."

"Ok, thank you very much. Goodbye." Anna hung up the phone and shifted in her seat a bit. She only had the strength to take short, shallow breaths. "He wants us to call Marty to pick us up," she said, looking to Mark.

He took the phone and started dialing. For a minute his vision blurred and he nearly forgot the number. Wiping his eyes Mark asked, "and where am I telling him we are?"

"Outside Monroe. Marty needs to bring Vinnie and take us to St. Francis in town."

He nodded as the phone was ringing.

"Hello...Mark?"

"Yes, it's me."

"Are you guys alright? I heard that New Orleans is totally underwater and..."

"Marty, I really can't talk right now. I will explain everything to you later. Right now I need your help."

"Anything, Big B."

"Agent Kroner says we are about 50 miles south of you on route 34. We need you to come pick us up. I think it's just south off 165. We'll be looking for your truck and wave you down."

"Who's Agent Kroner? Why doesn't he just give you a ride?"

"Marty, there's no time to explain. My cell phone is about to die. Just come get us. Make sure to bring Vinnie and I will talk to you then. Hurry..."

Just then the phone's battery went dead.

"They're on the way. I guess it will take them about an hour or so. Are you sure you're alright?"

"Yes, just a little wobbly," she said trying to stand.

Mark helped her up and they moved to a spot in the shade.

"I will be just fine when I know we are all safe and back together again," Anna said, her eyes glistening in the morning sun.

Mark loved just looking at her, remembering the first time they met, her long blonde hair in the sunlight at the beach. It was cropped a little shorter now, and her face had a few lines, but those brown eyes still danced as she spoke and added volumes to her speech.

They found a new resting spot facing the road where Marty should be meeting them. Sitting on a dew drenched stump atop a grassy knoll, Mark said, "Anna, while we've got nothing to do except sit here and wait, explain to me just what you saw at the parking garage. You said you thought you remembered what happened."

"I think you may have some explaining to do too, Mister!" Anna said laughing.

Mark looked at her with an expression suggesting he wasn't in a mood for banter.

Anna continued, blushing a little, "Well, okay, first maybe I should explain to you a little more about my journey here. As I told you I was placed in the witness protection program in Carol Stream. There I started to work at a Catholic Parrish helping with the children. Most were orphans and, of course, that is where I met and eventually adopted Vinnie. While there, I became close friends with this nun, Sister Amyra, who helped me recognize my spiritual gifts and how to utilize them for the good of others. She was, I believe, the daughter of the chief of a Cree Indian tribe and had many mystical powers that she revealed to me."

Mark nearly laughed out loud, but then he remembered that

his own mentor and guru was a stereotyped martial arts master who loved Carolina BBQ and "Fred Frinstone." He sighed, "But what does this have to do with what happened at the garage?"

"Let me finish. Once I moved to New Orleans, her spirit continued to guide and protect me. There are many negative forces in New Orleans and I guess she has always been there to shield me from them. In the garage, the first thing I remember was a flash of light and an object coming toward me in slow motion. It was as if time had stopped. Then I heard a voice, her voice, say turn to the left...NOW! As I did I saw the object slide past the necklace you gave me and hit the pavement. Then I heard you shout, "Get down!" It was then I saw something I could not comprehend. You were standing in one place, but something like fire erupted from your body and was propelled upward toward a man with a rifle. It struck him and he was incinerated. Then I heard Sister Amyra's voice again. It said that you needed my help, to enter the portal before me, find you and pull you back through it. If not, you would surely die. So I did what she said. I was so exhausted that I got confused as to how to get myself back after saving you. The portal had closed and I didn't know what to do. Once again, Sister Amyra came to the rescue opening a new portal for me to walk through and rejoin my body. Somehow, I believe that is how we came to this place. Since you were holding my physical body when I entered the second portal, we must have been transported as one."

"Sopie, you're talking about traveling through space—like through a wormhole. I had no idea that was possible."

"Well," she said, "I had no idea that you were the Atomic Fireball or whatever your crime-fighting name might be. So how about explaining to me just what you were doing all that time?"

Mark laughed, "It seems you and I have had quite similar experiences. I, too, had a mentor, Master Bennie Hana." Before Anna could interrupt, Mark said, "Yes, that's his *real* name. He helped train me in both the physical and spiritual realm since my crippling accident in LA."

"I assume, then, that what I saw was real and not just a scene from a bad sci-fi movie?"

"Very much so," laughed Mark. As the shooter started to reload, I astrally projected my spirit and entered his body and he disintegrated. Problem was that once he died, he tried to pull me into a netherworld and I could not break away from his grip. However, thanks to you and Chivas..."

"Who's Chivas?"

"My faithful golden retriever that died a long time ago—or his spirit, I suppose. Anyway, thanks to you and Chivas I was able to eventually get free once I tricked him by evaporating my spirit. And here we are."

"Yes, here we are!" Anna said smiling with a new admiration.

"It almost seems as if we were made in each other's image, like twins," continued Anna.

"I would say so...more like twin flames?" Mark replied.

"Twin Flames? I kinda like that," said Anna. "It's a lot catchier than the Atomic Fire Balls." She smiled. "What is a twin flame?"

"Master Bennie explained in great detail to me, that one day I would meet my twin and that we would have a mission to complete it would be of great help to others and the planet." He put his arm around her. "I truly believe that *you* are my twin, Anna." He kissed her forehead. "We were always meant to find each other."

"Of course we were."

A gentle breeze blew as the two held each other near and warm.

Anna crinkled her nose like she always did when she thought too hard. "Maybe your Master Bennie is the twin flame to my Sister Amyra."

"Maybe."

As the two began to delve further into the morning's unlikely events, Marty's truck came into view.

"There they are. Come on, let's go."

Chapter Two

_______________

Marty's S-10 was a sight for sore eyes. Mark and Anna were both tired and shivering when he pulled up.

"Well, get in," yelled Marty from the old rust bucket. "Where's the bar?"

Hopping into the truck, Mark said, "I wouldn't exactly call this happy hour, Bub." When Anna was buckled in he patted Marty on his beefy shoulder saying, "Let's go!"

He told Marty to head to St. Francis Medical Center in Monroe, as Anna was instructed.

From the looks of him, hulk of a man as he was, you'd expect some sort of hesitation. You'd expect Marty to put up some kind of a fight or ask some kind of questions about where he was now, how they all got there, and where he was going. But Marty was a pussy cat, despite his pro-ball linebacker frame. His heart was loving and generous and Mark was glad to call him friend.

"Hi Mom," Vinnie said, giving Anna a hug. "Are you guys okay?"

"Yes, Honey we are alright. Just a little shaken up is all."

"Us too!" bellowed Marty, "What's with all of this cloak and dagger stuff? What's going on?"

"There is a lot we need to talk about...with both you and Vinnie, but first we need to get to the hospital and see a Dr. Dunleavy."

"Why? Are you hurt?" asked Marty.

"No, but we do need to get checked out and...." Mark paused, "look, there's not enough time to fully explain everything. You are just going to have to trust us, follow my instructions and not ask questions for now."

Without so much as a sigh, Marty complied. "Okay, what's first?"

"I need you to go in and find Dr. Dunleavy. He is there waiting for us to arrive. When you find him, tell him that we are outside in the truck and let him take it from there."

"Whatever you say," Marty responded, still puzzled.

As he whipped the truck into the hospital parking lot a little before lunchtime, Mark said, "Marty, go inside and find the doctor."

As Marty left, Mark felt the inside of his mouth fill with warm saliva. Barely in the nick of time, he opened the passenger side door and started to vomit. "Oh god." Out of nowhere, he felt all his guts start to squeeze against themselves. Mark felt sweat pool around his eyes and heaved again. "I am so sorry. I don't know what's happening...I never..." and again he erupted what appeared to be nothing more than blood and bile.

"Oh, gross!" Vinnie recoiled from the sudden outpour.

"Mark! What's going on? Are you alright?" Anna bolted from the truck.

"I think I'm okay now," he said wiping his mouth and trying to catch his breath. "Maybe just too much movement from Marty's driving." Mark tried to laugh, but they both knew it was a front. Mark had never been one for motion sickness, even if it were Marty at the wheel.

As Mark's convulsions eased, he saw Marty coming back to the truck.

"The doctor said for us to pull under the emergency canopy and he was going to put you two on gurneys and cover you up. I don't know what's going on, but I'll follow your cue like always." He threw his hands up and resigned to his place as the lovable sidekick in the front of the truck.

As they pulled up, a team of medical personnel came out with the gurneys and covered Mark and Anna with bloody sheets.

"What the fuck?" Marty exclaimed.

"Shhhh..." Mark whispered. "Remember, no questions."

Vinnie just cowered behind Marty and didn't say a word.

The medical team went flying into the ER with Mark and Anna lying motionless on the gurneys. Onlookers were horrified at the sight of the bloody duo being rushed into the operating room.

Once there, rejoined with Marty and Vinnie, they were told to sit up slowly by a familiar voice. It was Agent Kroner.

"Hello again, Ms. Sopoulos," he said, tipping his fedora.

"Well hello, it's been a long time."

"It could've been longer," he responded, trying to add as much levity to the situation as an FBI agent can.

"Agent Kroner, I would like to introduce you to my fiancé Mark." She gestured to the gurney next to her where Mark was struggling to untangle himself from the bloody sheet.

"Hi, how are you, Mark?" Kroner reached out a hand to greet him.

"Well, I was better, but I got over it," Mark said jokingly.

"Mom," Vinnie interjected, "Who is this?"

"I'm sorry, Honey," Anna said, "this is Agent Kroner with the FBI.

"FBI!" Vinnie and Marty chimed in.

"Yes, the FBI. He is an old friend and our meeting is another story for another day. I don't mean to be rude. There is a lot that

Mark and I need to tell Agent Kroner...a lot you and Marty just won't understand, but we will have time to talk about it all later, so please, just save your questions.

Grinning Agent Kroner said, "And this must be Vinnie. He was a tad bit smaller the last time I saw him."

"Pleased to meet you, sir," said Vinnie.

"And I'm Marty the transporter, reporting for duty, sir." He stood tall, puffed his chest out and saluted Agent Kroner.

"Quite a crew, quite a crew," laughed Kroner. He stepped back over to the gurneys to address Mark and Anna. "Ok...now, would you two mind explaining to me how you managed to travel 285 miles on foot, after being shot at in New Orleans? Oh, and why there's no trace of anyone at the parking garage except a smoldering corpse?"

"Corpse?" gasped Marty.

"Marty...Q&A later," Mark said.

"Okay, Okay…" Marty said turning a little green.

"That may…may take some…time," Anna slurred. She was having trouble speaking all of a sudden.

"I've got all the time in the world." Kroner folded his arms over his chest.

Anna was trying to sit up on the gurney, but didn't appear to be doing so very comfortably. Her arms were shaking and she kept shifting her weight.

"Ms. Sopoulos, are you all right?"

"Oh, I'm fine...just a little tired."

"Honey," Mark said, "your nose is bleeding."

"Maybe before we continue, we better have Dr. Dunleavy check you out."

"No, I just think I need to lie down..." Just then she began convulsing. Her body thrashed on the table like an epileptic.

"Mom!" cried Vinnie as he rushed to her side. He watched helplessly as his mother's eyes rolled back into her head, blood gushing from her nostrils.

"She's seizing!" Kroner yelled.

The doctor came running in and held her down. "I need a crash cart in here now!" More staff rushed in with a Medi-cart and started pushing Vinnie and Marty out of the way. Dr. Dunleavy started barking orders about milligrams of this and that, but then, as soon as it had started, the seizure stopped.

A hush fell over the room.

"Anna?" Mark peered over and saw his love, still as glass.

She sat up sharply with a violent gasp for air.

"Easy, easy, it's okay, Ms. Sopoulos." Dr. Dunleavy calmed her down and cleared out the staff that had rushed in. He gave her a thorough examination while the other men in the room stood horrified. There appeared to be no cuts or bruises, but he decided to order x-rays and a CT scan to rule out damage and a possible stroke. He also ordered the same for Mark since he had been exhibiting similar symptoms.

After about an hour, he came back flabbergasted.

"I have never seen anything like this. Both of you have stress fractures throughout your bodies that have already begun to fuse. That healing process normally takes at least three weeks.

Both of you also seem to be experiencing vertigo. For whatever reason, I do not know. The CT scans showed no signs of a stroke."

Scratching his head, he continued, "With this many fractures, I don't understand how either of you are conscious, let alone standing. I recommend bed rest and constant monitoring until we can see what is going on and how this could have occurred."

"Well, they can't stay here," said Agent Kroner. "I will have them flown to a secure location at Bethesda Naval Hospital until they recover. Will that be okay, Doctor?"

"If you move them quickly by Medevac, maybe."

"Then, that's what we will do."

"What about me and Vinnie?" Marty inquired.

"Oh, we we'll put you two up in a hotel nearby."

"I still don't understand what's going..."

"Due time, my friend, due time," said Mark.

Mark looked over at Anna smiling. "It will be okay, darling." She smiled back and nodded.

The two were hastily transported to a Medevac copter and placed aboard. Marty and Vinnie headed out driving the S-10 and promised to call Kroner when they arrived in Bethesda.

Kroner turned to Dr. Dunleavy and said, "Finish filling out the death certificates and I will be back in touch shortly."

An article appeared a few days later in The Times-Picayune of Greater New Orleans:

*In an apparent random act of violence in the aftermath of Hurricane Katrina, the bodies of a local music teacher and a social worker were found shot to death in West Jefferson last night. Mark Banos and Anna Sopoulos were reported as trying to rescue children from Charity Hospital when the incident occurred. According to local authorities, the shooter disappeared without a trace in the chaos. Currently there are no leads as to the whereabouts of the perpetrator. Similar acts of senseless violence have plagued New Orleans in the weeks following the…*

## Chapter Three

Almost a week had passed at the hospital in Bethesda. Mark and Anna were still recuperating from their ordeal in New Orleans. They shared a common room with a Marine guard at the door. The doctors had run every test known to man on them, with no conclusions.

"Mark, what do you think happened to us? I felt fine and then all these problems just showed up."

"I don't know, Sweetheart." Mark used the bed remote to adjust his posture. "I'd expect the force of the bullet to be the cause of some of your symptoms, but that doesn't explain why I'm in a similar condition." He sighed. "It's very strange," said Mark somberly.

Just then Marty and Vinnie entered with flowers, candy and balloons and a little bit of Mark's favorite contraband…

"Macallan!" he shouted.

"No, my name is Marty," he said, putting the gifts on the bedside table. "You suffered some head trauma. Remember? M-A-R-T-Y."

Mark pushed him aside and reached for the bottle.

Vinnie laughed. "Hi guys, how are we feeling this beautiful day?"

"Dry, very dry…" chided Mark as he opened the airplane miniature and downed it in one sip.

"Easy, old fellow." Marty put a hand on his friend's shoulder. "They'll have my ass if they find out you've been drinking." He quickly stuffed the empty bottle into his coat pocket.

The guard at the door just kept his eyes forward, expressionless.

"Just sipping and savoring," laughed Mark. "And you'd be having…?"

"Blue Moon, of course," whipping the bottle from his pocket as Mark and Anna laughed.

"Good thing I brought two for you as I hate to drink alone," Marty jested pulling another miniature from his shirt pocket. "How long before you all blow this joint?"

"Not long I guess, as everything appears to have healed," said Anna.

"Where are we going now? Looks like New Orleans is a cluster-fuck." Marty guzzled his beer at his usual pace.

"Well, that hasn't been decided for us yet."

Vinnie finished putting the flowers in the vase by the window. "What do you mean…decided for you, Mom?"

She smiled and reached her arms out to hug her beautiful boy. Kissing him on the forehead she said, "I guess it's time to let you in on what's been going on."

"That would be much appreciated," said Marty as he sat back unscrewing the top on another Blue Moon.

"Damn Marty," Mark laughed, "how deep are those pockets?"

"Deep as they need to be." He held his bottle up as if to cheers and then let out a loud burp.

Vinnie chuckled. He'd been spending a lot of time with "Uncle Marty" lately and the two had become good friends.

"Anna, why don't you explain your part of the story to Marty and then I will fill in the gaps," said Mark.

"Okay, well, I was forced to be married in 1977 to a hitman for the mob in my hometown of Columbiana, Ohio. I was engaged to Mark in 1975, but had to break it off with him as William, my husband, would have shot and killed him if I hadn't. My parents were killed later by William and I had no choice but to stay with him until I overheard a plot to murder the county prosecutor. I knew then, that this was my chance to escape. I contacted Agent Kroner at the FBI and was placed in the witness protection program. He moved me to a suburb of Chicago. While there, my name was changed to Karli Roberts, I adopted Vinnie and reconnected with Mark. However, the mob found out where I was, so I had to be moved.

For the first time since Mark had met him, Marty was both speechless AND not drinking his beer. He just sat there, mouth wide open, flabbergasted.

"I could not tell Mark at the time for fear of endangering Vinnie," Anna continued, "but somehow through divine intervention, Mark found me once again in New Orleans."

"Yeah, my divinely inverted ankle! Praise God, glad I could help," said Marty looking toward Heaven.

"Yes," laughed Anna, "Well ultimately, one of the mob's hitmen found me by following Mark and tried to shoot us in the parking garage at Charity Hospital while we were trying to evacuate the children."

"Wow! But how did you guys get away?" asked Vinnie.

"Anna, maybe you had better let me take it from here," said Mark. "Marty, I know you remember our trip to Treme, right?"

"Oh god, how could I forget!" said Marty.

"Why? What happened in Treme?" asked Vinnie.

"Let's just say Old Mr. B here is tougher than he looks," Marty said.

"Really? What happened?"

"He kicked some major ass is what happened!" Marty stood up out of his chair making exaggerated karate chop motions and fake kicks, all the while letting out high-pitched squeals.

"Simmer down now, Marty," Anna said in her sweetest Mom voice. "We wouldn't want you twisting another ankle, would we?"

Mark laughed as Marty grumbled and sat back down with his beer.

"Anyway," Mark continued, "I was trained in a little more than the martial arts."

"I already figured that seeing as how I witnessed a cripple take out three hoods."

"Without providing all of the gory details, Marty, let's just say I neutralized the shooter, but not in the benevolent fashion that I exhibited in Treme."

"So, you guys really do that cloak and dagger stuff?"

Any sign of jocularity faded from Mark's face. "Not by choice…only when we have no choice." The truth is, Mark still hadn't made peace with what he had done in New Orleans. He knew he wasn't in the wrong, but something about the power he'd exhibited still felt unsettling. Master Bennie had always talked about balance as being a fundamental principle in the universe, and Mark feared what action would be taken to balance the cosmic scales. "I'd do anything to protect the people I love," Mark said. He looked at Anna and reached out to hold her hand.

"Well, that still doesn't explain how you got to Monroe."

"To be honest Marty," Anna said, "we're not quite sure either. Let's just say it was good providence and leave it at that."

"Mom, I had no idea," said Vinnie with tears in his eyes. "What will we do now?"

"Whatever we have to, baby." She ran her fingers through his hair. "Don't worry, God will look out for us."

Just then Agent Kroner knocked at the door. "Okay if I come in?"

"Sure, join the party," said Anna.

"I see," said Kroner eyeing the two Macallan miniatures and Blue Moon bottle in the trash.

"May I speak to Ms. Sopoulos and Mr. Banos alone for a moment?"

"Sure. It's time Vinnie and I headed back to the Shitz-Carlton anyway. See ya chief!" Marty saluted.

"Bye, Mom. I love you." Vinnie reached down for a parting hug.

"I love you, too. I'll call you later."

"Okay," Agent Kroner said as the door shut, "amazingly, you guys are getting better and no one knows how. By all human knowledge and experience, you both should be dead by now. The only way you could have fractured your bodies as you did, was to sustain a force of 5 G's. Can you enlighten me as to how this is possible? How you healed from this and what happened in New Orleans that morning?"

"To be honest, we are not quite sure ourselves," said Anna. "As you have probably figured out by now, both Mark and I do possess what the world would consider supernatural abilities, but I have no way to explain to you exactly what happened. All I can say is that somehow we are able to do things that most humans cannot. When provoked, together we seem to be able to magnify that force exponentially, eliminating any threat before us. But, we are not a danger to ourselves or others."

Kroner snorted, "Tell that to what was left of the corpse in New Orleans." He turned towards the window and smacked his gloved hand against the sill.

"We are terribly sorry about that..." Anna looked to Mark. He just stared straight down. She wondered if he was even listening. "But we really had no choice," she continued.

Kroner sighed. He had to ask the questions the bureau expected of him. "So, are you telling me that you are aliens?" He turned to face them. "Where did you two come from?"

"No, absolutely not." If Kroner wasn't acting so serious then

Anna wouldn't have been able to contain her giggles. "We have merely been trained to harness the energies in nature to be used for good or if need be, not so good." She looked to Mark again. Still nothing. Although, she detected an uneasiness in him. The faintest hint of a grimace trailed across his face.

"Not so good?" Kroner echoed the euphemism with disdain. He stepped away from the window and closer to Mark's bedside. "You've been awfully quiet. What do you have to say about these 'powers' and how they can be used to obliterate a human being?"

Mark looked up at Agent Kroner with sad eyes. He said nothing.

"Yeah, I see it all over your face. You're the one responsible for that man's murder aren't you, Mr. Banos?"

Unflinchingly, Mark replied, "How long did you work as a field agent?"

"Excuse me?"

"You heard me, Kroner. How long did you work in the field before you stuffed your heart and soul in a DC desk drawer?"

"Mark!"

"It's Okay, Ms. Sopoulos," Kroner said. "Nearly 20 years in the field, Mr. Banos. And if I catch your drift…"

"If you 'catch my drift' then you know I'm going to ask you about your first firefight. The first time you had to make an unpopular choice. The first time you had to take a life to save a life." Mark sat up in his bed and took a deep breath. With trembling lips he said, "Didn't make you feel like much of a hero, did it?"

Agent Kroner pulled up a chair. When next he spoke, his voice was finally one that didn't belong to a G-man robot. "I'm sorry. Sometimes, when you've been doing this job as long as I have, you forget what it's like to be a civilian."

Mark rubbed his eyes. "I'm not an agent or a cop. I'm a musician. A teacher. This isn't easy for me to accept either and it sure as hell isn't easy for Anna. So please, Agent Kroner, before you continue with the third degree, try and put yourselves in our shoes. We may have different training and experience, but if you think our fears and uncertainties are any less human than your own, you are sadly mistaken."

Kroner took his hat off and massaged his temples. He sighed, "This sounds like science fiction, that's the problem. Yeah, I can see you two as just kids in way over your heads… and I'd write it off as just that if I hadn't seen that corpse with my own eyes."

"So, where do we go from here?" asked Anna.

"I'm really not sure. My gut says to keep you here for further study. My superiors would want to lock you up in some facility off the grid, I'm sure." He paced back and forth through the room. "But my stupid, dumb humanity says protect you and move you."

"Agent Kroner, I think you know deep down that Mark and I aren't the bad guys here. There are forces at work that none of us are fully aware of."

"I see that—but still, where could I put you that the mob or the U.S. government wouldn't be looking for you?"

"I may have a solution," said Mark. "I know of a place in rural Canada that I visited back when I was performing. No one would ever think of looking for us there."

"The Feds can find you anywhere."

"Not if you don't tell them we're worth looking for. And the mob sure as hell wouldn't find their way that far north."

Kroner popped his knuckles nervously. "Canada might be a good choice. You will no longer be in the witness protection program as I have no jurisdiction there. But, as far as any one knows, you two were shot to death in New Orleans. There's records of your stay at this facility, but I can classify those."

He turned towards the door and then back to the two of them. "Tell me I'm making the right choice."

"You know we don't have to," Anna answered.

Kroner nodded. "I will be able to get you set up there, but from that point on you will be on your own. Where is this place?"

Mark smiled a wry grin. "Meadow Lake, Saskatchewan. Home of the Flying Dust Nation.

Chapter Four

_________________

illiam Bakalar sat in his cell at Allenwood
Penitentiary as he had for the past seven years.
The stench of disinfectant filled the air. Nothing to do but wait.
Wait for breakfast, wait for lunch, stroll back and forth on a two
foot strip of grass, then...wait for dinner, then...wait for sleep to
once again take him away from this place. With consecutive
sentences he had absolutely no chance of getting parole. He
would just rot away in this cell waiting...waiting for death to
take him.

*But none of this was your fault.*

The cell reverberated with the screeching torment of the
voices in his head.

*It's not your fault, William.*

Sometimes they sounded sincere.

*You did as you were told.*

Sometimes they seemed to mock him.

*You were a hard worker and provided for your wife, and she
betrayed you.*

Other times, they simply tormented him.

"Dumb bitch!" he said aloud. "She ruined my life!" Often

times he'd thrash about in his cell. It happened so often that his original bunkmate tried to break his leg. That didn't end well for him. Now William spent all of his time in solitary. They tried the psych ward for awhile, but sedatives never kept him calm enough. Somehow, he always found some otherworldly anger that let him rip the gowns off other patients and use them to try and strangle orderlies.

"Stupid fucking bitch," he screamed again." William liked the sound of his own voice. It was, for the most part, the only one he heard these days.

He had no *real* conversational contact with anyone except the guards. They offered no companionship, except for maybe Robbie, who was on the take. He would smuggle cigarettes in to him and an occasional newspaper or magazine. That helped some.

"Hey Robbie, how are the Pirates doing?"

"Snowball's chance, still in last place. Time now for the post-season playoffs."

"Maybe next year, huh?"

"Yeah, maybe next year."

*If only you hadn't made the deal with the prosecutors, we could be free.*

William tried to shake off these thoughts. Tell himself they weren't real. But every now and again he gave in.

"Shut up," he said. But no one was there.

*Death would set us free. Don't you want to get out of your cage?*

"You don't know anything! I'll find my way out of here. And if I don't, I can run this place better than Figerino ever ran Youngstown."

*You should have taken the needle…*

"I said, shut the fuck up!" William slammed his fists against the wall until he blacked out.

One day as Robbie was making his rounds, he stopped by William's cell.

"I have a message for you from Mr. Figerino," said Robbie.

"Really? Figerino, huh? Thought he had forgotten all about me."

"Oh no, he never forgets about anyone."

"So, what did he have to say? Does he finally have a plan to put us back on top?"

"He said to tell you that your ex-wife and her boyfriend were shot and killed during the aftermath of that hurricane...Katrina."

William grinned like a Cheshire cat. He couldn't even stifle his laughter.

"Yeah, I thought that would brighten your day."

"You have no idea," said William still smiling.

"Well, he also told me that he is the only one who orders hits, no one else."

William's smile faded away. "What are you saying, Robbie?"

"He was a little perturbed that you went and did this behind his back." Robbie shrugged and rolled his cart closer to the cell door. This is where he normally stashed all the contraband. "Mr. Figerino said he told you that he would address the matter when he was ready. Now the Feds are questioning him about it, and he is none too pleased." Robbie bent down to pull something out from the false cabinet in the base of the cart.

"Tell Mr. Figerino that I'm sorry if I caused him any problems. But to be fair, it's not like I work for him anymore anyway, right?"

Robbie didn't say anything much, but he let out a mutter or two of disagreement.

"I just thought..."

"It's best not to try and do that," Robbie cut him off. He lifted a heavy looking old tin drum from the cart.

"What the hell is that?" William said. "What'ya got in there? Hooch from upstairs? That's a mighty nice surprise."

"Oh this? It's a surprise all right. Yeah, Mr. Figerino, see, he thought different." Robbie took the lid off the drum and the room filled with pungent fumes. "See, he thought it might be nice for you to be rejoined with your wife," Robbie uttered as he tossed gasoline on William through the bars.

"Robbie, wait, wait, stop this! What the fuck are you doing? I thought we were friends?"

*Let it happen, William. Set us free!*

"I think this will brighten your day as well." Robbie lit the match and tossed it into the cell.

"No, no, NOOO!" William screamed and squealed as he danced around his cell, slowly becoming a blackened lump of smoldering flesh on the floor.

*Yes…yes…YES! Let us be baptized by FIRE!*

"Mr. Figerino doesn't like loose ends," Robbie said as he stowed the gas canister and continued on his rounds singing *"Goodness, gracious…Great Balls of Fire!"*

---

ANNA SHOT STRAIGHT up in bed. Sweat pooled around her eyes and her hair was soaked. Catching her breath, she felt a sinister energy flood through the room like a gust from a hurricane.

Mark turned over at the sudden movement. Sitting up, he put a hand on her shoulder. "What's wrong, Sweetheart? Nightmare?"

Trying to compose herself, she said, "Yes, it was horrible." She pulled her hair away from her face and draped it over one shoulder. Her hands were shaking. The dark energy buzzed around her…taunting her.

"Oh Honey, I'm sorry." Mark kissed her forehead and smiled. "What was it? Tell me all about it." Then he put his fists in the air like an Irish boxer. "Point me towards him and I'll smack that monster under the bed so hard he'll think it's Tuesday!"

Without much humor, Anna said, "It *is* Tuesday."

Mark rubbed her trembling hands. This didn't seem like an ordinary bad dream to him.

"I saw a man being burned alive. And then…something… some shadow…"

"Shadow?"

"It sounds stupid."

"No, no…what shadow? What do you mean?" Mark sat up fully beside her and held her close.

"It was like the form of an evil spirit arose from him yelling at me. It said, *I'm not done with you yet…not now, not ever.*' And I woke up. It was so real."

Mark rubbed her back. "Well it's okay now. You're safe at home with me." He didn't mean to sound patronizing, but it sure did come out that way.

Anna pushed his hand away and shook her head. "I really think this was more than a dream. Some type of vision…or a warning." Anna became sullen and pensive. That nightmarish electricity she felt buzzing around her body had faded, but it left a chilling sort of vapor. It was like a spiritual residue, a slime that she could still feel on her skin.

Mark did away with his hush-little-baby tone and spoke more seriously. "A warning of what?"

"I'm not sure. But I have this feeling something is coming."

"Well, it's about time to get up anyway. Let me get you a cup of tea to settle your nerves."

The temporary residence set up for them in Bethesda was much better than the hospital room they shared. It was only a few days before they shoved off to their new home in Canada and this would certainly seemed like the Taj Mahal compared to the offerings in the Canadian wilderness surrounding Meadow Lake.

Mark stood up and buttoned a shirt before stepping out into the kitchen. "Should I wake Vinnie and Marty?"

"No," said Anna, "Let them sleep awhile. Marty is taking off today and he needs his rest before he drives back to Carolina."

"Yeah, he's probably right in returning there." He stepped into a pair of jeans. "Not much left for anyone in New Orleans.

They will probably need a lot of help in rebuilding the city, but art teachers would be low on the totem pole."

For the first time since waking, Anna smiled. "Better watch those ethnic slurs. Our new neighbors might not take too kindly to that reference."

Genuinely dumbfounded, Mark threw up his hands. "What?"

Just then Vinnie wandered in.

"Morning Mom, morning Mark," he said as he nestled close to Anna.

"What do you want for breakfast, Honey?" she replied, looking up at Vinnie.

"I want three eggs fried, country ham, grits and biscuits with sausage gravy," Mark piped in.

"And the people in Hell want ice water, Captain Cholesterol!" snapped Anna.

As Mark tried to recover, Anna looked back at Vinnie and said, "How about some lime yogurt and granola?" Anna stood up and put on her terrycloth robe hanging on the door.

"You're killing me," said Mark

"That's fine, Mom."

"Don't overcook the granola this time," sneered Mark as he went to the fridge to see if there was any pizza left.

"Who's killing you?" looking back at Mark, Anna just shook her head. She followed the boys into the kitchen and sat down at the table with Vinnie.

Just then a groggy Marty trudged in saying, "Man, you got any beer to go with that pizza?"

"I give up!" said Anna throwing her hands in the air.

"So what's on our social calendar for today?" asked Mark as he chomped down on the slice of cold pizza with one hand and put the tea kettle on the stove with the other.

"After you two finish your *breakfast* and clean the dishes, I guess we need to see Marty off and figure out what we need to get and pack for our trip," Anna said.

"Yeah, it's going to be a long drive back," Marty said. He sat down at the table and held up his hand as if he were holding something. Mark observed the signal and tossed him a can of Blue Moon from the fridge. "So I better get packed and head out. I sure am going to miss you guys." He popped the top and chugged the beer. "Ahhh…It just won't be the same without you," said Marty. He punctuated the sentiment with a celebratory belch.

"We will miss you too Marty," Anna laughed. She kissed him on the cheek. "You have been a great friend to us and I really don't know what we would have done without you."

"Yeah, I guess my party days are over now with the ball and chain," Mark joked. The kettle started to whistle and he poured the water over the chamomile tea for Anna.

Without smiling Anna said, "Watch it Bub, or that ball and chain might be around your neck." She took the mug from him and said, "Thank you, Honey," ever so gingerly.

Mark kissed her. "I hope so," Mark said tenderly.

"Awww," chimed in Vinnie, "An *Ozzie and Harriet* moment."

Anna and Mark just giggled. The two of them kept buzzing around in the kitchen fixing breakfast while Marty packed his suitcase into the truck outside. They all packed lightly so it didn't take long for him to return.

"Alright you three," Marty said, "Before the sewer gets too deep, let me get out of here."

"I have a feeling we'll be seeing each other again. Safe travels my friend," replied Mark giving him a hug.

Saluting Marty said, "One more for the road," as he reached in the fridge for a beer.

"Get the hell out of here!" Mark pretended to kick him out of the screen door.

"Aye Chief!" As he was climbing into the S-10 he yelled, "Tell Inspector Clouseau goodbye for me. It's been real...too real."

"Goodbye Marty," yelled Anna and Vinnie waving.

# Chapter Five

As Marty drove out of sight, Mark and Anna both started to realize that they were now on their own. A new family, heading to a new town with new adventures...a new life, a new beginning. They had been through so much to even reach this point in their lives. A beautiful fairy tale ending where they could live happily ever after. But like most fairy tales, the wicked witch cometh.

It wasn't too long after cleaning up from breakfast that a knock resounded against the door. "Agent Kroner," said Mark. "What a nice surprise! Would you like a beer?"

Kroner furrowed his brow slightly. "No thanks," he said gravely. "It's still a little early for me." He stood at the threshold awkwardly with his hands full.

Mark, a bit puzzled, realized that Agent Kroner was waiting to be invited in. He laughed. "Please," he said with a butler's bow, "do come in."

Kroner struggled to shift the items in his hands in order to tip his hat. "Thank you."

Anna appeared from around the corner.

"Hi, Ms. Sopoulos," Kroner said with another difficult shuffling and tip of the hat.

"Well hi!" She rushed over and threw her arms around him, nearly knocking everything from his grip. "Hey you know," she said, "we have been through so much together and we will no longer be in the witness protection program per se, so why don't we go by first names and stop with the formalities, huh? From now on, I'm just Anna and this is Mark."

"Fine by me, I'm...well..." he cleared his throat, "my name is Firkin."

Mark had started walking back towards the kitchen, but in hearing this news, he shot beer out his nose nearly choking. Turning back towards Kroner, trying with all his might to maintain his composure he said, "I'm sorry, did you just say Firkin?" Mark had seen and done the impossible. He had exercised more willpower and energy than most humans do in a lifetime. But this moment was the most testing for him—it took almost more power than even *he* had not to laugh.

"Yeah, I know..." Kroner said. "Had to live with ribbing about my name my whole life. It sure helped toughen me up in school. But you see, Kroner is Danish, and a kroner is the currency in Denmark. Since I am a watered down Dane, my dad was half Danish and my mother Welsh, that makes me a quarter Danish. Firkin refers to a quarter, so my immigrant parents thought it would be great to name me Firkin. Maybe not such a good idea since moving to the U.S."

"Oh, I think it's a lovely name," giggled Anna. "Can I take your coat?" She hung it on the rack by the door. "And what's all this you have with you?" she asked eyeing the large box and folders he held.

Kroner started to answer her but Mark cut him off. "I think I'll just call you *Big F,* if that's okay with you?"

"Fine by me, Mr. Banos...I mean Mark," smiled Kroner. "But my friends, few of whom I have, just call me F.P." The three of them moved to the kitchen and sat around the table.

Laughing Mark said, "I am afraid to ask what the *P* stands for."

"Well my mother wanted to name me after her great uncle Percy and..."

"Oh dear," said Anna.

"They named you Firkin Percy Kroner!" He slammed the beer down on the table and kicked his legs out with such force it threw the chair back, sending him tumbling on to the floor laughing.

Kroner just sat there and took it, obviously desensitized to this kind of behavior. "Yeah, got the hell beat out of me almost every day in grade school," he sighed. "As you can imagine, it didn't do much good to try and reverse the two like you did for your stage name, Tom Marks."

Mark was now doubled over on the floor gasping for breath at the thought of Percy Firken Kroner and all of its iterations. "Stop! You're killing me."

Anna tried to bring it down a notch, "Okay, now that we've been introduced...MARK STOP IT!"

Mark sucked in air and tried to compose himself as he knew that it was time to quit. He stood the chair upright and took a deep breath. "Okay, I'm sorry. I just couldn't help myself," he apologized.

"It's alright. I've heard 'em all before. It's nothing new to me," Kroner sighed again.

"Okay F.P., what's up for today?" asked Anna still trying to keep a straight, stern face.

"Well, you guys are all set to go to your new home. Here are your visas and green cards and all of the documentation you will need." He tossed a manila envelope onto the table.

Anna opened it and looked through the paperwork. When she found her visa she exclaimed, "Hey wait, this says Sopie Banos!" She looked to F.P. and then to Mark, confused.

"Mark said nonchalantly, "Well, don't you think we better

make this thing official before we leave?" He stood up and walked toward the fridge.

Before he could get there, Anna ran over and jumped into his arms saying, "I guess it's time you made an honest woman out of me." She kissed Mark deeply.

"Jeez, mom," Vinnie said. He appeared from the guest room, blushing. Then he just smiled and said, "Finally!"

Kroner couldn't even maintain his usual stoicism. With an unpracticed little smile he said timidly, "I may have arranged for a private little ceremony at St. George's this afternoon." He laughed, "So, I suppose you'd better get ready."

Anna's eyes grew wide as Mark set her down. "But I…I have no dress. I can't get married in jeans," she said.

Kroner blushed now too. "I took care of that as well…size 6?" He slid the large box he'd been carrying across the table towards her.

Anna looked inside to discover a beautiful wedding gown and veil. Tears welling up, she asked, "But what will Mark and Vinnie wear?"

Mark went into the bedroom and returned carrying two tuxedos on hangers. There came a knock on the door.

"Must be the florist," said Kroner.

Opening the door, Anna was handed the most beautiful array of flowers in a nose gay to carry down the aisle. She was just beaming.

Mark then knelt on one knee as he opened a small box containing two gold bands, as she had requested so many years ago. "Anna, will you marry me?"

"Yes, oh yes, of course I will!" as he placed the band on the left hand symbolizing betrothment. She put his ring on his finger tearfully saying, "For as long as we both shall live."

Anna continued, "You remembered."

"Of course I did. I'm Greek too, remember?" He stood up and hugged her tightly, picking her up in his arms like that day at the beach many years before. Mark the immensity of their love for one another in that moment, and he felt as if all of their time, past, present, and future, was shining brightly as one combined flame in that instance. Where many feel trapped in memories or secluded from their dreams, Mark and Anna felt what it was like to breathe eternity together.

Setting her down, he said, "Come on, St. George's is waiting for us!"

## Chapter Six

_______________

They arrived at the church around 4 p.m. The October sky was clear with just a mild breeze, unusually warm for this time of year. The leaves on the trees had just begun to change to beautiful fall colors. It was a perfect day...a perfect day for a wedding.

As they entered the chapel, Marine guards lined the aisle, drawing their sabers to form an arch for the couple to walk under. Finding their way to the altar, they were greeted by the priest who said, "Let us begin."

After a few words of introduction and prayer, he asked the couple to exchange vows.

"Do you Mark, take Sopie to be your lawfully wedded wife, for richer or poorer, in sickness and health, to have and to hold for as long as you both shall live?"

"I most certainly do," said Mark.

And do you Sopie, take Mark to be your lawfully wedded husband, for richer or poorer, in sickness and health, to have and to hold for as long as you both shall live?"

"Yes, of course I do," Anna said as she smiled sweetly at

Mark. Her voice sounded just like it did all those years ago when she had given the same response over the phone.

The priest continued, "A circle is the ancient symbol of wholeness and peace.

In the giving and receiving of these rings, you again acknowledge that your lives remain joined in one unbroken circle, wherever you go, you will always return to your shared life together."

Mark then removed the ring from Anna's left hand and placed it on her right; then Anna proceeded to remove Mark's ring and placed it likewise.

The two of them then shared their first communion as a married couple and the Priest then proclaimed, "I, now, pronounce you husband and wife, in the name of the Father and the Son and the Holy Spirit. Amen." Looking to Mark with a smile and a nod he said, "You may kiss your bride."

After the couple embraced, the two of them walked down the aisle hand-in-hand to a symphony of applause and music. When they reached the antechamber of the cathedral, they were greeted by their loving benefactor.

"Congratulations!" Kroner said. "May I kiss the beautiful bride?"

"Of course!" said Anna. She threw her arms around him and planted a big smooch right on his lips. "Thank you, oh thank you. It was such a lovely ceremony. How in the world did you put all of this together?"

Blushing brighter than the lipstick, he said, "Connections, ma'am. I am a Marine veteran and just pulled a few strings is all."

"Well, we can't begin to thank you enough," said Mark. The two men shook hands.

Vinnie, who had proceeded behind the couple, joined the three of them in the foyer. "Well, Vinnie, we are one big happy family now," Mark told the boy.

"What's wrong, Honey?" asked Anna.

"Nothing, Mom" said Vinnie. "Really." He tried to fake a smile.

"I can tell something's wrong. What's going on?"

"Mom, really, it's nothing. It's stupid, I promise."

Mark had a hunch at what might be bothering the boy, so he started fishing around in his pockets.

Anna kept pressing him.

"It's just that, now you guys are married, and you have changed your name." Vinnie tried desperately to explain without putting a damper on the celebration. "I'm the only Roberts, in the family," he said with a fake laugh. "Maybe, I wish…I don't know, it's dumb…"

Mark found what he was looking for and then put his hand on Vinnie's shoulder. "Oh Vinnie, you ARE a Banos, through and through, a name has nothing to do with it. You are as much my son as if I had raised you myself all these years. The truth is, I wish I had been there. Just know that Roberts, Banos, even Firkin," he cracked a smile towards Kroner, "these are just titles. You are the one who gets to create your own identity. But when you need a family to help you figure out who that is, you'll always have a mother and a father right here if you want one."

Vinnie looked up at Mark with a genuine smile. "Thanks…Mark."

The two matching Dapper Dans hugged each other with warmth and tenderness.

"But," Mark continued "I had already thought it might keep people from asking too many questions once we arrive in Canada, so...here, look closely at your visa." He handed the document over to Vinnie for inspection.

"It says *Vincent Banos*!" Vinnie said tearing up.

"I hope that's okay with you?" Mark asked.

"Okay? Yes, now everything is perfect." The trio hugged each other.

"Vinnie," Kroner interrupted, "you are going to bunk with me tonight. I have an evening out planned for your parents, if you know what I mean." He winked at Mark. "You two love-birds hop in that limo out front and don't worry about a thing. Everything's been taken care of."

"You've done way too much already," Anna said. "I don't know how we'll possibly be able to repay you."

Kroner shook his head. "Think of it as a little wedding present" he said as he ushered them outside to the limo.

As promised, a limo was waiting with a *JUST MARRIED* sign hanging on the back. The smiling couple entered the vehicle and waved goodbye to Vinnie and F.P.

Settling back, Mark asked the driver, "Where to?"

"The beautiful Eastern Shore of Maryland," answered the driver.

"Sounds good to us. I'm Mark Banos and this is my lovely wife, Sopie."

"Hi, I'm Chester. Pleased to meet you. You will find champagne in the ice bucket in the mini-bar as well as some hors d'oeuvres and canapés, but I would not fill up as you will be dining and staying at the Eastern Shore's finest—The Robert Morris Inn."

"Sounds absolutely divine!" Anna said as Mark popped the cork.

"Sopie, here's to us!"

"Yes, here's to us." She giggled as the wine bubbles tickled her nose. "Who would have thought that the pet name you gave me so many years ago would stick? I always knew your surname someday would, although it sure did take a long while."

"I guess we had better make up for lost time," Mark said and engulfed her with passion.

Chester smiled and rolled up the partition behind him.

Christening the back seat, they caught their breath and sipped some more champagne.

"I could get used to this," said Mark.

"You better. I'm going to be after you until our bones are too brittle to risk contact," Anna replied.

"That's not even funny...we came close to that."

"Yeah, I know, but let's not talk about that this evening. Let's just breathe in this experience so it will last a lifetime."

"And maybe a little longer..." said Mark.

They finally reached their destination, Oxford Maryland and The Robert Morris Inn.

Chester said, "Let me get your bags so I can check you into your room."

"Bags? We don't have any. We didn't..." started Anna.

"Of course you do. Everything has been provided."

Amazed, the couple followed Chester inside where he escorted them to the Admiral Suite.

"This was part of the original Inn when it was built in 1710," Chester said as they climbed the stairs admiring the murals. "I hope you will find the accommodations acceptable."

"Oh my," is all that Anna could get out of her mouth. A look around the room with its period furnishings was like a step back into another time. Astonished at its breathtaking beauty, she peered out the window to find an enchanting view of the Tred Avon River. "Oh my," she said over and over again.

Chester said, "Get unpacked and change. Your waiters will be up to take your requests for dinner in about an hour. Of course, you can dine below, but Mr. Kroner thought you might like private dining in your room tonight. By the way, they offer a fabulous, full Maryland breakfast including scrapple in the morning, if you two are up by then."

"Scrapple? What's scrapple?" inquired Mark.

"Best not to ask, just put Old Bay seasoning on it. Good-night all," said Chester, as he grinned and shut the door.

Mark and Anna began to unpack and could not believe their eyes. There were two polo shirts, two pairs of slacks, a golf jacket and a suit complete with shoes for Mark and a gorgeous dress, two blouses, two pairs of capris, shoes and a sweater for Anna.

"No PJ's?" asked Anna.

"You won't need them," grinned Mark as he scooped up his bride.

"Alright, alright! We'd better get dressed before the waiters come," Anna said.

"Okay, but I already know what I am ordering for dessert," he said slyly.

"Okay, Mister!" She playfully slapped his chest.

They dressed for dinner and had just finished primping when there came a knock at the door.

"Good evening. My name is Charles and I will attend to all of your needs this evening," he said, carrying in a bucket of ice with champagne along with a plate of fresh strawberries dipped in chocolate. Behind him were two more servers carrying a beautiful floral arrangement for the room.

"These are your wine stewards. They will offer you a wine that will pair nicely with your meal selections. While you enjoy your champagne, we will set up the table in front of the window overlooking the Tred Avon, if you would like."

"Very much so, Charles. You are so kind," said Anna. "I feel like a fairy tale princess," she said to Mark. They watched the wait staff work methodically, almost surgically to make the necessary preparations.

"And I suppose I am the frog," he said, taking a seat on the chaise lounge by the window.

"Oh, you most certainly are the frog."

"*Ribbet*! Then come over here and kiss me before I *croak!*"

Playfully she jumped on his lap and gave Mark a big kiss. "That's for being handsome, not for the pun."

Charles said, "Your table is ready Sir and Madam. Look at the menu and tell me your desire for an appetizer."

Without even looking both resounded, "Shrimp cocktail, please," giggling.

"Very good!" said Charles as he left them alone to look over the menu while he went to retrieve their appetizers.

"Oh Mark, everything looks so wonderful; I just can't decide. What do you think?"

"I'm leaning toward the Lump Crab Cakes. Maryland is renowned for its blue crabs and something tells me that this will be the absolute best."

"I agree with your logic. Crab cakes it is!"

Charles reappeared with the shrimp cocktails and asked them if they had decided on an entree.

Mark said," We will both have the crab cakes."

"Excellent choice, sir. That is one of our finest offerings."

The white wine steward stepped forward and said, "And may I suggest a New Zealand Sauvignon Blanc by White Haven to pair with your crab?"

"Oh that sounds wonderful!" said Anna.

"Very good." The trio disappeared.

"Does this view and eating shrimp cocktails bring back any memories?"

"It sure does. Our first dinner together that night at the beach. The candlelight glistened in your eyes then as it does tonight," said Mark reaching for her hand. "I love you so much, Sopie."

"As do I love you, Mr. Banos," she blushed.

As the last morsels of their appetizers were being consumed, Charles returned with their entrees.

"Oh, those look absolutely delicious!" said Anna.

"As expected" said Mark trying a first bite. "These are incredible."

"Thank you, sir. I will return later to inquire about dessert."

Mark looked at Anna, winked and grinned and they both laughed out loud.

"Mark, I cannot believe this is really happening. You know this had to cost a small fortune. Why in the world would Agent Kroner do all of this for us?"

"I haven't a clue. He is an extremely nice guy with extremely dry wit. But as to why F.P. would go to all of this lavish expense is beyond me."

Charles once again entered rolling in a variety of choices for dessert.

"Tonight we are offering your choice of Chocolate Cake with Vanilla Ice Cream and Chocolate Sauce, Lemon Cake with house-made Lemon Curd, whipped Cream and Berries, a Classic Tiramisu with White Chocolate and Kahlua Sauce or the famous Smith Island Cakes—Original or Red Velvet with Chantilly Cream."

"What would you like, Anna?"

"It all looks so good! I think I will try the Red Velvet Cake."

"Very good, Madam and you sir?"

"The original Smith Island cake for me," said Mark.

"Also a great choice."

After he served each their dessert, Charles said, "I will return in a bit to clean your table and turn down your bed."

As he left Mark said, "Good choice!" Looking in Charles' direction.

Anna just smacked him on his arm and gave him *that* look.

"Oops!" said Mark, and Anna just giggled.

Charles once again returned and as promised, cleared the table and turned down the bed.

"Will there be anything else, sir?"

"I can't think of a thing."

"Then I bid you goodnight."

"Charles, here's a little something for this evening."

"Oh no, sir, I cannot accept this. The bill has already been paid in full—a handsome gratuity included." And with that Charles left.

"How about that!"

"Unbelievable" said Anna as she turned her back to Mark and looked out the window.

Mark began massaging Anna's shoulders kissing her neck. She continued to look out of the window. He slowly unzipped her gown and turned her to face him. She knew his desires. They were the same as hers. Slowly, she began to unbutton his shirt, rubbing his chest. As she did, he slid the straps to her dress over her shoulders allowing it to drop to the ground. His arms encompassed her as he unsnapped her bra exposing her small but beautiful breasts. Mark gently kissed her neck and then her lips as he caressed her breasts. He, then, lifted her up in his arms and carried her to the marriage bed. Laying her down as if she might be one of the rose petals that adorned the mattress, he proceeded to make love to his one true companion, his twin flame, who he had waited for all these long years.

She surrendered willingly to the weight of his embrace and fell into the abyss of his passion.

Anna awoke to the sound of Mark saying, "Good morning, Sweetheart. Scrapple time!"

## Chapter Seven

—————————————

*A*fter making coffee in the room and dusting the sheets once again, the two showered together (of course they did), got dressed and ventured downstairs to find a magnificent breakfast buffet prepared. Eggs were made to order, but everything imaginable was featured.

Anna feasted her eyes on all the delectable choices while Mark somehow managed to find the one thing missing. "No grits," he grumbled.

Anna rolled her eyes at him. "No, but have your tried this scrapple? It is really good, especially with Old Bay and ketchup on it."

"No, not yet, let me try it." He plunged a fork into the strange little square of meat. The outside looked like a cooked sausage patty but the inside was soft and sort of mushy. He cut it like a piece of cake with the side of his fork and noticed the inside had a slight green tint to it. "Man, this is good," he said after the first bite. Shoveling more in his mouth he said, "I wonder what's in it."

Without much though Anna replied, "Chester said we better not ask."

With his best Dirty Harry villain impression, Mark widened his eyes and exclaimed, "But I gots to know!"

When the waiter arrived with their eggs, Mark asked, "This scrapple is good. What's it made out of?"

"Just pig and cornbread. All of the pig including the squeal, if you know what I mean."

"What about that odd hue that it has?"

The waiter looked a little distressed. "Are you sure you want to know?"

"Yes, absolutely."

"It's probably the mold from the hot dogs. We get ours locally and they use about anything they have." He chuckled a little bit. "You know, things that don't meet the quality standards for sausage links and such. Bits that fall on the floor. The scraps —I guess that's why they call it scrapple." He scratched his nose and smiled with his eyes closed. "Never touch the stuff myself, but folks sure do enjoy it!"

After the explanation, the meat wasn't the only thing with a green hue to it. "I think I'm done," Mark said, pushing his plate back.

Anna just laughed and continued to eat. "Aww, don't be such a Firkin Percy," she said chomping down on another bite.

"You're right. I probably ate a lot worse on the road," Mark said laughing. "I shouldn't have asked," he noted pulling his plate back in front of him. "So what's on our agenda after breakfast?"

"I haven't a clue," said Anna. "I guess the return trip."

As they finished up, the two caught sight of Chester coming through the door.

"You *kids* ready?"

"I suppose we are. Thank you for bringing us here. It was absolutely wonderful," Anna said with a smile.

"It will just take us a minute to pack and we'll be ready," Mark said. He stood and began gathering up his belongings.

"Oh, I've already done the bulk of that for you. You two

take your time and gather your personals, then just follow me to your transportation home."

After making sure they weren't leaving anything behind, they got up and followed Chester, but instead of heading to the parking lot as they expected, he led them to the docks.

"Here is your mode of transportation home," said Chester.

"What in the world?" they both exclaimed.

In front of them was a 42' sailboat with a captain greeting them, "Welcome aboard! I'm Captain Carl."

"F.P. thought you might enjoy leisurely travel back and avoid the weekend traffic."

"Un-Firkin-believable," Mark said.

Anna just grinned and hopped on board as Mark followed.

"We'll see you when you arrive in Annapolis," Chester said with a wave.

Mark gestured for Anna to lead the way in exploring the ship.

Before they took off, Captain Carl came down from the control room to greet them. "There are drinks in the cooler. Feel free to sit back aft, or wander around the deck after we head out on the river." The Captain shook their hands and said, "Pleased to have you on board!"

After setting sail, the couple sat back, just enjoying the experience, passing by the beautiful homes toward Bachelors' Point. Easing toward the Choptank River, they were then on their way, heading toward the Chesapeake Bay. All Mark and Anna did was sit back and enjoy the panoramic view. Not a word was spoken during the two-and-a-half hour trip, just the solace of holding one another's hand as they basked in the beauty of the bay.

Mark finally broke the silence. "One day, we have got to get one of these."

"I think we will. Nothing beats this. It's so relaxing, just watching the waves break along the side of the boat."

As they approached the landing in Annapolis, Mark stood up to say, "Land Ho!"

Anna joined him and felt something in the air change. A sudden chill blew through her bones, one that didn't match the air or temperature of the day. A vision of a dark fog appeared to her and, suddenly, for the first time since their wedding, Anna was reminded of her night terror from weeks ago. Her skin crawled and buzzed with that same sinister, spiritual energy she had felt that morning. Anna thought she was going to be sick.

Mark sensed something was off with her. "Honey, are you all right?" He placed his hands on her shoulders. Her eyes looked as if they were fading away to darkness. "Sopie? Sweetheart can you hear me?"

But she couldn't. A dizziness plagued her like it did after New Orleans. The shadowy fog rolled in, billowing up from the water…it was coming for her, trying to pull the air from her lungs. The sunlight and glistening waves dissipated; the sounds of the bay faded into nothingness, and all that emerged in its place was the disquietude of nightmares. She was screaming in her mind, but nothing emerged from her lungs but a cold silence.

"Captain Carl," Mark yelled. "Help, someone help! Something's wrong." Staring into her eyes, Mark watched as his wife began trembling and going limp. He was losing her…again. Despite his extraordinary abilities, he never seemed to feel powerful when something threatened Anna. Only vulnerable. Only insufficient. "Sopie, please, answer me!"

But she couldn't. The black fog had covered the boat at this point. It engulfed them and echoed with cruel laughter. She felt old scars and bruises pulse across her body. The soreness from her micro-fractures and the impact of Pete's bullet reverberated within her. She could taste the blood in her mouth from William's fists. The fog smelled like hatred. She could barely hold herself up. All that she knew existed in this world was the darkness, her body and its excruciating pain, and her husband. Mark was always there, always and forever.

And even though she felt like she was dying, fading away into an empty portal, when she saw it coming, she felt a strength surge from within her. The smoke billowed upward and pushed hard against the main sail of the boat. It shifted with its heavy weight and swung towards Mark with the force of a meteor.

*Move…*

She felt the grinding sensation of her bones struggling against each other. The searing of her scar tissue burned against her flesh.

*Make…him…move…*

She used the pain and drew power from it. She used the fear and made courage from it. And even though her tongue was made of sand, even though her mouth was filled with blood and ash, she screamed.

"Move!"

Mark, instinctively, fell flat on the deck and pushed Anna down with him just as the main sail passed above them.

Carl yelled, "Are you two alright down there? I thought I heard yelling?"

"Yeah, I'm fine. Just a little damp is all," Mark said as he brushed himself off. "You almost took me out with that thing though!"

Carl looked down at his passengers. "Sorry, I wasn't expecting that. I was turning starboard and the main sail went the other way. Must've got stuck on the rigging. I'd better check that out when we dock. You sure you're okay?"

Mark looked to Anna who was gasping for air. She was wild-eyed, like waking from a nightmare.

After a few moments she realized where she was. "Yeah," she said. "Yes, Captain, thank you, we're fine here."

"That was close," Mark said.

She just nodded.

"What happened to you just then? You had me really scared. Are you sure you're okay?"

"I'm fine, really. I uh, well I guess maybe I just got a little seasick or something. Little vertigo is all, I promise." Anna embraced Mark.

He could feel her body still shaking. Whatever she was selling, he wasn't buying it. But before he got a chance to ask any more questions, he heard shouting in the distance. From the dock they could see Vinnie and F.P. waving. "Welcome Ashore!" they yelled as the couple disembarked.

"Hi Mom." Vinnie ran to hug her. "Have a good time?"

"Oh, it was more wonderful than you could ever imagine." Seeing her son made Anna feel almost like herself again. She mustered a real smile now that she was back on land. "I will tell you all about it when we get back."

"I hope you two had a nice evening," said F.P. as Chester once again opened the doors on the limo.

Everyone got in the back as Mark said, "I can't believe that you did all of this for us. The wedding, the clothes, the inn, the sailboat...how can I ever repay you?"

"The look on your faces is repayment enough." He patted Mark's shoulder and smiled. "I don't often get a chance to make people I care about happy. Money well spent." Kroner spoke with genuine sincerity. It's true, he'd developed quite a long relationship with Anna through her time in witness protection, but it was over the past few months since she had reunited with Mark that Kroner noticed something special. He couldn't quite put his finger on how the two of them worked together, but it was almost like they spread a sense of peace and happiness wherever they went. Kroner liked that and wanted to see more of it in the world.

"Well, the government must pay you very well," Mark said. "I know this had to run you a small fortune."

"Oh, the government does pay me well, but not that well.

They did, however, provide me the necessary connections I needed to pull this off. My father actually paid for this."

"Your father? Why would...?" Anna started.

"Well, he didn't pay for it directly. He's been dead many years." Kroner crossed his legs and adjusted his seat as the car picked up speed. "Let me share a little story with you. Back in 1943, during the war, my father was a furniture maker in Denmark. An old school friend, Ingvar Kamprad had moved to Sweden and had started a mail-order business. He wanted to add furniture to his line." The three of them could tell that Kroner didn't get to tell this particular story often. He became more animated and started talking with his hands. "He contacted my father to come up with plans for modular furniture that could be easily assembled by the customers when they received it. This way, he could save a fortune in shipping costs as the furniture could be shipped flat. My father agreed to create the templates for the venture for 10% of the company's profits. Mr. Kamprad agreed and began selling furniture five years later. The name of the company, still very much in business globally today—"

"Don't tell me…"

Kroner smiled. "The name is IKEA."

Anna's jaw dropped.

"You're shitting me, right?" asked Mark.

"I shit you not," replied Kroner. "Sorry ma'am."

"It's quite alright. I am getting used to it," Anna laughed. "So why do you even work?"

"Oh, I love my job. As soon as the Vietnam conflict had ended, I enrolled in the academy and have been working with the Bureau ever since. It's very fulfilling work. Especially when I get to do something special like this," Kroner said.

"So, is there a Mrs. F.P?" asked Anna.

"No," he said laughing, "for her sake." He folded his arms and sighed. "My career is my wife. I have never had time to build a long term relationship. Maybe that's why this was so important to me." Kroner smiled and nodded at the happy couple. It's true, he had his doubts after seeing the crime scene in New Orleans. Whatever the two of them are is very powerful indeed. But after spending his whole life sorting out monsters from mice, Kroner had developed a sixth sense about this sort of thing. As far as he was concerned, Mark and Anna were something unique. Something above even his pay grade. So, he decided he'd keep an eye on them, but not try to control or meddle in forces he would never understand.

"Well, here we are," Chester said as the car slowed to a stop.

"Here where?" asked Mark.

"Dulles International," Kroner said. "We'll fly out to Canada together on my private jet. That way I can help you three get settled and maybe still have a little time for some trout fishing."

Vinnie, who had been quiet for a while, felt his ears perk up. "Did someone say fishing?"

They all just laughed as Kroner stepped out of the limo. "Let's hop aboard!"

## Chapter Eight

_a_board the jet, the happy family buckled up to prepare for their flight. The captain's voice echoed over the loudspeaker.

"Welcome aboard! We'll be cruising at 28,000 feet over sunny skies. Make sure all baggage is secure, seats are in an upright position and seat belts are fastened. Once the plane has reached its altitude, you may get up and move around if you wish. Enjoy your flight. Next stop, Meadow Lake, Saskatchewan, Canada."

"I didn't even know they had an airport in Meadow Lake, let alone one that would accommodate a jet," Mark said.

"Oh, I believe you will end up with more than one surprise when you arrive," Kroner said.

"I suppose you're right. I just remember the area around the hotel, although I did go to the Cree reservation once for a party. We ended up ski-dooing. Almost broke my neck on one of those damn things," Mark said reflectively.

The captain's voice once again came over the loudspeaker.

"We have now leveled off at 28,000 ft. You may now move

around the cabin if you wish. ETA is 1800 hrs or 6 p.m. Central Standard Time."

"Wow!" Mark chuckled. "That's only four hours of flight time. That's fast. It took us 33 hours to drive from Meadow Lake straight through to the beach in Carolina, taking 20 minute naps at rest areas and gulping about six boxes of 'No-doze' with 10 gallons of black coffee."

"That's what made you the healthy boy you are today," Anna grinned, squeezing his hand.

"Hey, would you folks like something to drink or eat? I have sandwiches and a full bar," F.P said.

"Would you like something Honey?" said Anna.

"Blue Moon, please," Vinnie said, testing the waters.

"I don't think so!" Anna shrieked. "How about a coke and a ham sandwich?"

"Ah, Mom. Uncle Marty let me have plenty of them…"

Anna's eyes widened. "Vinnie!" Then she thought about how "Uncle Marty" came into the picture in the first place. "Mark!" she yelled.

Mark felt his face go white. Before Anna reacted, he wondered which he was more likely to survive—a free fall from nearly 30,000 feet, or the wrath of his wife.

"Kidding! I was just kidding," Vinnie laughed. "Oh, you should have seen your face, Mom!" He slapped his knee and giggled some more. "But sure, Coke and a sandwich sounds nice, thank you."

Anna took a deep breath. "And you Mr. Banos? Now that a knuckle-sammich is off the menu?"

"Well, Mrs. Banos, I will have Vinnie's Blue Moon, but nothing to eat. I'm still full of scrapple."

"You are definitely full of something," quipped Anna.

They sat back, enjoyed their refreshments and settled in for the rest of their trip.

In a quiet moment, Anna thought again about what had happened on the boat. She felt a bout of fear and anxiety hit her. "Do you really think this place is remote enough so that we won't have to worry about being found, F.P?"

Leaning forward Kroner lit a cigarette and offered one to Anna.

"No thanks," she said. Although, it sure did smell good, especially as worried as she felt. "Believe it or not I finally quit."

"Wish I had. No, that's not right. If I really wanted to quit I would. Guess it's one of my few personal comforts." He took a long drag. "Kind of like an old friend."

"Yeah, I know what you mean, but I stayed so busy in New Orleans that there just wasn't time to sit down and smoke." She took a deep breath and remembered all the long mornings with tea and cigarettes in Chicago. "Plus they were getting so expensive."

"You got that right. At this rate I will be broke in about 50 years or so," Kroner grinned.

Anna laughed, but she still felt an uneasiness that was easy to see.

"Look, to answer your question about being found, I don't think you will have to worry about it anymore. I was going to wait and tell you this once you got settled, but..." Kroner took another long drag on his cigarette and continued, "you're ex-husband, who we discovered ordered the hit, is no longer in the picture."

Anna sat up straight, a little stunned. "What do you mean he is no longer *in the picture*?"

"The Bureau believes that he pissed off Leonard Figerino when he ordered the hit without clearing it first." Kroner paused. "He was killed while in solitary."

"Oh my," Anna said, "How did it happen? Wasn't he isolated from the other inmates?"

Kroner cleared his throat. "Are you sure you want to know?"

"Yes, I'm sure." Anna thought back to all the abuse he gave to her. "The bastard surely deserved whatever he got."

"Well ma'am, they torched him in his cell. Someone poured gasoline on him and lit a match."

And then it hit her. That nightmare from weeks ago, it wasn't just some figment of her imagination. "Oh my god!" said Anna turning white. "It's not that he didn't deserve it," Anna muttered, feeling nauseous.

Kroner started to speak again, but Anna couldn't understand the words. She closed her eyes and thought of the nightmare, the creeping smoke, the sensation of evil she felt when it approached. "You will have to excuse me a moment." Anna rushed to the restroom.

"I knew it was going to be too graphic for her," said F.P turning to Mark.

Mark narrowed his eyes and thought back to Anna's recent episode on the boat. "I don't think it's that." In all the excitement he had forgotten the kinds of burdens Anna carried within her all the time. He was starting to piece together some of the things that could be bothering her. "The morning you came over she had awakened to a nightmare about a man burning. I believe she might be reliving that experience. Sometimes being a psychic is no walk in the park. God knows the images she carries inside her."

"I am beginning to understand that," Kroner said.

When Anna returned, they continued the trip in silence. Anna just gripped Mark's hand tightly and looked out of the window. She couldn't quite grasp what was happening yet, but she knew Mark was patient enough not to press her.

The captain's voice broke the silence, "Buckle up! We're preparing to descend to our destination...Meadow Lake, Saskatchewan."

Once they landed, Anna cleared her mind, put a smile on her face and exclaimed, "Here's to our new home, a new life, and new beginnings!"

But sometimes, despite our best efforts, our past continues to haunt us...no matter how far we run.

# Sopie

## Chapter Nine

They all followed Anna off the jet. Chester had already loaded the baggage into the awaiting SUV.

Kroner gestured toward the vehicle. "I hope you like it. You will need a sturdy mode of transportation up here."

"You're kidding, right?" Mark looked back and forth between Kroner and the car in amazement. The thing was brand new and fully loaded.

"Just a little wedding gift. I hope you don't mind," said F.P. grinning. "Well, we have to have something to go trout fishing in, don't we?"

"Oh no," said Anna. "You are not going to stink up my new car with fish."

"A few months up here and you'll get used to it," laughed Kroner out loud.

The group piled in to the SUV and began driving through the complex labyrinth of back roads, gravel, and winding dirt paths to find their new home.

Arriving at the cabin Kroner said, "It's not much, but it's home."

Looking at the amazing structure in the wilderness, even as

night approached, Anna was overwhelmed. It overlooked the lake and was absolutely breathtaking. She managed to squeak out a humble "Thank you" as her reactions on the jet were now totally dispelled.

"How can we ever thank you?" asked Mark.

"Sopie just did," said Kroner grinning. "I guess we had all better get used to using your new name as to not arise suspicion."

"That's probably a good idea," Sopie replied.

"Well, come on inside and get unpacked." Kroner motioned toward the entrance.

They walked up the steps on the wrap-around front porch and entered the cabin.

Again, all Sopie could say was "Oh my, thank you," as she wiped the tears from her eyes.

The room revealed a huge den with a panoramic view of the lake, a full kitchen with granite counter tops and a service bar as well as an area to place an office already connected to Wifi or the Saskatchewan equivalent (smoke signals), and a half bath. There was an upstairs with four bedrooms, each with walk-in closets and two full baths.

"Wow, Mom! This is unFirkinbelievable!" exclaimed Vinnie.

"No you don't!" she said, then turning toward Mark with that look of death.

He turned to look at Vinnie sternly. It didn't last long. He tried to contain his giggles but he kept busting out laughing as he said in a low voice, "There will be no Firkin in here, young man!"

"That's when everyone just lost it, including Anna as she laughed and said, "I just give up; I just give up," shrieking loudly as Mark grabbed her and began to spin her around the room.

Kroner just grinned, knowing that he had totally made the right choice in sharing his benevolence. He had not been this happy in years.

When everyone regained their composure, Kroner said,

"Mark, when you get unpacked I want you to take a closer look at the kitchen."

"Ok, Firkin," trying his best not to piss his pants as he started to get unpacked. He then went downstairs to the kitchen.

"What did you want to show me, F.P?" Mark asked.

"Do you see anything in the kitchen that might require your attention?"

"No, is there a leak or something?"

"Something."

"Well, I can tell you that Sopie is gonna love this stainless steel cookware hanging from the ceiling. It certainly makes it accessible. And those knives...are they Henckles? Wow, you went all out here. Even a turquoise Kitchen-Aid mixer. I am not much of a cook myself, but I really appreciate..."

Just then Mark spied a box on top of the service bar.

"Open it," Kroner said with a smile.

Mark looked inside and the tears started to flow. It was a mixed case of scotch. None like Mark could ever afford. There were six bottles of Yamazaki Japanese whisky, three 12 year, two 18 and one 21 year, just like the one Master Bennie had given him on his 21st birthday. Further down were five Macallan 18 year and one Macallan M. Mark was speechless and the tears of gratitude continued to flow.

Finally, after placing the box on the table ever so gingerly, Mark said, "I thought the M stood for Mythic…" In truth, he had never seen a bottle. He had been careful not to even try to afford to dream of a bottle.

Kroner looked at him seriously and said, "It does." With a laugh and a hearty pat on the shoulder he continued, "So let's crack it open!"

"Are you shitting me?" Mark said. "That bottle costs more than $6,000. It's a collectible."

"Only if you're not a scotch drinker, and I believe we are! Scotch is made for collecting in a body, not a bottle."

"But...."

"Come on, I can buy more. Sip it slooowly."

As they savored the scotch, Sopie walked into the room.

"Are you boys having a party?"

"I'll say," said Mark. "F.P. bought us some incredible scotch. Scratch that—magical. No, wait, unbelievable? I just can't find the word…"

"Us? But I don't drink scotch." She raised her eyebrows and flipped her hair sarcastically.

"I knew that," said F.P. "Look in the wine cooler.

Sopie opened the door to the cooler and could not believe her eyes.

"The Seeker! My favorite New Zealand Sauvignon Blanc."

"I knew that, too."

"How did you ever find it? I have been looking for it for over two years."

"You got to know where to look." He opened a bottle and poured her a glass.

"Oh, this is better than I remember. Just smell those grapes."

"I have one last little surprise for you," said Kroner.

"Oh no, you have done too much for us already."

"This I don't think you will mind. Open the china cupboard and look inside."

Anna slowly moved toward the cupboard and opened the doors. Inside were all of her dolls, including Effie, cleaned and restored. The collection she thought was lost forever in New Orleans had come home.

Wiping the tears from her eyes, all Anna could manage to get out of her mouth was, "UnFirkinBelievable!"

---

<h1 style="text-align:center">Chapter Ten</h1>

Mark awoke to an unfamiliar smell. Fresh coffee brewing and...waffles?

He quickly threw on his robe and went downstairs to find his bride in the kitchen preparing breakfast.

"Good morning, Sweetheart," Sopie said. "Sleep well?"

"The most peaceful rest I have had in sometime," said Mark sipping from the cup of coffee that Sopie had just handed him. "I guess you do cook--and not just lamb stew."

"Of course, I do," Sopie said flippantly. "It's just the first meal that I have prepared for us together."

"Together..." Mark repeated and savored the word, "as long as we both shall live."

Smiling from ear to ear, Sopie grabbed and hugged him, then leaned her chin up and kissed him.

"Hi Mom, morning Mark. Do I smell the special waffles?" asked Vinnie.

"What does he mean...the special waffles?" said Mark.

"You'll see," said Sopie.

Just then F.P. stumbled downstairs, fully dressed of course. His bed was made, too. "Morning all."

"Morning F.P.," they all responded.

"Any of that coffee left?" he asked.

"Sure," said Mark filling his cup.

"Are those waffles I smell?" asked F.P.

"Sure are," Sopie replied with a smile.

"I haven't had homemade waffles since I was a child. Mama always let me sit and watch and lick the spoon out of the mixing bowl when she was done. Is that chicken frying too?"

"Yes sir!" said Vinnie, "Louisiana chicken and waffles."

"Well, that is one delicacy that I have not yet tried," said Kroner.

"Remind me sometime and I will tell you about the time Marty and I went to Willie Mae's Scotch House in Treme. But it looks as if this is going to be every bit as good, if not better," Mark said.

"Have we got any Crystal, Mom?"

"Of course, we do."

"What's Crystal?" Kroner asked.

"You gotta get out more," laughed Sopie.

"They all yelled together...Weezyanna Hot Sauce!"

They all sat down to a delicious breakfast of chicken and waffles. All of them had maple syrup on the waffles, except for Mark, who used a mountain of white sausage gravy that he prepared just for the occasion. They all eyed his plate in astonishment.

"What?" He gobbled up every morsel.

After finishing the dishes, they retired to the back porch and just sat and enjoyed their coffee and the view. They all reclined, rocking back and forth, not saying much.

Kroner broke the reverie saying, "Well, if we want dinner, we had better get going to the fresh market."

"Fresh Market? They have a Fresh Market up here?" chimed Sopie with anticipation.

"Certainly, it's right down there in front of you," Kroner said pointing toward the lake.

"I don't see it."

"What he means is, it's time to go fishing," said Mark.

"Can't get any fresher than that!" F.P. stood up and stretched.

"Well, I guess we better grab our gear and get started," said Mark. "Coming Honey?"

"No, I need to start getting this place in order, but Vinnie's free to go."

"Great!" Vinnie jumped up and ran inside to change.

The three grabbed their rods and tackle and headed down to the lake.

"What types of fish do you think there are in this lake, F.P.?" Mark studied the water as if he could see through it and find the answer himself.

"There's Northern Pike and Walleye, but I got my taste set on Lake Trout."

"Man, that sounds good."

It was around one o'clock when they wet their first hook. After casting for about an hour, with no luck, Kroner said, "Let's switch from spoons to flys. I think the reflection with the sun is too much to lure 'em in. This time of year, trout is usually near the surface though, so we just gotta keep at it."

They switched to fly fishing and had barely cast out before Vinnie landed his first one.

"I got one!" he yelled pulling in a beautiful Lake Trout.

"Me too!" yelled Mark.

Before long they had pulled in nine of the Lake Trout and one Walleye.

"Whew!" said Kroner. "This is quite a haul. We'd better get them up to the cabin and see what the Mrs. has in mind to prepare them.

Upon arriving, the proud fisherman cleaned the fish and placed them on a platter for Sopie to fix.

Sopie said, "I have an idea, but you're going to need to filet them."

"Alright," said Mark. He fetched a shining new filet knife Kroner had equipped the kitchen with. Returning with prime cuts, he noticed that Sopie was mixing seasoning.

"What you making?"

"An old Cajun fish recipe that I think you will really like."

"What's in it?"

"Two tablespoons of Tony's Creole Seasoning, one tablespoon each of garlic powder, onion powder, paprika and black pepper. You take olive oil and rub the fish, then rub the seasoning, add some panko and drizzle more olive oil. Then bake it at 475 for 12 minutes. I thought I'd fix some Jasmine rice and asparagus to go along with it."

"Sounds fantastic!" they all chimed in.

"I love the 12 minute part. I'm starving!" grinned Vinnie.

After all were through and had their fill, Sopie started to look for volunteers to clean up.

"All right," she said, "KP time. Vinnie, would you be a dear and take out the garbage so the fish doesn't stink up the house?"

"Sure, Mom," he replied.

"Okay, you other two bums get into the kitchen."

"Aye, Aye Chief," they both saluted.

After clean up, they retired to the back porch to spend another lazy evening looking at the lake, enjoying wine, scotch and Cheerwine, which Mark had introduced to Vinnie as the official drink of North Carolina.

Kroner stood up and yawned. "I think before I go, Mark and I should head into town to secure some firewood for the winter months. It gets mighty cold up here and when the power goes out you had better have a backup system."

"I hope you mean *if* the power goes out," said Sopie.

"No," Kroner laughed, "unfortunately, I mean *when*. Power outages are common in these parts, and they last for weeks, not days."

"Mark, Sweetie," Sopie said with a bit of venom, "you

could've let me in on this little tidbit of information before we *moved* up here!"

"It'll be fine," he said, "just more blanket time." Mark leaned in for a kiss, but Sopie pushed him away.

"Maybe for me and Vinnie. *You* will be busy stoking the fire, Paul Bum-yan."

"That's not the only fire I will be stoking, Honey," as retorted, hugging Sopie.

Again she swatted him away. "Get out of here you horn dog…but hurry back."

"Sorry," Mark said, "I think you're stuck with me tonight."

"He's right," Kroner said. "The sun's almost set—better get an early start tomorrow so we don't get lost coming back." He rose from the chair. "We better get some shut-eye. Night all," Kroner said with a tip of his hat.

The next morning, after coffee and buns, Mark and Kroner headed for town while Sopie and Vinnie stayed behind.

Vinnie went to retrieve the fishing tackle that was left outside yesterday. As he was gathering up the tackle, he noticed a large dark shadow out of the corner of his eye. It was a huge black bear ripping through the garbage that Vinnie laid beside the trash can last night.

Frozen in his tracks with fear, Vinnie looked toward the cabin and spotted his mom.

She returned the looked and looked again. All Vinnie could manage to get out was a soft, "Bear!" Sopie glanced left to spy the animal in the trash. The bear had not noticed them…yet.

There was no point in running…a bear can outrun anyone. No need to play dead either. That might work sometimes, else-where with other types of bears. But black bears in Saskatchewan don't play that shit.

Sopie grabbed a loaded 30-30 that was by the door and raced out. The bear now realized that it had been spotted and rose on its hind legs and began to growl. She aimed the gun at the bear and fired. The bullet left the barrel, but was suspended in mid-air. Vinnie and the bear froze like statues. This moment in time just stopped; but she was still able to move and observe. "*Strange*," she thought as she continued to look on as if a spectator.

An image and then a voice appeared before her. It was Sister Amyra.

"What are you doing my child?" Amyra asked.

Confused, Sopie answered, "I am trying to protect my son." After a moment, she thought maybe she should be the one asking that question. "What's happening…how are you here? How are you doing this?"

"This is not important and you know it." Amyra folded her arms over her chest. Her long robed sleeves blew in the breeze. She always wore strange garments. Today's was some combination of a nun's habit and a traditional Indian sari.

"You say you're trying to protect a child. The bear, too, is trying to protect her children by providing food. There is another path you can take. Do not fear."

"What path is that?"

Amyra stepped closer to where the bullet spiraled in its fixed position. "One that is more true to who you are. You are a lover, a mother, a kind woman. Do not fight with forces you cannot hope to overpower." Sopie watched closely as Amyra stood in front of the bullet. Suddenly it spun faster and faster until it changed form and shape. The metal became water and split into many particles. Then these droplets evaporated into mist. Amyra blew the mist away like steam. "TAME the bear."

Sopie dropped the gun. "Tame the bear?" She glanced from Vinnie who was frozen with fright, to the wild animal who was a statue of ferocity. "I don't understand."

"Your husband was taught a great many things, using the bear's strengths to overcome his adversaries. You are his twin, but not the same. You are the mirror of your twin flame and as such, you need to approach things in your own unique way." Amyra chanted something under her breath and looked to the sky. A purple glow emanated from the center of her forehead as she used her arms to trace a smooth circle in front of her. A black hole appeared from a sonic boom and stabilized into a violet humming doorway. "Enter this portal to talk with the bear's spirit and see if there is a compromise that can be made. Remember, violence breeds violence, so see if you can find another solution. Do not fear; no harm will come to you."

Sopie did as she was instructed and entered the portal. Her body felt like it was trapped in a vacuum, but only for a moment. There was silence, an intense shock of cold, and then nothing but an intense déjà vu. The bear's spirit was now moving toward her and started to speak.

At first all she could hear was unintelligible cries from the animal. But as she concentrated, the noises conveyed meaning—they became words. "Why did you just shoot at me?" The bear said with a pitiful growl.

"I was just trying to protect my son." Stunned by the question and even more by her answer, Sopie added, "I'm sorry. I was scared and didn't think."

"Protect him from what? Me? I was not trying to harm him. I just wanted to eat and take some food back for my cubs. I am so hungry...I could eat a bear," she said now grinning like a...well you know.

"But you are eating our garbage and making a mess. Is there nothing to eat in the forest?"

"Nuts and berries...do you want nuts and berries every day?"

"No, I guess not. I'll tell you what. When I leave this portal, I will go inside and get the leftover fish from last night's dinner and bring them to you, if you promise not to hurt me or my son...or make any more mess. Deal?"

"Oh, that's a great deal. Thank you for your generosity."

The portal closed and Sopie was back in her present. Everything happened so quickly that the shot still rang out, even though Amyra had vaporized the round. The bear fell to the ground, petrified and Vinnie started to run when Sopie yelled, "Stop!"

"Mom! You just shot at a bear and MISSED! Run!"

She was trembling, but she knew what she had just felt was real. She had no reason to fear. "We have come to an understanding, just come with me." She moved towards the door of the cabin.

Vinnie followed in a haze, not knowing what would happen next. Sopie went to the refrigerator and got the rest of the leftover fish and headed back outside.

"Mom! What are you doing?"

She continued toward the bear holding out the fish. She placed them in the bear's mouth so she could carry them back to her cubs. The bear walked away, turning to look back one more time in gratitude before heading into the forest. Sopie looked around to see a totally stunned Vinnie, but there was no sight of Sister Amyra. She had vanished into the wind.

That afternoon as Mark and Kroner arrived to unload the wood from town, Mark asked, "And what have you two been up to all morning?"

"Oh, nothing special, just washing up the dishes and taking out the garbage," Sopie said nonchalantly.

"Mom...tell him about the bear!" said Vinnie excitedly.

"Oh, that. There was a bear eating last night's fish, but she went away," Sopie said. She continued to fold clothes as if she had just told Mark about buying milk at the store.

"A bear! How did he come to eat last night's fish? Vinnie, did you not secure the lid to the trash can?" Mark growled angrily.

"Well, I didn't think..."

"You didn't think? This is not the city. There are wild animals looking for food and we don't want to start a restaurant."

Hanging his head, Vinnie said, "I'm sorry, I just didn't know. We could have been killed. But Mom is really brave. She shot at the bear and then she went inside and got it some more fish. She put them in its mouth and then it walked away. She said they came to an understanding."

"What the..." Kroner started.

"Vinnie just meant to say, once I realized that she was hungry and needed to feed her cubs...well honey catches more flies, or bears, than vinegar."

"But how did you know?" asked Mark.

"We'll talk later. Right now you three boys have wood to unload and stack. I will start dinner."

As they stacked the wood Kroner wiped his brow. "It's about time I headed back to the States."

Mark laughed. Starting to feel a little overworked on your vacation, F.P.?"

"Something like that," Kroner said with a smile. "I've got a lot going on. Looks like you three can handle things from here. Best if you get to know the folks in town by yourselves and they get used to you being a part of their community." He gazed out at the rolling hills and wilderness around them. "It's not like the city. Here, everyone knows your name and they look after one another." Looking to Mark, Kroner said "It'll be a lot different from the places that your wife has lived up until now, so help her adjust. I know you are kinda familiar with this type of existence, being from Carolina and all. But even though she is not the innocent she once was, she still has much to learn about nature, things around her and how to use these things to help herself and others."

He took a few steps toward the larger woodpile and spoke more softly so only Mark could hear. "There is much more to Miss Sopie than meets the eye, and I don't mean her psychic abilities. She has a harmony and balance with nature...I can just sense it. And speaking of nature, why don't we try fishing once more before I go...say 6 a.m.?"

Mark just listened and nodded, eternally grateful for the love and generosity Kroner had provided.

## Chapter Eleven

_____________________

Six o'clock came early, as it seems to everyday. The "boys" had invited Sopie to tag along on their sunrise serenade, so all four marched forth, gear in hand, to go and sit quietly watching the sun break through the clouds as they anticipated their first bite.

"I think I got a nibble," said Vinnie softly. Then it hit!

"You got her son...easy," Mark whispered as he went over to help Vinnie.

About that same time Kroner felt a snag and reeled in a huge pike.

Then Sopie hooked one and reeled in a nice trout.

Mark, still helping Vinnie with his catch, didn't notice he had left his line in the water.

Getting Vinnie's pike reeled in, Vinnie yelled, "Mark, your rod!"

Looking over, Mark saw his rod fly into the lake. Reacting, not thinking about the 40 degree surface temperature, Mark jumped in after it, racing to catch the swiftly fleeting rod. Grabbing hold, Mark suddenly realized that the rod was not the only thing moving out into the lake. That damn fish was pulling them both.

"Let go of the damn rod," Kroner yelled, but by then the fish did an abrupt jump out of the water and swam back toward the shore, tangling Mark's legs in the line. Now Mark was totally helpless, floundering in the deep water of the lake. To make matters worse, some huge shape was swimming toward him as Mark struggled to free himself. Bigger than any fish and even bigger than Mark himself, it was, yet again, a Canadian black bear swimming right for him.

Sopie now had jumped in the water, ignoring the cold, and began swimming toward Mark and the bear. Again, Sopie spoke to the bear's spirit. "What are you doing?"

The bear replied calmly. The water wasn't cold to her. "I am trying to help save him." The bear looked straight at Mark as it went underwater to lift him up in the air on her back and then swam back to shore.

Once on shore, Mark gasped for breath, but managed, "RUN! I will hold her off as long as I can," indicating the bear.

"Mark, there is no need to fear. She was just trying to save you from drowning. It's Okay," said Sopie. Vinnie and Kroner couldn't utter a word. They just stared in total silence.

Then Sopie tossed the bear one of the pikes they had just caught saying, "Thank you," as the bear walked away into the forest.

"Come on," Kroner said, "let's get you two some dry clothes before you freeze to death."

Mark held Sopie close to him after they cut the line around his ankles. "You okay?"

She nodded. "I'm fine," she said through chattering teeth.

But as they walked inside, her legs started to feel weak. She stumbled, chilled more than she realized.

"Mom?" Vinnie helped her up.

"I'm fine guys, I'm fine," she repeated. But a dizziness came over her suddenly. And even though the sun was pouring through the clouds now, when she blinked, she swore she caught a glimpse of that same black fog moving in on the lake. "Let's just get inside, okay?"

———

After resting into the afternoon, recovering from the morning's hypothermic adventure, Kroner announced, "Time for me to go."

Mark said, "Not until you share one more glass of scotch with me. I have been saving the Yamazaki 21 for a special occasion with a special friend. The last time I drank it was on my 21st birthday with another very special friend. I can only hope that we become as close."

They saluted and downed the shot. Then F.P. said, "Take care of him Lil' Miss City Girl. I think you'll end up doing just fine up here. Chester's outside waiting for me, so I best be on my way."

They all hugged each other with love's embrace. And as Kroner got in his car and drove out of sight... They all waved and said, "Goodnight."

———

## Chapter Twelve

The next morning at breakfast, Sopie looked over at Vinnie and said, "It's about time we make a decision about completing your high school education. You have missed so much since this *adventure* began and we need to decide what to do."

Mark interjected, "I am afraid that there is not the kind of opportunities here for education that you are accustomed to." He took a bite of toast. "Even if he enrolled at the local high school, there aren't many courses that he hasn't already taken. The only other choice is the Indian school on the reservation, but I'm afraid you'll find the same shortcomings there."

Vinnie listened and nodded. He had always been a patient conversationalist, even at his age. "Look Mom, I have been thinking about what I should do already and I think it would be a better idea for me to study at home, be tested on the material and graduate that way.

I really only need to finish four classes to graduate and this way I could finish by June and look forward to attending college."

"Oh my…" Suddenly Sopie felt a rush, like all of life caught up to her at once. "I hadn't even thought about college yet. What are you thinking about majoring in?"

"Well," Vinnie started, "I really believe I want to be an engineer."

"You mean drive a train?" said Mark with a little snort.

"No," he laughed, "a mathematical engineer. Basically a problem solver."

"Well, you certainly do well in mathematics," Sopie said. "You had already finished Calculus when you were a sophomore. And that other one too—"

"Linear Algebra," Vinnie said.

"That's right, Linear Algebra." Sopie smiled wide at her bright boy. "Your teachers said you were a prodigy."

"I can't even spell math," Mark said. "Mathematicians solve problems that you didn't know you had by applying techniques that you don't understand. They should call them Mathemagicians!"

Laughing more Vinnie said, "Well, what do you think, Mom?"

"If you promise to do your work every day, we'll try it and see."

"Thanks Mom." As he headed for the door, he added, "Be back in a few."

"I hope this works out," Sopie said sighing.

"Oh, I think it's a great solution. He's a bright kid. I think he'll stick with it." Mark took a sip of juice. "Besides, he's taking advantage of the fact that he's got two licensed educators in the house. We'll have to double-check the logistics of it with some of the folks on the school board up here but he should be fine."

"Speaking of which, we need to start showing our faces in town and get to know some folks around here. Why don't we run into town once Vinnie gets back?" Sopie suggested.

"Yeah, I guess you're right." Mark stood up and cleared the dishes from the table. "We don't want people to think we're anti-social. Or worse…Polish."

"Oh my God." Sopie smacked her forehead with her palm. "How many times do I have to tell you that those jokes aren't funny? They never were!"

Mark put his hands on her shoulder and began to massage her neck. He leaned forward to kiss her cheek.

"Oh…don't think you can…get out of…Okay, that feels nice."

Mark kissed her again and whispered in her ear, "How many Polacks does it take to give a back massage?"

"Oh get the heck out of here!" She stood up and smacked him playfully.

"Ouch, ouch, Okay, Uncle!" Mark ran around the table, but Sopie kept chasing him and slapping him.

Vinnie returned from his walk to a kitchen of hysteria. "Mark telling Polack jokes again?"

---

MEADOW LAKE IS BASICALLY the large town in the area. Even though the population is under 5,000, surrounding villages house under 100 with Greg Lake housing 23. It's what you might call a *little* remote. Yeah...

Heading into town on route 55 was a long twenty-minute drive. It required negotiating a two lane rural highway surrounded by forest, a far cry from the city life that all of them had grown accustomed.

Arriving into town, the trio first stopped at the co-op grocery to pick up a few necessities. It was a nice surprise to see a well-stocked grocery store up here. It even had a bakery and deli. The produce was fresh and the meat was cut to order.

Gathering up a few items, they checked out at the register.

"That'll be $37.52." The clerk smiled. "Aren't you the Banos' that moved in near the lake?"

Mark, fumbling with his change, replied, "Well, yes. Was it that obvious?"

The young man laughed. "As you might have noticed, we are a small town. It's not hard to know everybody because there aren't too many of us, eh?"

"Well, I'm Mark, and this is my wife, Sopie, and my son, Vinnie. Now you know everybody," he said with a grin.

"Pleased to meet you. My name is Henry. So, you are touring the town, eh?"

"Yeah, and we're getting a little hungry. Could you suggest a couple of places to eat some lunch?"

"Sure, we have the usual quick stuff, McDonald's, KFC and A&W. Then, if you want Pizza, there is the Fidrock Cafe, a little run down, but serves great pizza. There is also the Eatery on Main for sandwiches, salads and pizza. My personal favorite is Garfunkel's Gourmet Grill. The taco wraps and Poutine fries are to die for."

"Thank you very much, Henry," said Sopie. "You have been a huge help. Are these places right around here?"

Laughing Henry said, "Everything is right around here, Meadow Lake is not very large."

"Thanks again," Mark said lifting his sacks. "Hope to see you again soon."

"Good-bye, hope you all enjoy your new home. Come back and see us."

Loading the groceries in the car Mark asked, "Are you all hungry?"

"Yes, I am getting a little hungry. Breakfast just didn't hold me this morning," Sopie said.

"No, but I did!" grinned Mark, as Sopie smacked him on the arm.

"I'm famished, eh?" Vinnie looked at them mischievously.

Mark said, "Okay, Mr. Funny Guy, that's what we used to do when I was in the band up here, making fun of the Canadians from Cananada. But now that we live here and want to be a part of their culture, we had better start to realize that we are the foreigners, not them. So try not to make fun." He put his arm around Vinnie. "Although, it was funny."

Sopie punched him again.

"Alright. Where to Mr. B?" asked Vinnie.

"Pizza or Taco Wraps?" asked Mark.

"Taco Wraps sound interesting," said Sopie, "What are you in the mood for, Honey?"

"Taco Wraps sound good to me, too," said Vinnie.

"Then Taco Wraps it is," said Mark swinging into Garfunkel's parking lot.

Going inside they found, as expected, a small family restaurant with a buffet. Seating themselves, a waitress approached.

"Hi, Mr. Banos, I'm Sylvia and I will be your server. May I take your drink order?"

"I think just water with lemon for all of us, thank you. Does everybody in town already know my name?" Mark said laughing.

"It's not hard to figure out. We don't have many newcomers to the area. I'll be right back with your drinks."

"Well guys, it appears as if they already know us. Now, all we have to do is get to know them and who they are," Mark said grinning.

"They certainly are friendly enough," Sopie said. "I believe I am going to like it here." She eased back into the booth.

Sylvia reappeared carrying their drinks and said, "Have you had time to think about what you would like to order?"

"I believe everyone will have the Taco Wraps and Poutine fries, right guys?"

"Oh yes, that came highly recommended, so of course we will," said Sopie.

"Can I get chili cheese fries?" asked Vinnie.

With a puzzled look on her face, Sylvia said, "If that is what you want."

While she was gone, the manager approached the trio.

"Hi, I'm Terry. Are you enjoying your move to Meadow Lake so far?"

"Very much so," Sopie told her. "The people here are all so friendly. I think it is going to be a great fit for us."

"I am so glad to hear that." Terry smiled. "Are you planning on working in Meadow Lake?"

"I am sure that we will get involved with something," Mark said. "As soon as we get settled in, that is." He realized how cryptic he sounded. Mark wondered just how strange the three of them appeared to the townsfolk.

"What type of work do you do?"

"Mark teaches music and I work with children and tutor."

"You know, there are a lot of needs at the school in the Flying Dust First Nation. Drop by again, once you get set up, and I will be glad to discuss the possibilities."

"Sounds great!" said Mark. "Thank you."

"Yes, thank you. We will be in touch soon." Sopie shook her hand.

"Enjoy your lunch," said Terry as she left.

"Well, that was nice of her."

"It sure was," Mark said.

The food arrived and Mark and Sopie dove in, but Vinnie had a strange look on his face.

"What is it, Honey?" she asked and then looked at his plate with fries and this huge wedge of cheddar cheese sitting on top.

"The cheese isn't melted and the fries are almost frozen." Vinnie was trying to figure out just how to attack his lunch. Mark and Sopie just started laughing and then Vinnie just joined in. "Well, you asked for chilly cheese fries!" Mark said.

Getting Sylvia's attention Mark said, "Would you mind bringing him a regular order of Poutine fries?"

"Are they not chilly enough?" The three of them began to roar with laughter.

"He meant chili as in hot dog chili, like they serve down south in the States. Sorry," said Sopie.

"I'm not sure what you mean by hot dog chili. We only use catsup, mustard, relish and onions on our hot dogs. Never heard of hot dog chili…"

"It's fine, we don't have taco wraps down south either. They're delicious!" Sopie took another bite.

"Glad you like them. The fries will be right out."

Looking at Vinnie, Mark said, "Good thing you didn't order a chilly cheese dog."

"Right," said Vinnie ginning. "What's for dinner?"

"Chilly pork chops!" said Mark and Sopie together.

"Enough!" Vinnie said.

## Chapter Thirteen

*S*ettling into their new home, routines replaced novelties, chores took the place of adventures and Mark and Sopie eased into their new roles as husband and wife, Mom and Pop.

Vinnie dug into his school work so he could finish his high school courses by the following June as he had planned. He studied hard and was well paced to complete his requirements. A driven and bright boy, he seemed to be able to accomplish the tasks before him with relative ease.

Mark and Sopie met with Terry, from Garfunkels, concerning the possibility of teaching at the Flying Dust First Nation school. Sopie and Mark both applied and were accepted at the Kopahawakenum Elementary School. Sopie was hired as a Special Needs Education Assistant and Mark as a general music teacher, both teaching across grades K-4. It was again, low pay, but employment that would turn out to be rewarding. They were to start the first week in January, right after the Christmas break.

"Isn't this exciting, Sweetheart?" asked Sopie warmly. "Our

first Christmas together as a family." She held up her glass of egg nog for a toast.

"One of many to come," said Mark, clinking the glass. "I purchased something to mark the occasion." He held up a Christmas tree ornament with the year 2005 stamped on it.

"Oh, it's so beautiful! Our first Christmas together ornament," remarked Sopie. "I think I will place it here, near the top."

Mark then admired the fresh pine they had set up in the den and all of the ornaments they had decorated it with as a family. He started to sit in his recliner and meditate on the beauty of the lights and the glistening trimmings.

"Look!" Sopie said excitedly, "It's already starting to snow. How beautiful." She peered out the window overlooking the lake and settled into a dreamlike gaze. Maybe, just maybe, all the darkness of their collective past had settled. Maybe this was finally the place where they could find peace and tranquility.

Mark snuck up behind her and interrupted her daydream with a musical interlude. *"I'm dreaming…of a White…Trash Christmas."*

"Oh, stop! Don't *ruing* this for me," Sopie said with a pout.

"Sorry, just an old habit from my nightclub days." He kissed her on the cheek. "Oh look, mistletoe!" He kissed her again. "Oh, look! More mistletoe."

He leaned in for another smooch but this time she pushed him away. "Someone's been adding to their nog a little bit, huh?"

He grinned. "Maybe just a tiny smidge."

She rolled her eyes playfully. "Well, if you must sing, I'd better let you open up my Christmas present. It is Christmas Eve after all." She went and pointed to a large box under the tree.

Mark followed. "Okay, but what is it?"

"Open it and see silly!" She laughed and had a seat on the couch.

Mark acted like opening the paper was a real struggle and then he peeped in so no one else could see. He liked to make a big production with these sorts of things. The paper soon went flying. "Oh, I can't believe this. It's a handmade Art and Lutherie!"

"Is that a good one?" Sopie genuinely didn't know. She usually picked gifts based on intuition. In this case, she picked the instrument from the shop that she imagined would look prettiest in Mark's hands.

"It's one of the best...thank you." He stood her up and gave her a tight bear hug.

"Sing me something, now that you have a fine guitar to accompany that fine voice."

He smiled and sat by the fireplace. "I think I remember one." Starting to strum softly a chord here and a chord there, he plucked the intro to *their* song.

*"If a picture paints a thousand words, then why can't I paint you?"*
Instantly Sopie felt the warm sands of Atlantic Beach between her toes and the golden-salt sunset pouring through her hair.

*"The words could never show the you I've come to know..."* Mark sang his truth with Sopie hanging on every word, and ending, *"Then one by one, all the stars would all go out and you and I would simply fly away."*

Tears rolling down her cheeks, Sopie managed a whimper, "I had forgotten how beautiful you sing," she said giving him a big kiss.

"Turn about is fair play, now you get to open your present." He handed Sopie a large, heavy rectangular-shaped box.

Sopie opened the box, eyes beaming. "Oh Mark, it's beautiful! Thank you!" she said as she opened the box to reveal a handmade winter coat, parka, and gloves made by Flying Dust First Nation. Trying it on and spinning around she said, "Oh, I just love it!"

"I guess Santa must have forgotten me this year," pouted Vinnie. He had been reading in his room, but the sound of the guitar must have roused his interests.

"No," Mark said matter-of-factly, "I think I saw some switches and coal outside when I came in." He grinned.

"You are kidding, right?"

"No, I am serious...have a look outside."

Vinnie reluctantly ventured outside and spied the coal and switches on the stoop. He was about to turn around and come back inside when he spotted something unusual in the driveway. He did a double take as he ran to the Volkswagen Camper Van.

"Is it mine?" Vinnie said in disbelief.

"Sure is!" said Sopie twirling the keys, "You might need these."

Vinnie gasped as he opened the door and sat in the driver's seat, still not able to believe his eyes.

"We thought this would suit your needs here as well as when you go off to college. Merry Christmas, Honey."

"Merry Christmas," Mark echoed. "Look on the passenger's seat. There's a little something extra you might need."

Vinnie then saw the small, wrapped package laying on the seat. "May I open it?"

"Of course, you may," Mark laughed. He was always shocked at how polite and well-rounded Vinnie had grown up to be. Especially with the kind of instability he'd known as a child.

Ripping off the paper, Vinnie discovered a brand new TI-89 Titanium graphing calculator.

"Man, will this ever help me in advanced mathematics! Thank you all."

"You are very welcome. You deserve it, the way you have been working on your studies. Merry Christmas!"

"Merry Christmas to us all...God Bless us everyone."

"Okay, Tiny Tim, let's go inside and bless that fine Christmas goose that Scrooge got us," said Sopie.

"Watch it missy or I'll cook *your* goose!" Then Mark let out a hearty, "Ho-Ho-Ho" as the trio headed for the warmth of the cabin with the glow of Christmas in their hearts.

## Chapter Fourteen

The first day of school after the Christmas break found everyone scurrying around preparing for the children to arrive the next day. Ms. Hogan, the principal, held meetings in the morning with the teachers, allowing them to work in their individual rooms in the afternoon. Other than casual introductions, everyone was too busy that first day to socialize and get acquainted with the newcomers. Ernest, the janitor, was hastily putting the last bit of spit and shine on the school, as well as making himself available to move anything the teachers needed to get started.

Mark had the most to do as his room wasn't anywhere near prepared for music. He spent most of his first day putting together bulletin boards and lesson plans. He had to check out all of the equipment as well to make sure it was functional.

Sopie, on the other hand, spent her afternoon assembling the individual education plans for the resource teacher that she would be assisting. Jennifer White had just moved up there from Toronto at the beginning of the school year, so she was fairly new as well. But she was not new to the job. At 53, she was a seasoned veteran working with students that had challenges and her IEP's were obsessively detailed for the semester, but allowed for significant adjustment based upon the student's progress. It looked as if Sopie would be involved not only in helping with the students, but doing a lot of the menial office duties.

Mark would have his own menial duties at the school. Since he would only teach five classes each week, he would have arrival as well as dismissal duty. Essentially, this meant that he made sure the kids got on the right bus—or if they were getting picked up, it was a parent or guardian grabbing them. Even in quaint little towns like Meadow Lake, monsters do still exist.

Mark would also be on lunch duty and recess. In addition, he would be responsible for two music programs each year. Still, it was nothing like teaching high school. Plus, he would be working side by side with the love of his life...that would be a win-win any way you look at it.

The remaining members of the cast were, Jane Martsey, the kindergarten teacher, who was, by appearance, at least sixty, but a very kind and gentle woman. There was Eva Baker, who taught first grade, a young vibrant individual who was pretty and single. She was so desirable, in fact, that the gym teacher, Rocky Rhodes (yeah, that was his real name), had his eye on her. Then, there was Joannie Whitcomb, who taught second grade and was the in-between of the other two ladies. She was middle-aged and not as pretty as Eva, but a strict disciplinarian. The remaining grades, third and fourth, were taught by Sky Roma and Luna Sinclair, respectively. Both of them were in their forties, married, a little chubby, and were Meadow Lake Aboriginal women.

The teachers worked without a break until around five o'clock when Ms. Hogan said over the intercom, "Please try to wrap up whatever you are doing so we can go home. Earnest still has a few floors left to clean, and we don't want to hold him up any longer than need be. See you all bright and early tomorrow morning!"

The next morning came earlier than either Mark or Sopie expected.

"This schedule is going to take a lot of getting used to," Mark said. He was still wiping the sleep from his eyes and yawning. "But, like anything else, once you get into the groove, the school year will fly by." He was trying to convince himself just as much as Sopie.

"I certainly hope so." Sopie stepped out of the car and into the parking lot of the school. "I'm already ready for summer vacation," she said shaking her head.

"Cool thing is, we are here, everyday together." Mark smiled and shut her car door for her.

She put her arms around his neck. "Awww, you not tired of me yet?"

"No ma'am, not today, not never." Mark kissed her.

She pushed him away and feigned embarrassment, adjusting her bun to maintain professionalism. "That's a double negative, Mr. Banos!"

"No, it's a double positive, now and forever." He grinned like a fox.

"You better get on duty before I jump those old crippled bones of yours." She took his hand and they walked together towards the front door.

"Whatever you say m'lady...wouldn't want to gross out the little kiddies, eh?"

"Get to work you." She playfully shoved Mark in the direction of the entrance, blowing him a kiss.

Mark prepared for the first buses to arrive and Sopie made her way to the resource office. "Good Morning, Jenny," she said. "What's up for this morning?"

"First thing we need to do is sort through the IEPs and make copies for all of the teachers that have their students involved in classes here. Next, before stuffing them in the teachers' boxes, we need to attach this resource calendar with appointment times so they will know when to send the students to meet with us, so that we can help each student individually, eh?" Jenny was rifling through a stack of folders and papers on her desk all while explaining.

"I'll get right on it." Sopie moved quickly to try and match the efficiency of her supervisor.

"No real rush." Jenny's hands kept working, but her voice relaxed. "Everyone's going to be moving slowly today to get the children back in the groove. Kind of an organization day, so pour yourself a cup of coffee and relax." She smiled.

Sopie hesitated, but then took a minute to unpack her backpack and take off her coat. "Do we have any tea?"

"Certainly, the teabags are over there next to the creamer." Jenny was flagging individual files with post it notes and sliding them into various trays on the left flank of her desk.

Sopie found the tea and flipped the switch on the coffee maker for hot water. "Thanks." As she watched Jenny more closely, Sopie realized that she wasn't watching the frantic movements of a stressed worker. Instead, every motion of Jenny's, while quick, was practiced and methodical. Her dexterity came from years of experience. Sopie knew then and there that she was in good hands.

Alternatively, Mark had to spend the first week getting to know his students, not his boss. As he only taught one class per day, he had plenty of time to do his planning and visiting with the other teachers in the lounge when he took breaks—which was often.

Rocky Rhodes, the gym teacher and the only other guy in the school, had the same type of schedule with the exception of teaching two classes a day since the students had gym twice a week. The two of them chatted in the lounge frequently. After getting to know each other a little bit that first week, Mark asked him, "Have you ever considered offering martial arts classes as an option, either during class or after school?"

Rocky didn't think long. "Nope," he said. "I really don't know anything about it. The closest I came to that was wrestling in high school." When he said that, Mark immediately took notice of Rocky's broad shoulders and meaty neck. In a lot of ways, he reminded him of Marty. Only difference was that Rhodes probably curled a bit more than twelve ounces at a time.

"Well," Mark said as he sipped some coffee, "maybe you would let me help out. I used to be pretty good at it." He thought back to when he trained near D.C. for a while. Then, of course, he thought back to the first time he met Master Bennie Hanna. "It can really shape up the discipline of a child." He laughed. "I know it had a life changing effect on me."

Rocky looking confused. "Now don't take this the wrong way, I mean..." Rocky cleared his throat, unsure how to approach the subject. "I don't mean any disrespect, but don't you hobble with a cane? How can you teach martial arts?"

Mark laughed again. He had become so adjusted to maintaining one outward appearance while simultaneously manipulating his balance and mobility via inter-dimensional portals that he nearly forgot how strangers saw him. "Yeah, I can see how you might think that." Mark finished his donut and tossed the paper coffee cup. "Are you free right now?"

"Yeah, I don't have any classes until two."

"Well, let's *hobble* on down to the gym and let me show you what an old man can do." Mark winked at the whipper-snapper and put on his best old geezer impression.

"Well, alright," shaking his head, "lead on, old man."

Once in the gym Mark asked, "Do you have some thick tumbling mats?"

"Sure."

"Would you mind getting a couple? I don't want us to get hurt."

The coach just scratched his head and pulled out a couple of mats. "Okay, now what?"

Laying his cane aside, Mark said, "Pretend you have a knife and come at me with it."

"Are you sure?" Rhodes watched as Mark, somehow, scrambled onto the mat. At once, it looked like an old man floundering on broken legs, and, at the same time, like some kind of illusion.

"I'm sure," Mark said with complete sincerity. "Don't worry, I won't hurt you."

Rocky's jaw dropped. "You won't hurt...you are kidding, eh?" The more closely he watched Mark, the more it looked like some sort of old school silent film. The old man moved in a jumpy kind of way…like slices of film were missing from the reel. Rocky just shook his head.

"Come on," Mark bellowed, "attack me."

As Rocky lunged forward, he made a stabbing motion like he had a knife in his hand. Mark didn't move an inch. And, for the briefest of moments, Rocky was worried that his mammoth fist would spear right through the old man's ribcage. Then, right before Rocky landed the blow, he felt himself lifted gently and placed on his back on the mat.

"I told you I wouldn't hurt you." Mark stood above him with his arms folded.

The coach lay there in total amazement. He never saw Mark move an inch.

"How did you do that? It's some sort of trick, eh? Let me try again." This time he rushed at Mark, attempting to tackle him.

Mark only had a split-second to react, so the blow was not going to be as gentle as before. Mark allowed his life force to leave his body and hit Rocky squarely, just as Master Bennie had done so many years ago, propelling him backward to the mats.

"Oomph!" Rocky went sailing. As quickly as he'd hit the floor, he tried to stand. His body hadn't even processed that he'd been hit yet. Rocky staggered and fell again.

"I am so sorry." Mark rushed over. "Don't try to get up yet. Give it a second. You didn't give me a chance to prepare so I wouldn't hurt you." He kneeled down and put a palm on his chest. "Are you okay?"

"Yeah," Rocky said with a gasp. After a few moments of

trying to catch his breath, he forced a laugh. "I guess I just got my ass handed to me by an old crippled guy." He tried to sit up, but wasn't quite ready for that yet. "At least, I thought you were crippled. What gives?"

Mark sat beside him, cross-legged. "Well, you can't always judge a book by its cover. After my car accident a few years ago, I had to make a lot of adjustments, both physically and mentally, to continue with not only martial arts but everything I do in life. That's one reason I believe this could really boost confidence in the children and teach them that they don't have to fight to solve their problems, but if they do, they will have the abilities to overcome the bullies." Mark smiled with a bit of embarrassment. "But if you don't mind," he said, "let's just keep this between us. Others knowing about it tends to invite trouble." Mark held his hand out to help the young man sit up. "So what do you think? Wanna start a martial arts club?"

"If you promise not to embarrass me again," Rocky said laughing.

"Oh, the children won't be learning anything like this. They will just concentrate on the basic skills and the discipline."

"I'm all for that. Let's do it!" The two of them hobbled out of the gym together and took a much needed coffee break…again.

SOPIE FINISHED her work for the day and met Mark outside where he was just finishing afternoon pickup duty.

"Long day?" asked Mark.

"Long day," concurred Sopie. "This is going to take a bit of getting used to after living in luxury." She sighed.

"Yeah, back to reality," said Mark. "Let's go home and eat. I'm starving." He grabbed Sopie's hand as they left for home.

The next morning, Sopie was greeted by Jenny and a little boy. "Hi, Mrs. Banos," Jenny said in her teacher voice. "This is

Marcus and he is in the 4th grade this year. Isn't that right, Marcus?"

The little boy just stared up at the two strangers with wide eyes.

"He will be your first resource student and needs help in understanding his math work, especially fractions." Jenny smiled wide at Sopie, then Marcus, then Sopie again.

*Oh boy!* Sopie thought. *Math… Great!*

"Hi Marcus. I'm Mrs. Banos. So you're having a little trouble with fractions, eh?" Sopie said, falling into the Canadian colloquialisms.

The timid boy finally spoke to her. "Yes ma'am." He looked down at the table with embarrassment. "I just don't get them."

"Well," she said sweetly, "let's see first what you do get." Sopie fished out a sheet of addition problems from a file cabinet. "Try your hand at these."

About a minute later, Marcus handed her the work. Sopie looked it over and said, "Great! There all correct. Let's try this sheet."

He worked for another minute and handed in the sheet.

"My! It looks like you know your subtraction facts, too."

Handing him a third sheet with multiplication problems, Sopie said, "Now don't worry if these take a little longer."

But a minute later, he raised his hand indicating he was finished.

"All correct. Okay, one last sheet. This time division. Take your time."

But again, Marcus handed in the sheet, almost before Sopie could sit back down at her desk.

"I don't get it. You know all of your fundamental math skills, and I might say, better than most children your age. What seems to be the problem with fractions?"

"I just don't get them," said Marcus. He felt good about finishing the worksheets flawlessly, but all the more frustrated that this didn't lead to a discovery regarding his trouble.

"Well, let's see...do you like pizza?"

"Yeah!" said Marcus.

"But you couldn't eat a whole pizza, could you?"

"Sometimes."

"But other times, you might want to share it with a friend, right?"

"Well…" Marcus had to think hard about this because he *really* liked pizza. "Maybe. If he was a really good friend."

"Okay, so you have a whole pizza. If you cut it in two pieces, what would each of you have."

"A half."

"Right, you still only have one whole pizza, but since you cut it in half, you now have two halves. What if two more friends show up and want pizza? What do we do then?"

"Tell them to go home."

Sopie stifled a laugh. "Marcus…" she said seriously.

"Okay, we would cut each of our pieces in half so they could have some."

"Yes, now you have four pieces out of that same whole pizza, a *quarter* of a whole pizza each. A fraction of the whole pie. When you *divide* the pie among your friends each gets some, but not more than the whole pizza," explained Sopie.

On a piece of paper, Sopie wrote down the math connotations for whole...1/1, half...1/2 and quarter...1/4.

"See," she continued, "fractions are no different than division, except you only have one thing to divide, not more than one. The line under the top number means the same as the box you put around the number you want to divide, in this case the top number is *divided* by the bottom number."

As if a light bulb just went off, Marcus beamed and said, "I've got it… I've got it! It's the same as division, just kinda backwards. Thanks, Mrs. Banos." The little boy who came in with a shadow of shame and embarrassment now shined with excitement. He hugged Sopie.

"You are most welcome, Marcus." Sopie felt the warmth of

the hug and remembered when Vinnie was that age. An uncontrollable smile appeared on her face. "Make sure you check in with Mrs. White before you go back to class."

Sharing lunch duty with Mark, she reveled in her first victory.

"I just couldn't believe it. Me teaching a child math! Maybe some of Vinnie rubbed off on me," said Sopie as she ate.

"You underrate yourself. You are fabulous at everything you try and you are great with children. They just get you," encouraged Mark.

"Well, what about you, Mr. B? I hear the children really like their new music teacher. And what's this I hear about starting a martial arts club? Do you think you are up for that?"

He laughed. "You might want to ask Coach Rhodes about that."

Sopie's eyes widened. "What did you do to him?"

"Nothing..." he said looking sheepish at Sopie's glare. "What?" He threw his hands up like an innocent man.

Just then, a fight broke out at the 4th grade table. Sopie jumped up and ran to stop it.

Then a milk carton was thrown by one of the boys, missed its intended target and hit Sopie in the chest, adding a splash of chocolate to her favorite white blouse.

Sopie, with controlled disappointment, placed a hand on each of the boys' shoulders and quietly said, "Stop." A sudden quiet fell over the cafeteria and the two boys were overcome with a sense of love, peace...and regret. They stopped fighting and turned to one another, told each other that they were sorry and shook hands. Turning to Sopie, the one who threw the milk said, "I am so sorry, Mrs. Banos. I didn't mean to…" The young lad began to tear up.

"It's okay," she said softly. Sopie kneeled down to see him eye-to-eye. "But there are consequences for our actions. I am afraid you will both have to go and see Ms. Hogan." She gently escorted the boys to the office.

Returning shortly thereafter, she resumed eating with Mark.

"Looks like you diffused that situation with ease. What did you do this time?"

Without much thought, she said, "I just loved them." Sopie finished her sandwich.

"Oh, that."

"Yeah, that," grinned Sopie.

As the semester rolled on, Mark resumed teaching his daily music classes and aided Rocky in implementing basic martial arts instruction once a week in his physical education classes. The children loved karate and they loved Mr. B.

Before the teachers knew it, they had reached the end of February and the 100th day of school mark. They had planned a feast for all of the parents and children at the school. The children performed a ceremonial "tea dance" and Mark had them sing and echo the Cree song, Tanisi (The Hello Song) once in English and then in Cree:

*"Hello! (Hello!) tânisi ! (tânisi !)*
*How are you? (How are you?) tānisi kiya ? (tānisi kiya ?)*
*I am fine. (I am fine.) namôya nânitaw . (namôya nânitaw .)*
*Come on in. (Come on in.) pihtikwê . (pihtikwê .)*
*Sit down. (Sit down) api . (api .)*
*Have some tea. (Have some tea.) maskihkiwâpoy minihkwê .*
*(maskihkiwâpoy minihkwê .)"*

And then the children sang in unison:

*"It's nice you come to visit tâpwê miywâsin ê-pê-kiyokawiyan .*
*Where have you been? tânitê ê-kî-itohtêyan ?*
*Please tell me what you've been doing. mahti âcimo kîkway ê-osihtâyan .*
*Please tell me a story. mahti âcimostawin ."*

Then, the Elders of the Flying Dust First Nation gave a

blessing for the feast and offered thanks to the Great Spirit and the feast began.

"Oh Mark, that was just lovely. You did such a great job with the children. I am so proud of you," said Sopie.

"Believe me, when you have kids that are this great to teach and hungry to learn, it's a piece of cake. Speaking of which, I am going to have to get another piece of that Bannock Bread and a couple of those Feast Day Cookies. They are so good and so homemade."

"Watch your waistline, Mr. B."

"Just adding a little to it so you can help me watch it."

"I give up!

---

NEXT THING THEY KNEW, the school year ended. Mark's spring program was a resounding success, with a mixture of traditional English and Cree folk songs. It was well-received by all of the parents in attendance. The Banos' were also being well received by the Flying Dust First Nation as the two of them got involved in the reservation community affairs as well. Many of their students lived on the Cree reservation, so it was hard not to become acquainted with tribal politics.

During this time, Vinnie had been working hard on completing his studies, and had graduated high school by June as expected. He had already been accepted by the University of Toronto, by early decision in March, pending his graduation. His dream of being able to pursue a mathematical engineering degree had finally been realized.

"I'm going to miss my little chipmunk," said Sopie. "I don't know if I like you being 2000 miles away."

"Awww Mom," said Vinnie, "I'll be just fine. I'm sure that I will have plenty of work to do so that I stay out of trouble."

"Still, it's a long drive. Make sure you stop like we mapped out for you. That way you will be rested by the time you arrive."

"Believe me," interjected Mark, "you need to take breaks to keep from dozing at the wheel. Although, that never seemed to bother your mom when it was me driving up to see her."

"I worried!" said Sopie.

Mark furrowed his brow.

"Well, I did. Besides, you had been traveling for years and were older than Vinnie."

"Yeah, an old man…" He looked at Vinnie. "I was twenty."

Turning her attention back to Vinnie, "Are you sure you have everything packed and loaded?"

"Yes ma'am. Clothes, TV, computer, TI-89, snacks and scotch."

"Scotch!" said Sopie.

"Sure," he said nonchalantly. "It's going to be a long drive."

"You can't drink and drive, young man!" She shook her head. "What am I saying, you can't even drink yet!"

"I got stops, eh? And this is Canada, Mom. You're talking to an eighteen-year-old adult!"

"Mark," said Sopie.

"Your mother's right, Vinnie, no drinking behind the wheel." He nodded sternly. "You're of the age now to start making mature decisions…so make sure you stop and climb in the back first."

"Right, Mark. Good fatherly advice," said Vinnie.

"Good fatherly advice my foot. MARK!" yelled Sopie.

"WE'RE KIDDING!" they yelled back.

"Still flabbergasted she said, "Okay, you two had me going. Come here and give your mother a kiss goodbye."

"Bye Mom," said Vinnie, "I will be in touch soon." He hugged and kissed her goodbye.

"Come on, I'll walk you to the van," said Mark. "Here is a little something for the road," as he handed Vinnie a fifth of Macallan 18 and a fifth of Chivas. "The Chivas is for any old time, except driving. The Macallan—save for those special little celebrations. Drink it slow, as you won't be able to afford to buy more. And don't you dare add ice to that 18 boy, or I'll whoop you," said Mark grinning as he gave Vinnie a final hug.

"Bye, Mark and thank you for everything." He fired up the VW and headed out for his long journey.

Mark and Anna turned back toward the cabin, arms entwined, both sad and glad as they watched Vinnie drive away. He had been a huge part of their everyday lives and now it would be just the two of them.

## Chapter Fifteen

The fall had replaced the moderate warmth of summer in 2006. It had almost been a year since their move to Meadow Lake. School had begun once again and Mark and Sopie got into the groove of their daily schedules. Both really missed the day-to-day interaction with Vinnie, as each morning, they looked toward the stairs to check and see if he would amble downstairs for breakfast...and each morning, both would let out an audible sigh.

Mark's Karate Club classes were growing to the point where they were going to have to be offered after school. As he did in his music classes, he kept everyone mesmerized and instructed to each individual's needs and addressed their techniques only after assessing their limitations. By doing this type of individualized curriculum, his students were able to achieve more than they thought possible, while Mark never forgot the fun factor.

Sopie's success was demonstrated in a similar manner. She treated each child as an individual, adjusting the curriculum as need be, for each child's abilities. This approach had never been tried at the school before, and its success overflowed to the other classrooms. Soon, everyone was using this individualized instruction as the preferred method for teaching. Test scores soared and academically, The Flying Cloud First Nation excelled for the first time in its history.

It was late November when they received a call from Vinnie, one that put sadness in their hearts. He had decided to stay over Christmas break this year so he could finish a project that, if successful, would propel him into the next school year's honor's program.

Hurt, but with understanding, Sopie said, "While it makes me very sad that we won't be together this Christmas, I totally understand and appreciate your dedication to your field of study. After all, Christmas is just another day. We'll see each other soon." She hoped her son couldn't hear the change in her voice as tears welled up in her eyes. Every mother lives two emotional lives—constantly amazed and filled with pride at the accomplishments of their children, constantly torn to shreds as the people they love the most grow further and further apart.

As school closed for Christmas break, Sopie was having a Blue Christmas. Even though Mark was there with her, Vinnie was her son and had been such a huge part of her life. She might not have made it through those years in witness protection had it not been for Vinnie.

"It will still be Christmas," she sighed, "It will just be different this year."

Mark tried his best to reassure her that everything would be all right. But even he couldn't seem to cheer her up. No amount of egg nog, mistletoe, or dancing Santas could lift her spirits.

But one day, after a long walk around the lake Sopie caught sight of a familiar VW camper. It was Vinnie! She ran to the door, losing her scarf and hat in the process. She turned the lock with trembling hands and lunged through the door.

"Hi Mom! Surprise!" Vinnie stood in the living room wearing a hideous Christmas sweater.

Mark clapped the boy's shoulder and lifted a glass of nog. "Look what the cat dragged in!"

Sopie ran to her boy and squeezed the life right out of him. "You devil, you!" She was fighting back tears. "But you're my little chipmunk and I love..." Sopie stopped mid-sentence as she saw someone else out of the corner of her eye.

Vinnie smiled and gestured toward an attractive young lady next to the Christmas tree. "This is my good friend, Angel."

Startled Sopie said, "Pleased to meet you." She extended a hand.

"Hi Mrs. Banos, I am pleased to meet you as well." Angel smiled and revealed a near perfect set of pearly whites. Her voice was reminiscent of her namesake.

"Quite a surprise, right Honey?" Mark looked at Sopie to try and figure out if she approved. Her face seemed to still be beaming from the shock of seeing her son. "Let me show you where to put your things, Angel." Mark grabbed one of her bags for her and headed towards the stairs. "And then we'll go to the back porch to get acquainted. I will get a fire going in the chiminea."

"And I will make some hot cocoa," said Sopie.

"Thank you both so much for welcoming me into your home." Angel looked to the surprised couple and continued to smile. "It's really beautiful here."

"Yeah, thanks, guys," said Vinnie as he and Angel hustled upstairs following Mark.

Sopie was in deep reflection, stirring the hot cocoa when Mark returned.

"I wonder why Vinnie told us he wasn't coming and then just showed up like this, with a *friend?*" Sopie narrowed her eyebrows toward the mug.

"I don't know. He probably just wanted to get one over on the old folks at home." He squeezed Sopie around her waist.

Mark kissed her neck. "I'm going outside to start the fire."

After a bit, Vinnie and Angel came back downstairs and joined Mark and Sopie on the back deck.

"So, we haven't heard from you in a while." Sopie's excitement had worn off and now her concern was becoming more defined. "How are your classes going?" she asked.

"Great Mom." Vinnie pulled out a deck chair for Angel. Having a seat he said, "I am really loving all of my classes. They are a lot more challenging, but it's amazing what I have learned in such a short time."

"Are you in school as well, Angel?" Sopie zoned in on the unexpected guest. She was beautiful, but what mysteries was she concealing?

"Yes, this is my second year at the University." Angel didn't appear to be nervous. She spoke as if she were someone with nothing to hide, oblivious to the motherly eyes trying to penetrate and dissect her. "I am studying communications and broadcasting."

"That's something we could use up here," interjected Mark with a snort. "The only reception we can get is the government channel and old Mr. Wizard reruns."

"Hey," Vinnie said, "don't hate on the Wiz."

"So, how did you guys meet up? In class?" asked Sopie. She was still staring at Angel. Maybe if she looked hard enough she could see her spirit, her truth, her soul's thoughts…

"Well, not exactly. We actually just ran into each other one day," Angel said giggling.

"Yeah, I was walking with my iPod in my ears, listening to this new album my roommate downloaded, I was just getting with the groove and the next thing I know, I find myself on my back with this beautiful girl on top of me." Vinnie laughed as Angel blushed.

"You see I was roller skating to class and..."Angel started.

"I get the picture." Mark smiled and put a hand on top of his wife's. "Sound familiar, Sopie?" He sensed that she was uneasy. But when Sopie heard the story, Mark felt the uncertainty melt away from her.

Sopie's mind wandered back to Atlantic Beach. And in that

moment she saw a little bit of herself in the young couple. "Another hit and run," she laughed.

Vinnie and Angel just looked at each other and shrugged.

"Well, after I recovered, I asked Angel to join me for coffee. She said she would prefer tea. That ring familiar too, Mom?"

"Oh yes, go on."

"We seemed to have so much in common. We talked for hours, missing our classes before we realized it."

"Yeah, we paid for that one," said Angel.

"Of course we did. Anyway, we became great friends and just started to hang out with each other anytime that we weren't studying. It sure has made college life a lot more bearable," grinned Vinnie.

"Yup, yup, yup…" Mark took a long sip of his cocoa.

"So, as Christmas approached, I asked Angel if she would like to go to my home for the holidays."

Sopie looked a bit confused. "Angel, please don't misunderstand, Mark and I are more than happy to meet you and have you here with us. But, to be honest, when I thought Vinnie wasn't coming home for Christmas, I was a wreck." She laughed. "So, I guess what I'm saying is that I hope you're not causing that kind of grief for your family this holiday by spending it with us."

Angel smiled like she had inside, still calm, still full of peace. "Well, Mrs. Banos, I don't think that's something we need to worry about. My parents aren't with us anymore."

"Oh my goodness, I'm so, so sorry, please—"

"Mrs. Banos, it's fine." Angel sort of tilted her head to the side. She wasn't concealing any kind of pain or embarrassment, she just didn't seem to have any. "You couldn't have known."

Vinnie reached over and took her hand. "Angel's parents were killed in a car accident a few years ago and I…" He looked at the lovely vision sitting next to him and almost lost his words. "I didn't want her to have to spend Christmas alone." Vinnie smiled at her, studying her eyes with his own. To him, her stare looked like a quantum equation, one that would never have a fixed answer, but one that he would never tire of trying to solve.

He came out his trance and looked back towards his mother. "I figured I'd tell you that story about having to stay on campus for the holidays so that by the time I got here, you would be so glad to see me that you wouldn't mind me bringing a friend."

"Oh Honey," said Sopie, "any friend of yours is a welcome guest in this home. You don't have to make up stories." Turning to Angel, Sopie said, "It's so nice to have you stay with us for the holidays, Angel. Just make yourself at home. Everyone is welcome here." Standing, she said, "Come on inside, and you can help me with dinner. We can leave the boys to be boys for a while."

"You want me to help?" asked Mark.

"Not on your best day," said Sopie jokingly. "You stay here and catch up with Vinnie and I'll call you when it's ready."

Mark smiled a knowing grin. When the ladies went inside he looked at Vinnie and said, "See? Never let them know you can cook or clean and they'll never ask you too!"

Sliding the screen door back open, Sopie said, "I heard that!"

Vinnie just laughed. After a while, the boys replaced the cocoa with Macallan. Inevitably, Vinnie asked what Mark thought of Angel. The old man sipped his scotch and said, "I think she's beautiful. She's calm and warm…she seems knowledgeable and ambitious…I get nothing but good feelings from her." He put his glass down. Vinnie was about to speak when Mark said, "But, none of that matters."

Concerned, Vinnie's eyes widened. "But…you just said…"

"I said what *I* thought of her. But the only thing that matters is what *you* think." Mark raised his eyebrows. "So, ask yourself truly, how do you feel around her?"

Before Vinnie could answer they were summoned to the dinner table. It didn't matter though because Mark and Vinnie both knew exactly what he was going to say. They all sat down to a lovely dinner of pork chops, cooked with shallots and balsamic vinegar along with mashed potatoes and peas. After saying grace, they dove in.

"This has always been one of my favorites, Mom."

"I'm glad you are enjoying it."

"The vinegar and shallots really bring out the taste."

"Thank you, Angel."

She took another bite. "No, thank you for the recipe!"

After dinner, the men cleaned up and then they all went back on the porch with coffee and tea.

"Constant Comment is one of my favorites for this time of year. The flavor of the cloves and cinnamon is just right with this nip in the air," said Angel. "Oh look, it's beginning to snow."

"Always perfect here at Christmas," Sopie sighed snuggling up to Mark.

Vinnie scooted closer to Angel as well, putting his arm around her.

"Wouldn't want you to get a chill," he grinned as she smiled back.

A peaceful and still silence fell over the back porch as they rocked away the evening.

Sopie began to sing quietly,

> *Silent night, holy night*
> *All is calm, all is bright*

Mark joined in,

> *Round yon virgin, mother and child*
> *Holy infant, so tender and mild*

And all ended with,

> *Sleep in heavenly peace.*
> *Sleep in heavenly peace.*

"That was so beautiful. I am so glad I decided to come," said Angel.

"And we are so glad you did, too," said Mark, "but it's time for us old folks to hit the hay. Make sure you two put the fire out before turning in."

"Goodnight, Mr. Banos," said Angel standing.

"That's Mark," he laughed and hugged her. "And Goodnight."

"Goodnight Mom...Mark."

"Goodnight Vinnie, goodnight Angel—and before you say it, I go by Sopie."

Angel laughed a little at the strange name. "Okay then, goodnight, er...Sopie."

As Mark and Sopie ascended the stairs, Mark said, "Me thinks the kids are becoming more than just great friends."

Putting her arm around Mark, Sopie whispered, "Me thinks so, too."

<hr>

CHRISTMAS VACATION CAME and went as it always did...too soon. After bidding goodbye to Vinnie and Angel, Mark and Sopie headed back to the cabin to de-decorate and prepare for the second half of the school year.

"It was a wonderful Christmas," said Sopie sighing.

"Yes, it was. Our second," Mark said grinning widely.

"But, it was a different Christmas having Angel here. I guess my little chipmunk is growing up."

"He's supposed to. It's just easier for them than it is for us," said Mark. "Okay, let me haul this tree outside and we'll get this place back in order."

"Are you sure you can handle it by yourself?"

"Yeah, as long as I drag it."

"Across my nice rug? I don't think so, Mister. Let me help you."

# Sopie

## Chapter Sixteen

The second half of the school year had become quite routine. Everything fell into place like a well-oiled machine. Sopie and Mark both spent an incredible amount of time at school as well as at the reservation, helping with community affairs and celebrations. They got to know the children and their parents on a personal basis and became a big part of the community that they served. Mark, of course, entertained at the functions and Sopie was the activities organizer. She also chaired several fundraising events for the tribe.

This is not to say that they shunned their neighbors in town. They were always ready and willing to lend a helping hand, whether it was to build a neighbor's garage or help the local Girl Scout troop hold a bake sale. They were the town's staunchest supporters, no matter what the cause. Need help? Call Mark and Sopie Banos.

Vinnie would soon be home for the summer, marking the end of his freshman year. And for a time, a very short time, things could go back to the way they used to be.

"Hi everybody!" Vinnie said as he paraded through the door.

"Oh, there is my little chipmunk," said Sopie as she planted kisses all over him.

"Awww Mom. Hi Mark."

"Hey buddy, how is life treating ya?"

"Good, everything is good. It's nice to have a break, but I am ready to get back to the grindstone. I brought home some books on statistics and differential calculus for the summer, hoping to get a jump on classes in the fall."

"Differential Calculus? I thought that was a junior course?" Mark took a look at the thick textbooks Vinnie was lugging.

"It is, but in college you can take courses out of order as long as there are no prerequisites. So...when's dinner? I'm starving."

"Oh, I bet you are. That's an awful long drive. Maybe an hour? See if you can find a snack to hold you over until then," said Sopie.

"Okay, thanks Mom. After I grab a bite, I'm going upstairs and get my stuff put away. Then I'm going to Skype Angel and let her know that I got here in one piece."

"Okay, Honey. I put fresh towels in your bathroom, made up your bed and straightened your room, but it's up to you to keep it that way."

"Alright, I will."

When Vinnie disappeared up the stairs, Sopie said, "You know, Mark, he seems different somehow. More mature, more sure-sighted pertaining to his goals."

"Yeah, he's not three-years-old, playing with the stove like he used to," laughed Mark. "Don't overthink it, Sweetheart. It's just that your little chipmunk is growing up."

"But I don't want him to..." pouted Sopie.

---

F.P. Kroner returned that summer for a visit or a "lengthy sabbatical" as he preferred to call it. He had recently retired from the FBI and had decided to come visit his old friends once more.

"So, you finally retired from the Bureau, eh?" asked Mark.

Punching Mark in the arm he said, "Yeah, I never thought I would. I always figured to die with my boots on, so to speak. But you know, I got to thinking one day, I sure would rather be in Meadow Lake fishing than in some swamp tracking down a criminal. So, here I am. I do hope I am not imposing on you."

"Imposing? How could you be imposing? After all, you bought this place for us as well as everything in it."

"True, but it was a gift, and it is your home now, to do with as you please."

"Well I know, but you are welcome wherever we are...always. You have become a dear friend, and I don't mean that because you spent a lot of money on us. We truly love you and are so glad that you came up to see us."

"Oh yes," said Sopie. "We really are glad to have you here with us. We have really missed you. Come sit down on the back porch and tell us what you have been up to."

After finding a comfortable seat, F.P. lit up a cigarette saying, "Hope you don't mind. Never did kick the habit. Figured there's no point trying now."

"It would be like me trying to give up scotch and cigars," laughed Mark.

"God knows that ain't happening," grinned Sopie.

"You asked me why I finally retired...well, the job just got to me finally. The last creep we were chasing had raped and killed six little girls ranging from 11 to 14. I just couldn't stomach the graphic images anymore. Without getting more into the gory details, I decided that after we nailed that one, I would just quit...and so I did. But enough of that, how are you doing in college, Vinnie? Are you home for the whole summer?"

"Yes sir, I will be here until my classes start up again, some-time in August. Oh, and school, it's fantastic! I am learning so much and have met some really nice people."

"I can think of one, in particular," said Sopie, ribbing him.

"Awww Mom." Vinnie blushed a little.

"Anyway, we are really delving into some practical applications for mathematics, especially in the communications area, which my friend, Angel, is a whiz."

"Oh, I'm sure!" Sopie kept egging him on.

"Mom stop!"

Sopie rolled her eyes and looked at Mark. "Okay, fine."

"Well, I sure wish you could come up with a way to fix this lousy TV reception that we have up here. I am getting tired of watching Mr. Wizard reruns," said Mark.

"Well, why don't you hook the signal up to a Wifi server and transmit the channels that way? Sorta like Tesla tried to do with electricity...wireless."

F.P. and Mark just looked at each other. The solution was so simple. Why had no one ever tried it?

F.P. said, "You know, the lad may be on to something. Mark would you mind pouring us a scotch while I mull this over."

When Mark returned with the drinks, F.P. started to speak. "Vinnie, I think you have a great idea. If you..."

Sopie popped her head out from inside the house, "Excuse me for interrupting, but I wanted to let you know that dinner will be ready in about ten minutes."

"Okay, Mrs. B," F.P. said. "Thanks. Now as I was saying, if you think you can make this work and can build a prototype to demonstrate that it works, I would be willing to shell out a few bucks to fund the project and get it up and running. I need a hobby in my retirement anyways. I can't spend all of my time fishing. I'm afraid I would get hooked. Say, that's pretty good for an ex-FBI guy, eh? You in?"

"Certainly, Mr. Kroner."

"F.P, my friends call me F.P."

"Okay, F.P. Er...what does the F.P. stand for?"

Sopie raced onto the deck and she and Mark both echoed, "Don't ask, just don't ask!"

After finishing a lovely dinner of local trout, F.P. said, "Oh, how I have missed this. This is really living. Maybe we can wet a couple of hooks tomorrow?"

"I don't see why not," Mark said.

"Let's just not have a repeat of last time," said Sopie.

"Right Boss!" Mark grinned and kissed Sopie on the cheek.

Vinnie hurried upstairs to Skype with Angel as the two men reassumed their positions on the porch, enjoying a little more scotch and smoking some panetellas.

"You know Mark, I really like the way that boy thinks. There may be quite a bit of money to be made in this if Vinnie can get his idea off the ground. God knows, the folks up here could really benefit from it. I believe that if we can show that it works here, it will be viable across Canada. I will need you to come into the business with Vinnie and me though."

"Me? What can I do that would help? I don't know anything about TV, communications or Wifi."

"Well, somebody's got to watch!" F.P. joked, which is a rarity. "Seriously, you are the best communications guy I know. People believe what you say. You impress people with your integrity. We need a front guy. Me, I am meat and potatoes, just the facts, ma'am. And Vinnie is really smart, but excuse me, geeky. Not a bad thing, but when you're selling a clock, people want to know if it keeps time, not how it was built."

"I kinda get your point," said Mark.

"So, you in?"

"All the way."

"Great! I love it when a plan comes together. See you in the morning. We got a date with some fishies."

## Chapter Seventeen

-----

*B*efore the couple could blink, two more Christmas seasons had past and they were on the door step of their fifth together that winter in 2009.

Vinnie was now a senior at the University, and Angel had graduated the year before. Vinnie had moved off campus to a small apartment, so Sopie and Mark thought they would surprise him this year by coming down to Toronto for the holidays.

After ringing the doorbell, soon everyone got a surprise.

"Hi Mom! Hi Mark! Come on in. Why didn't you call and let me know you were coming? I would've...er, straightened up."

"Turn about's fair play," Mark said in his usual dry fashion. "After all, you surprised us a few years back."

Looking around the apartment, Sopie asked, "Did we come at a bad time? Do you have company?"

"Well...er...no...and, yes." Vinnie rubbed the back of his neck and let out a little nervous laugh.

A second later Angel came out of the bedroom wearing a robe. She had obviously put on a few pounds. "Hi Mr. and Mrs. B. It is really great to see you."

"You too," said Sopie a little apprehensively.

Sitting down in the living room, Sopie continued, "So tell me, what have you two been up to since we last saw you?"

Blushing a little, Vinnie started, "Well, there's been a few changes. For the good, mind you, but changes. The first change is that Angel and I have become pretty much inseparable since my sophomore year. What we thought was just a great friendship has turned out to be a little more...actually, a great deal more. And...I have asked her to marry me."

"That's fantastic!" said Mark, "This calls for a drink!" He jumped from the couch and headed to the kitchen to find some glasses.

"Mark, wait. I think they have more to tell us," said Sopie. Her motherly intuition kicked into high gear the moment she walked in the door.

"Well, I guess you have already noticed that I have gained a little weight," said Angel.

"Well...yes," said Sopie, "My guess is it is not from eating donuts."

Laughing nervously, Angel continued, "No...It looks like we are going to have a baby in a few months."

"A baby! That really is fantastic! Now can we have a drink?" asked Mark. "Well, er, I guess all of us except you, Angel." Mark hugged her. "You're drinking for two now! I'll make it a double." He winked.

Sopie folded her arms. "Not quite yet, Sweetheart," she said, starting to lose her patience. "Are you two sure you are ready for this responsibility? A child needs a lot of love and care from loving parents."

Vinnie stepped closer to his fiancé and put an arm around her waist. "He will have every bit of that from us," he said calmly. "We will raise him just like you raised me." He smiled with truth and a bit of naiveté.

Sopie knew he was sure of the decision, but she couldn't help but feel an awful pressure. There was a creeping uneasiness that clouded around her ever since they all moved to Canada those years before. And despite the fact that they had been safe and happy, despite the fact that she and Mark and Vinnie had all thrived and flourished in their new homes…Sopie couldn't help but feel a darkness looming.

She thought of the old days. Of Youngstown and William, of her own struggles as a single mother, and all the pain and violence she once knew intimately. She looked at Angel and blurted out, "I just don't want you to feel trapped the way I felt, when..." then she hesitated.

"What do you mean, Mom?" Vinnie furrowed his brow. He clung to his love even more tightly than before.

"Well, it's just that...and I know I never told you about this before, but…."

"Honey," Mark tried to interject, "maybe now's not…"

"Mark…please." She patted her husband on the knee and he got the signal. "Vincent, when I was in high school, I got pregnant. I felt that my whole future was going to change. Then I…well, then I lost the baby." She started to tear up. "It felt like I'd never recover. Then I met Mark and..."

"And that's a story for another day," Mark interrupted. "What your Mom is trying to tell you, I think, is that this is a big responsibility and you both will have to work very hard together and place your child's needs and wants ahead of your own. You won't have much 'we time' anymore."

"And what will you do for money?" Sopie's voice had hit a higher pitch. Very rarely was she this unsettled. But there was a feeling in the air that she couldn't shake…this was more than just worry. "You have got to finish school," she said.

"Oh, I fully intend to graduate." Vinnie pulled out a kitchen chair for Angel to sit. He leaned up against the counter. "In the meantime, Angel has a great job with a broadcasting company here in Toronto."

"They already assured me that I'll have a job waiting for me no matter how long I go on maternity leave."

"And when I graduate it looks like I will be heading up the Wifi company. F.P. loved the prototype I showed him, and Mark has already laid the groundwork for installing it in the rural areas surrounding Meadow Lake. I know it's going to take off across Canada and we are going to make some mega bucks."

"Don't count your chickens before they hatch." Sopie ran her hands through her hair. A million thoughts rushed into her brain at once. "What are you going to do for money in the meantime?" she asked.

"There is enough allowed in the business plan for my salary for the first two years to get the company up and running. I've got a good feeling about this, and so does F.P. Otherwise, he wouldn't have sunk his money into it. He's a pretty sharp guy."

"You can say that again," said Mark. "And it sounds like you two have already thought this through like the mature adults you have become." He rubbed Sopie's back and tried to release a calming energy into her body. "I am very proud and I love you both very much."

Sopie felt the echoes of a million doubts reverberate in her mind. Something about the happiness she and the family had experienced these past five years just seemed too surreal. It was like she'd been placed in a dream world and now she was filled with the anxiety of waking up.

But she also felt Mark's hand on her spine, the love emanating from within him and from within herself. Wasn't that real? Wasn't that true love once enough to foil the mafia's plans for her? Wasn't their devotion one that defied the expectations of time itself? Who's to say that Vinnie and Angel hadn't been made for each other as she and Mark had?

With a deep breath, Sopie finally said. "Me too, I also love you both, very much."

In saying this, Sopie pushed back her impending fears and tried to deny her anxieties. While she was emotional and uncertain, she knew that whatever was truly bothering her wasn't coming from her own son.

"Congratulations. I wish nothing but the best to you both and my new grand..." And then it hit her like a brick…the excitement of it all. "Did you say 'raise *him*'? I'm going to have a grand*son*!"

"Yes, Granny, you are!" ribbed Mark.

"Oh, shut up, you," said Sopie, arms crossed.

"Drinks now?"

Sopie glared.

"Soon?"

"Oh, go ahead Grand Sot. Maybe our new grandchild will call you Sot-Sot."

"What?"

Ignoring Mark, Sopie said, "Well, I guess he could call me Nan and Mark, Granddaddy. That's sounds nice."

"For an old codger that's 100," retorted Mark. "How 'bout Nan and Big Guy?"

"Oh, I like that," said Angel, "Big Gut."

"No, Guy!" said Mark, as he crossed his arms and frowned, "Big Guy…"

"Yeah, that's fine with us," laughed Vinnie and Angel.

Sopie then asked Angel, "Have you thought of any names yet?"

"Vinnie and I thought, if it was okay with you, we would name him Thomas Sopoulos Banos."

"That's a mouthful!" said Mark, "How 'bout Sonny Boy?"

"He's not a dog, Mark," said Sopie again losing patience.

Mark just grumbled and finally got up to fetch some libations.

"Wait," said Vinnie, "I like Sonny. We could call him that as a nickname."

"I love it!" said Angel, "Sonny it is."

"Well this is going to be a very Merry Christmas. One filled with surprises," said Sopie.

"Yes, God Bless this house and everyone in it," said Mark as he finally got to lift his glass.

SOPIE'S BIRTHDAY came right after Christmas on the 29th, and Mark had held onto a couple of surprises just for the occasion. Of course, he would never be able to top the one that she got when they arrived that year.

"Angel, Sopie loves red velvet cake, but as you might have guessed, I'm not a baker, or much of a cook for that matter. Could you possibly bake a cake for her while she and Vinnie are out shopping this morning?"

"Not a problem, Mr B. Cakes are one of my specialties. You watch me and I will have you being able to bake one in no time."

As Angel got the ingredients together, Mark watched intently. "Say, this doesn't look too hard at all."

"It's really not. Just measure all of the portions and have everything ready before you start. Then you put everything in the mixer and pour it into a pan to put in the oven. As long as you don't stomp on the floor while it's baking, you're good."

"What happens when you stomp?"

"The cake falls and you then made shoe leather."

"That doesn't sound good."

"It's not. Don't stomp."

When she got the cake in the oven, Mark said, "Well, that was easy. Now all I have to do is wrap this gift."

"Would you? I am all thumbs when it comes to these things."

"Sure, I'd be glad to."

Vinnie and Sopie, arriving back home from shopping, came into a festive apartment decorated with a "Happy Birthday" banner and balloons.

"Oh, I love it! This is a surprise."

After enjoying a wonderfully prepared birthday dinner, the beautiful red velvet cake that Angel had baked was brought out with lit candles on it. (It's not polite to tell a lady's age, eh? So, I won't say how many.)

"Oh, this is marvelous! Red velvet cake is my favorite. Did you bake this Angel? I know Mark didn't."

"Well, he helped."

"If he helped it would be butter*scotch* icing," ribbed Sopie.

As everyone sang, Sopie blew out the candles. Sopie remarked, "Oh, this is so good. May I have another piece?"

"Watch the waistline, Sweetheart," said Mark.

"Oh, I'm just getting it to where you can see it, so you can keep an eye on it for me," said Sopie beginning another Banos banter.

"Okay, enough, if you're not nice to me, you won't get any presents."

"Presents! You got me birthday presents. Awww, how sweet. Gimme!"

Opening the first, she had *that* look. It was a T-Shirt that read:

*Limited Edition*
*Vintage 1956*
*All Original Parts*

"Very funny, Mr. B."

"Here, open this one."

Ripping into the large rectangular package, revealed a beautiful seascape painting of *their beach.* "Oh, Mark it is so precious. It is just as I remember it," she said kissing his cheek.

"Yeah, when we go back one day, you can wear your new t-shirt over your old black bikini."

That got him punched.

"What?" He feigned innocence like a pro.

Angel extended a brightly wrapped box to her. "Vinnie and I have one more gift for you."

Upon opening it, Sopie tearfully said, "Thank you both. I will treasure this always." She revealed to Mark a teacup with "Nan" inscribed on it.

ARRIVING BACK HOME from their trip to Vinnie's, Mark and Sopie were drained, both physically and emotionally. They talked about the joys and apprehensions they felt during the entire 2,000 mile trek. While they had a great time, they couldn't help but worry about the young couple and their new baby. It was truly a life changing trip for everyone.

At one point, Sopie tried to share with Mark the sort of feelings she had. "Do you ever just feel like, sometimes, things are *too* happy?" She felt the words were a little silly now that they had been uttered.

Mark's eyes got wide and he rolled his head like he did when he's felt especially sassy. "Uhh…NO!" He laughed. "What in the heck do you mean, *too happy?*"

She shook her head. "Nothing. Never mind, it's stupid."

Mark looked at her and then back at the road. "No, no it's not. I'm sorry, it's just a long drive. I'm tired."

"It's fine."

"Yeesh," he said. "Now I know I'm in trouble if it's *fine.*" Mark tried to make a silly face at her. "Come on Honey, what did you mean? Talk to me."

She rubbed her forehead. It felt like she'd had a headache for days now. "I really don't quite know how to explain it. It's just that, everything seems to be going so wonderfully for us up here. Since we escaped Katrina and got married, it's like we've been living a fairy tale."

Mark listened intently, trying to find the problem. "I'm still not sure I understand what's wrong."

Sopie laughed. "That's just it! Nothing! Nothing has gone wrong, AT ALL, since we've lived here." She turned in her seat to better face him. "For people like us, with the pasts we have… don't you find that just a little odd?"

Mark kept one hand on the wheel, but put the other on her

leg. "Honey…I know we've been through a lot. Especially you. And, I mean, I get it."

Sopie cocked her head to the side. "You do?"

He laughed. "Of course I do. It's like you hear about those guys that come back from war and all of a sudden they don't know how to live in society."

Sopie's face scrunched up. "You're saying I have post-traumatic stress?"

"No, no, no. I mean, not really. Well, sort of. It's just that if you live your whole life in a war zone, peace can seem a little strange, you know?" He looked over at her with soft eyes.

She leaned back against the passenger side door of their SUV. "I guess maybe that's it." She sighed and stayed quiet for a long time. They were almost home. Almost back to their perfect cabin nestled in their beautiful acreage that was almost magically gifted to them. It's not that Sopie wanted to find fault in any of it. For the first time in her life, she truly was happy. And despite her initial shock, she really was happy for Vinnie and Angel. The problem was that Sopie was a trained psychic—she had a bloodline trait that worked like a second-sight. And even though she was happier than she had ever been, she wasn't truly at peace.

Even though it had been years, she often thought of William Bakalar. Vividly. She often thought of that nightmare years ago and the visions of smoke that plagued her. While these thoughts and feelings had dulled, they never truly disappeared. And maybe, just maybe, Sopie felt that they were no longer simply looming at a distance, but drawing ever closer.

Evidently she had lost herself in deep reverie. Before she realized it, the car came to a stop.

"Home sweet home, Sweetheart." Mark rubbed her back and leaned over for a kiss. "I don't know about you, but I've gotta piss like a Russian racehorse!"

As the two started toward the front porch of the cabin, they noticed the door ajar. Sopie felt the hairs on her neck stand up.

Looking to Mark, she said, "Didn't you lock up before we went to visit Vinnie?"

"I am sure I did," Mark said with bewilderment. He motioned for Sopie to stand behind him. Calmly, Mark inhaled and collected his energies, preparing for whatever threat might be lurking in their home.

Slowly pushing the heavy door and peering in, they discovered an elderly gentleman watching their TV. Without turning away from the set, the stranger said, "Hello Tommysan."

## Chapter Eighteen

——————————

"**O**h my God!" Mark exclaimed.

"Not God, just Bennie." And there he sat—after all these years, Master Bennie Hanna had resurfaced in Mark's living room. Still not turning in the chair to face his hosts, Bennie simply threw up a half-hearted wave. "How come Frintstones not on TV up here," he said with obvious frustration. Bennie kept pushing buttons on the remote trying to find his favorite show. "All I can get is government channel and Mr. Lizard!"

While Sopie turned on some lights, Mark walked over to the recliner Bennie had claimed as his own. "That's Mr. *Wizard*," Mark said, correcting him, "and there are no real channels up here. That's it."

Finally averting his eyes from the screen, Master Bennie barked at his former student as if they were back in the gym. "You need to fix!"

Mark laughed. "We're working on it."

Bennie just grumbled in his seat and turned off the TV.

Mark looked back at Sopie. She threw her hands up and just started to take off her coat as if everything were perfectly normal. "How in the world are you here?" Mark sat down in the chair beside Bennie. "And why are you here? And don't say Carolina Barbecue because, obviously, we don't have that either."

"No, no, trout will do, he-he. I actually come up here to visit relatives of Amyra."

Sopie's ears perked up. She was about to head to the kitchen for a glass of wine, but this she could not ignore. "Wait, did you say Amyra?" Sopie stepped closer to Master Bennie. "As in, Sister…"

"The one and only," said a voice from the kitchen.

"Amyra!" Sopie exclaimed as a figure approached from the kitchen carrying cheese and crackers.

"Hope you don't mind me fixing us a little snack," she said. The woman seemed to glide across the floor because of her strange but fashionable garb. Just like the last time Sopie saw her, Amyra wore an odd combination of flowing robes that concealed most of her body, giving her the grace of a rainbow jetting across the sky. "It has been a long journey for us."

"I don't mind at all," said Sopie still in a state of shock. "But how did you get in and how did you know we were here?"

"Me know much," said Bennie. "That one, not so much" pointing toward Mark.

Amyra, my twin sister, is Cree. This place her home. We hear of a new couple that teaches at school and helps with charities in Flying Dust First Nation. Bennie say, "Can it be?" and then they tell me name and I know it be!"

"Right, right," said Mark not convinced. He smiled and rolled his eyes.

"Amyra…" Sopie reached out and hugged her mentor with such force that the snack platter almost went flying. "It is so good to see you again. How have you been?"

"Very well, my child," giving Sopie a motherly kiss on the forehead.

"I didn't know you were from Meadow Lake," Sopie said with genuine surprise. "What a coincidence."

"Yes, coincidence," said Master Bennie. He waggled his eyebrows at Mark.

"There's no coincidences where Master Bennie is concerned. So what's up?" Mark said. Maybe it was the long drive he had just completed, or maybe it was a severe lack of scotch in his system, but Mark didn't quite feel up to the sort of headache that usually accompanies Bennie. Truthfully, he was fully content living in the fairy tale Meadow Lake had turned out to be. And as much as he wanted his Sopie to be happy, Mark had hoped that it wouldn't necessarily have to involve their usual brand of excitement.

"Always impetuous." Bennie wagged his finger at Mark. "There is plenty of time to talk of these things. Now, I have heard of someone here that has possession of some Yamazaki 21." With a big smile, Bennie shot up from the chair and started to rub his hands together with excitement. "Should we not seek this person out and see if he is a generous soul?"

"Ok, voodoo man." Mark wanted to be angry, he really did. But there was something about Bennie's presence that cast a ray of calm over his soul. Maybe what Sopie was saying in the car had some truth to it—maybe the two of them did have some higher purpose they were leaving unfulfilled in this particular chapter of their lives. "You know…I don't know *how* you know, but you know that I have some Yamazaki 21 and...." Mark said mellowing, "of course, we will share it, my old friend," betraying his annoyance with a wide grin.

Before the men went to the kitchen, Mark stood and shook Amyra's hand. "It's a pleasure to finally meet you, ma'am. I've heard so much about you."

Amyra smiled. "And I you."

Mark laughed and pointed to Bennie. "From him? All lies most likely."

"Oh," Amyra said with a cocked eyebrow. "So then, you're *not* a very talented and enlightened student?"

Mark looked to Bennie with genuine surprise.

The old master was already pulling out a barstool in the kitchen. "Ahh, don't give Bennie puppy-dog eyes." He patted the bar top. "Less mush-gush, more scotch!"

Mark smiled and nodded at Amyra and then sat at the bar with Bennie, pouring the golden nectar with great care.

As he did so, it gave Sopie and Amyra time to reacquaint.

"I have often wondered how you were doing," Amyra said. "You left Carol Stream in such as hurry, without even saying good-bye."

"I'm sorry for that," Sopie said with a tinge of embarrassment. "I was in the witness protection program and was moved to New Orleans, by the federal marshals, to ensure mine and Vinnie's safety." She shook her head, thinking back to that frightening time. "A hitman had discovered our whereabouts and was closing in. I couldn't even tell Mark, but somehow he found me."

Amyra smiled. "When the universe makes plans, they will always be fulfilled." She ate a cracker with cheese. "You know what would be excellent with this?" she said with a mouthful of food.

Sopie nodded and disappeared into the kitchen. Coming back with a bottle of sauvignon blanc and two glasses she said, "No reason the boys should be the only one with a tasty beverage."

Amyra laughed. "You always were a talented psychic!" She took the glass Sopie offered her and savored a long sip. "Be that as it may, you have not realized your full potential. Not like Mark has." She set her glass down on the table and leaned forward. "I did not have the time to share everything with you that I needed to."

Sopie's eyes narrowed. "I'm not sure I understand."

"You will," Amyra said with a smile, "but not tonight.

Tonight we celebrate the reunion of old friends." She held out her glass and Sopie clinked it with her own.

"Cerebrate indeed!" Master Bennie yelled from the kitchen. "I'm drinking frowers from Heaven!"

The women laughed. "I suppose we better have a real meal instead of just a liquid dinner." Sopie walked into the kitchen and pulled some trout out of the freezer for dinner. Fixing it in her wonderful Cajun style, she added red beans and rice.

After they had sat down at the table and had given thanks, Master Bennie yelled, "Oo-Wee, I guarontee!" doing his best to imitate a Cajun chef he had seen on TV years earlier. "Fish hot ...very hot!" He waved his hand in front of his mouth as if he were trying to put out a fire. "Good though—and these red beans and rice with the andouille sausage are wonderful." He shoveled another spoonful into his mouth. "Much hotter than food prepared in California and much hotter than expected."

"So, you don't know everything?" ribbed Mark.

"No," he said wiping his mouth, "but way more shit than you!" The old Asian Master whacked Mark on the head with two fingers.

They finished dinner and retired to the deck out back as they watched the sun disappear with a satisfying silence.

Sopie broke the silence and said, "Maybe this is the perfect ending to our little story." She thought about the doubts filling her mind earlier that day and how silly they seemed now in the reflection of the sunset. "Good friends, good food, and a beautiful home with this magnificent view. Vinnie is in his senior year at college and he and his fiancé are expecting our first grandchild later this year. We both have interesting and fulfilling jobs in a loving community. Who could ask for more?"

Bennie interrupted. "As seasons change, so does the cycle of life. Enjoy these moments, it will help you overcome the trials ahead."

"Trials?" Sopie looked at Bennie and then Amyra. "What do you mean, trials?"

"We will talk tomorrow, my child," Amyra repeated. "For now, let's just enjoy this beautiful evening and then get some rest."

Showing Bennie and Amyra to their rooms, Mark and Sopie retired as well.

"What do you suppose they meant by trials?" asked Sopie.

"I don't know, but I do know Master Bennie, the master of riddles. When he says something, take heed and listen carefully." Mark took off his slippers and climbed into bed. "He does have a very serious side to him as well. I don't think they traveled all this way just to see relatives. He has something important to share with us and we will just have to wait until morning to see what it is." He leaned over to kiss Sopie. "But," he said softly, "you may have been right. You know, about things being a little *too* perfect."

"Oh, Honey," she said, "I don't know what I was saying, really." She sighed. "I think maybe you were the one who was right. I mean, why would I find fault in this life we've finally built together."

Mark turned out the light. "Maybe you're not finding fault," he said solemnly, "maybe we've just been too blind to see it."

Sopie rolled over and placed her head on his chest. "I hope not…" she whispered.

That night, Sopie re-entered the familiar territory of nightmares. Again she saw the recurring vision of the man burning alive. Just as she had seen years before without knowing, she watched as her ex-husband writhed in flames, roasting alone in a prison cell. His screams echoed so loudly through her chest she thought she'd explode. And just like in the visions she'd had before, a sinister smoke poured from William's bones. Suddenly, the smoke took form like it had during her honeymoon and that day on the lake. And before Sopie knew it, she was the one in the cage, flames surrounding her, screams had turned to hideous laughter as a black entity arose from the burning corpse. A voice, an unfamiliar voice, one that never resounded from

William's throat, taunted her. "We will be together again, Sweetie." The flames closed in around her and the cell itself was made from smoke. "Soon," the demonic voice howled, "very soon."

Sopie jolted awake, trying to scream, trying with all her might to shout—but nothing came out. She felt like she was convulsing in the darkness, wrestling with the shadows and choking on blackness.

"Honey," Mark shot up and turned on the light, "Sopie, are you okay?"

Trying to scream, putting such immense pressure on her lungs that she nearly passed out, Sopie finally managed a cough. It was thick and wet. She kept coughing and then gasping until she had caught her breath. When she finally realized where she was, she saw Mark. He didn't move and was completely silent. He simply stared at her in disbelief. Sopie looked down into her palms. They were spotted with blood and speckled with…*ash.*

---

DAWN BROKE and all sat down to a lovely breakfast. Sopie had gotten used to preparing more than yogurt and granola, even after not getting a sound night's sleep. Pancakes and sausages were on the menu this morning with fried eggs.

"Anyone like a cup of coffee?" Mark asked.

"Tea. May I have tea?" said Bennie.

"A man after my own heart," Sopie said.

"What no Twinkies?" asked Mark.

"No room," Bennie retorted sharply.

They settled in on the back porch to once again enjoy the morning sounds of the forest, when Amyra broke the silence. "May I borrow Karli for a few days? Since school will probably not begin for a couple of weeks due to the unusually high accumulation of snow, I would like to take her to the reservation to introduce her to my people."

"Okay by me," Mark said. "I'm sure Bennie and I can find our way around. Maybe we will even go do a little ice fishing."

"Or you do fishing," Bennie said with a laugh, "I ride in boat!"

"Not unless it's an ice boat, Sensei," said Mark laughing.

"By the way," Sopie said to Amyra, "you need to get used to calling me by my new name."

"Oh, that's right," Mark said. "It's Sopie now. We had it changed again to help make sure no one could find us here. Everyone in Meadow Lake knows her as Sopie Banos."

"Yes, I am afraid my real name, Karli Anna Sopoulos is a thing of the distant past. Although, Mark has always called me Sopie as sort of a pet name." She reached out to take his hand. "And I truly love my new last name and the man who shared it with me," she said beaming. "Even if he is a bit of a goof sometimes."

"I can see that," Amyra said. "The love and the goof." She smiled. "I know you two are very happy." Amyra stood and stretched. "Pack a few things and we will leave on our way shortly.

"Good thing I bring my hat and vest for fishing, just in case," laughed Bennie.

Amyra and Sopie left a short time later as Mark and Bennie gathered their gear to do a little fishing, and swapping lies.

"You remember last time we go?" asked Bennie.

"You bet I do. We caught some nice ones and had a great day at the pier," said Mark.

"Yes, you much younger then; me too." Bennie looked out at the ice that covered the lake contemplatively.

Mark began to saw a hole in the ice. "Well, let's see what a couple of old farts can do!" Bennie's thoughts were visibly interrupted. He scowled at Mark. "Old farts do nothing but smell. Why you say this?"

"It's just an expression," Mark laughed. "Forget it."

"Say what you mean and mean what you say." Bennie

fumbled around in the tackle box to prepare his line. "All not understood, although I understand all."

"You didn't understand Sopie's fish was going to be hot…" Mark liked to chide Bennie when he had the chance.

"Don't be plick! Me know," Bennie said laughing.

---

AMYRA AND SOPIE arrived at the reserve a short time later.

After parking the car, the two women hiked up a narrow dirt road towards a large hut on the hillside. "I want you to meet my father," Amyra said. "Well…he's the one who raised me as a child."

Sopie admired the simple frame structure. It was a modest but very well maintained ranch-style home with bright red shutters. Amyra referred to it as *Kikinaw* which means "our home" in Cree.

"My father's name is Chief Machk." Amyra grinned. "Do you know what that means?"

Sopie laughed. After spending so much time in the Flying Dust Nation, she had learned a fair amount of traditional Cree vocabulary. "Bear," Sopie said, fully aware of the irony.

Before the women could reach the top of the snow covered hill, the front door of the large hut swung open as if by magic.

"Ta'nsi!" shouted Amyra.

"M'on na'taw, Amyra," shouted back a booming voice. A very tall man who looked like leather filled the door frame. "Who is this you have brought with you?"

"This my dear friend, Sopie Banos."

Sopie nodded and extended her hand. "It's a pleasure."

"Oh, I have heard much about you and your work at the school. I am very pleased to meet you."

"Kinana'skomitin," said Sopie thanking him in Cree.

Amyra continued, "I will be staying a few days to show Sopie some of our ways.

"You have a good teacher, Miss Sopie. Pay close attention and you will learn much. "Ki'htwa'm ka-wa'p mit n," said the old chief, meaning he would see Sopie again soon.

"Come," said Amyra, "We have much to do." Amyra gestured for Sopie to enter the hut.

---

MEANWHILE, back at the ranch, our heroes weren't having much luck. After a long, laborious afternoon of just sitting and waiting over a hole Mark had cut in the ice, Mark said, "Come on, I have another idea for supper."

"Liquid supper?" Bennie said grinning.

"No, but that would be an excellent start."

Mark pulled out the Macallan M for the occasion. Master Bennie, upon seeing the bottle, said, "What you do, rob bank?"

"No, I have a very generous friend. I am just trying to extend that generosity to another great friend, to whom I literally owe my life." Mark poured each of them a shot in two rock glasses.

"God gave you life, I just tried to keep it going," said Bennie humbly accepting the glass with a slight bow.

They talked...and drank, for the next two hours. After about six shots of Mr. M, Mark said, "Hell, I almost forgot, we were supposed to eat dinner."

"What you fix?"

"Me not fix shit, we go," said Mark doing his best Bennie impression.

Bennie, not amused, said, "Where we go?"

"To get the best taco wrap this side of L.A."

"Sound good," Bennie said from a fog, "but I can barely walk."

"It's a good thing that we're driving then, because I can't walk either."

The two ambled out the door stumbling to the SUV and

poured themselves into the car. After fumbling with the keys, Mark finally started the engine and pulled off.

"Wee, wee wee!" shouted Master Bennie.

"Are you having that much fun?" asked Mark.

"No, Dumbass—ass--asan, I have to wee-wee!"

Mark veered to the side of the road. Bennie fell out of the car and rolled into the ditch. He stood up, finished his mission and fell back into the seat as Mark proceeded down the road.

About five miles before town, a deer jumped out in front of them and Mark swerved to miss it and ended up in the ditch once again.

"Whew, that was close. I can't believe I missed both of them."

"There was only one," said Bennie.

Mark, confused, recounted the scene in his head. After running the numbers he argued, "I distinctly saw two."

"How many fingers I hold up?" asked Bennie, extending his middle finger.

"Two, why?"

"Me drive. You can't see."

Pushing the car out of the ditch, Bennie started off just as a RCMP pulled up alongside, motioning them to pull over.

"May I see your license and registration?" requested the officer.

"I don't have license," said Bennie.

"What?" said Mark.

"I don't usually drive, but since you are drunk..."

"Have you guys been drinking?"

"No, we sip it slooow..." said Bennie.

"Okay, out of the car. I am going to have to issue a sobriety test." The officer produced a portable breathalyzer from his vest pocket. "Blow until you hear a beep."

Bennie did as instructed and nearly passed out.

"Holy crap, you just blew a 0.28! I am going to have to take you to jail."

"Do you have taco wrap at jail?" asked Bennie.

"What? No!"

"Then we not go...we go get taco wrap." Bennie gently touched the officer's forehead.

The officer said, "Well, you two drive carefully and have a nice evening. Be sure to be on the lookout for deer. They pop out when you least expect it." Then, he hopped back into the cruiser, pulled off and waved at the dynamic duo.

"Thank you officer, we be careful," said Bennie as he drove away.

"That was a neat trick," said Mark. "You haven't taught me that one, yet."

"Not for you to learn. Wife will learn, though, and keep you straight." Bennie laughed as he buzzed down the highway onto the next adventure.

---

## Chapter Nineteen

---

Amyra woke Sopie around 4 a.m. "Come, it is time for us to begin our day with meditation to clear our minds." After an hour she said, "Let us eat." And she led Sopie to a meager breakfast of yogurt, nuts, fruit and tea, which suited them both perfectly.

Then she said, "There is much for you to take in over the next three days. These things will not take time to learn because you already have the power within you. I just need to introduce them to you and explain the dangers involved. Let me start by explaining a little about who you are."

"Who I am?" Sopie looked confused. Sure, she had worn many names in her day, but she always felt like she was sure of who her true self was.

"Yes, dear. I know that you know you are an intuitive psychic, but you are so much more. You are not like most mortals. You have a twin, a mirror of yourself." Amyra smiled. "But you know already, you have found your twin flame in Mark. When you were created you two were conjoined souls."

Sopie had heard Mark use the terminology before, but he never truly explained it to her. She always liked the idea though.

"One soul," continued Amyra, "but separated at birth so you could experience the joys and pains of individual lives before coming back together and ascending to your rightful place. I and Master Bennie were at one time just like you and Mark."

Sopie scrunched her face. "And now?"

Amyra took Sopie's hands into her own. "We have ascended."

Sopie stared into her strange teacher's eyes and knew she was speaking the truth. She had seen her perform incredible miracles like that day with the bear and the bullet. "But if you have ascended, why are you here now?"

"We came to help you in your journey and then we will go back. Notice the necklace I wear. It is just like yours. Master Bennie wears one as well. It is the symbol of the twin flame."

"Then why doesn't Mark have one?"

"He did. He gave it to you to symbolize your bond. He will receive his own once he comes back with you to help another couple. You don't need to understand everything about this, but one of your main missions here was to be reunited so that the planet could heal. When you two were reunited on Earth, you emitted high frequencies that sent a healing power to the planet. If it were not for this, the planet would have died millenniums ago."

Even though Sopie had a high tolerance for accepting things she didn't understand, even this was a bit much for her. "Jeez," she said. "Now I know you're really just yanking my chain." She laughed.

"Oh?" Amyra held her hands close together as if in prayer. "Let me show you something." Closing her eyes, Amyra concentrated hard on one thought—Bennie. Suddenly, a glowing light enveloped her hands. A soft, purple hue emanated from them.

"What are you making? What's happening?"

Amyra did not open her eyes. "I'm not making anything. I'm simply changing the wavelength of the radiation constantly emitting from me. This way your mortal eyes can see what is always there."

Sopie studied the light closely.

"What you're seeing is the frequency of my heart. The electrical impulses emitted from each heartbeat, charged by the ultraviolet radiance of the stars, magnetized and grounded by the metallic core of this planet." She opened her eyes. "These are the healing frequencies. And they magnify exponentially when twins are reunited on Earth." Amyra placed her glowing hands on Sopie's cheeks.

In the span of a breath, Sopie felt a charge of love like she had never felt. Kindness and warmth rushed through her body. She felt an uncontrollable urge to heal and help, an undeniable and unquestioning love.

"Now do you believe a force like this exists? You have felt it all along, have you not?"

As if in a trance, Sopie responded with a simple, "Yes."

"And do you now see why this force is crucial for the health of the universe? How this force is the only thing that can balance the evil and cruelty in this life?"

Again, all she could say was, "Yes."

In an instant, the room went dark and the glow dissipated. "Good," Amyra said curtly. "Then perhaps now we may proceed."

Sopie blinked and shook her head as if waking from a beautiful dream.

"Do you understand that Mark has some significant powers of his own?"

"Yes," she said, clearing her throat. "He saved my life. He became…" she had to think hard about what she saw and try to describe it. "It was like…like a giant fireball. And he destroyed the hitman who was trying to kill me. And yet, somehow he can do all this, even though he is crippled."

"Oh, he has made the necessary adjustments to compensate for the deficiencies of his body. He is actually capable of moving from one dimension to another so that he can move from one place to another quickly. An adversary may see him in front of him and a split second later he is behind him. His body would not be capable of this if he stayed in this, the third dimension."

Sopie nodded and listened intently, trying to understand.

"He also has Chi power, a powerful spirit force that can literally move mountains and he has the ability to astrally project at will."

"I always knew he was amazing," said Sopie.

Amyra smiled at her student's ignorance. "You have some amazing powers as well. I believe you also saved his life on one occasion, did you not?"

"I think I may have."

"See? That is what I am speaking of. You have the power, but do not realize what you have or even if or when it is working. This we need to explore more deeply."

Amyra stopped for a moment and sipped on some tea, then continued, "I know you have walked through the portals as my spirit was there on one such occasion.

"With the bear?"

"Yes, dear. Portals literally stop time, long enough to sort out results of a situation before making a hasty mistake. As you have experienced, you can also travel through time and space…" Amyra's face grew dark. "But heed this warning: there is much danger in doing so."

"Danger, what do you mean?"

"When you traveled from New Orleans after the shooting, did you and Mark not suffer injuries as a result?"

"Yes, we did. The doctor said we had micro-fractures throughout our entire bodies. Neither Mark nor I had any idea what would have caused it. Was it due to us traveling through the portal?"

"Yes, I am afraid so. You see, you can use the portals for time and space travel, but only so many times in one human life. If your body experiences the shock too many times, you will surely die."

"That is serious. I believe I used it the first time to rescue Mark when he came back from trying to find me in Carol Stream…although, at the time, I could swear I was dreaming." Sopie remembered a vision where Mark's car nearly careened off the side of the road. In the vision, she floated like a ghost through his windshield, grabbed the steering wheel, and adjusted the car to save him. "And the second time in New Orleans…that was a jump of hundreds of miles!"

"The distance and magnitude of that experience is surely why your bodies experienced such trauma."

"Oh my god, the third time was with the bear… how many portal jumps can a body stand?"

Amyra's face was graven. "I have never seen a body survive a fourth."

Sopie felt the blood drain from her face. She felt as if she could faint at any moment. She took a deep breath and said, "Well, I am so glad you showed up when you did. I might have used it again and..."

"Perhaps…but, remember what I said, it only causes injury to the body when you use the portal for time and space travel. With the bear you merely projected your senses into the spirit realm, but stayed in the same location. There is no danger in this as long as you don't travel. The spirit can astrally project and heal itself through meditation, but the body is frail and cannot regenerate in the same way."

Sopie nodded.

"The other two instances did involve time and space. So beware, you can only use the portal once more for travel, no matter what the reason."

"Okay, I will remember."

"Remember this as well. You and Mark are twins, a reflection of each other. You see each other's strengths and weaknesses. If you lie, he will know and vice-versa. His powers are aggressive powers while yours are that from a gentle soul, a yin and a yang. That is why he had to spend years developing his powers as he had to overcome ego and his aggressive nature. You already have the powers that you possess, which are different from his. The two of you will complement each other to accomplish your mission."

"What is our mission?"

"You will figure that out once it is time. Enough for today. We will eat some supper and rest now. We continue tomorrow.

As Master Bennie woke, he placed a hand to his head. "Oh, my head feel funny. Not good for Bennie to feel this way. Walk like man with stroke."

"Here take this," Mark said, handing him a drink of scotch. "What that?"

"Hair of the dog," said Mark. "It'll fix you right up...or kill you."

"Ah, dog hair good. I remember. Time for meditation. Got to heal chakras."

So they entered a state of meditation for the next several hours, then ate some breakfast.

"Feel much better now. Dog hair and meditation did trick."

"Breakfast didn't hurt either," added Mark. "So what's on the agenda for today Sensei, more fishing?"

"I think I need to rest today. Old bones," said Bennie laughing.

Mark said, "Well, I think I will bake a cake for Sopie for her return. She loves red velvet cake. Let me see if I can find the recipe Angel typed up for me."

While he was busy in the kitchen, Bennie flipped on the TV to watch another thrilling episode of Mr. Wizard. Mark, after locating the recipe, began putting the ingredients together in the KitchenAid mixer. He turned the mixer on but nothing happened. Then he noticed he had plugged it into the bottom outlet, which was controlled by the wall switch.

He had just started to flip the switch when Bennie said, "Mark, quick, come see. Mr. Lizard show us how to make a hydrogen bomb."

Mark hurried in the living room just as Mr. Wizard launched a can into the air.

"Say…that's pretty cool. We could do that."

"No," Bennie said very seriously, "Mr. Lizard say not to try at home."

"Oh hell, what does he know? Besides, he just says that to keep kids from trying it. We are grown adults. It will be great."

"You got what we need?"

"I believe I do. I gave Vinnie a Gilbert's chemistry lab once and if I am not mistaken, it had some hydrogen pellets in it. Let me go look."

Mark came back a few minutes later with the pellets and a test tube in hand.

"Oh," Bennie said, "I not know you part-time chemist!"

Mark laughed. "Now all we need is a coffee can."

He then proceeded to empty the remaining contents of the can into the coffee canister.

"Now, I will take an ice pick and make a small hole in the top so we can light it. We don't have boards to put under it, so we will just prop it up using the test tube. I need to put the pellets in the test tube and add some water to release the gas, place it under the can and then light the top."

Bennie looked around nervously. "Mr. Lizard do this outside. Sure you want set off in the house?"

"What?" Mark said. "You want to go out there? But it's warm in here…and our booze is in here."

Bennie nodded. "Is nice house. But, then again, is nice house. Maybe too nice for bomb to go off?"

Mark just brushed him back and mumbled something about

lilly-livered chicken-hearts. Then he lit the lighter at the hole in the top and said, "Move back!"

A few seconds later, the can blew up in the air, as expected. What was not expected was that the trajectory was strategically located toward the wall switch, which turned on the power to the mixer which was set to high. The mixer began throwing red velvet cake batter all over the kitchen, from ceiling to cabinets to floor.

"Holy shit, Batman. Look at this mess!" Mark examined the kitchen and saw batter seeping into every crack and crevice.

Bennie nodded and said, "Batman think he go back and watch some more Mr. Lizard. I told you not to try at home."

"Thanks for the advice. You could lend me a hand."

"We'll clean up later. Rest now. I'm exhausted from all of the excitement. Too much for old man."

Mark just shook his head.

---

Sopie awoke to another peaceful morning of meditation at 4 a.m., followed by breakfast and more teachings with Amyra.

"Today we will start developing another hidden talent that you have—psychokinetic energy."

"Psycho what?"

"Psychokinesis, the ability to move objects with your mind."

"Whoa! That would take years for me to develop."

"Not so, you have this ability, which has lain dormant for years. All you need to do is believe you see the object move and it will move. Remember, Jesus said, 'With the faith of a mustard seed you can move mountains.'"

"We will start small." Amyra pointed to some objects in the yard behind the hut. "Use your third eye to envision this stick moving from the ground to the top of this rock. Do not over think it. Just imagine it so."

As Sopie followed Amyra's instruction, the stick flew up atop the rock.

"Oh my, I did it," said Sopie excitedly.

"See, you have always had this power. You used it once before when you were angry, but probably don't remember."

"How do you know?"

"Remember when you were all alone and had no one to talk to but your doll?"

"Yes, but..."

"I, or should I say, my spirit was there in the doll much like it was there in the portal when you went to confront the bear. When William came in and threw Effie across the room, you became so enraged that you, by using psychokinetic energy, threw him against the wall, knocking him unconscious."

"As much of a bastard as he was, I still feel bad about that."

"You would. You have a gentle spirit and do not enjoy confrontations. But if you are provoked, these powers become unleashed. My purpose today is to help you control this power, so that you can use it at will and not just when you become angry."

"Cool beans."

"What?"

"I'm sorry, that's an expression my students use when they think something is neat or special."

"Oh," said Amyra quizzically. "Now I would like you to try spending the rest of this day moving different objects at will to practice your new found skill."

"I will. Thank you so much."

"My pleasure, Atayohkan."

"What did you call me?"

"Atayohkan—your Cree name. It means spirit power or spirit being," said Amyra. "Cold Beans, eh?"

"It's…well, you'll get the hang of it," Sopie said with a laugh as she continued to work on her skill as instructed.

That evening she was invited to a special rite called the

"Wihtikokansimoowin" or the Wintigo-like dance. It was based on the mythical creature called a Wintigo that devoured humans and whose hunger was never satisfied as it grew exponentially as it ate. Most were fearsome giants growing to fifteen feet with yellowish skin and red eyes; a story that would make bad children behave.

The Wintigo was believed to have been a human being who had resorted to eating human flesh. Once he did, even if it was because of starvation, an evil spirit would take him over and transform him into the Wintigo. The human that he was became frozen inside the Wintigo and the only way to kill it was to kill the human as well. There are some stories that have the human surviving upon the death of the Wintigo...but at this particular ceremony, the elders didn't tell it that way.

The dance had one warrior lead the dance imitating the Wintigo, while the other braves imitated the hunters. This was believed to ward off the evil spirits of the Wintigo. After the dance, there was a huge feast.

"Amyra, thank you so much for allowing me to share this. It was very special for me."

"I'm glad. Rest now, my child. We have much again to do tomorrow."

<hr>

Meanwhile, the boys at home were cooking dinner and drinking a little scotch. Of course they were.

"I'm thinking pike tonight. That okay with you?

"Sounds good, partner," Master Bennie said as he leaned back in the rocker on the back porch.

"Well, don't forget, we still have a mess to clean up from this morning. After dinner you gotta help me with KP."

"Aye, KP," said Bennie. "Who's KP?"

"KP, you know, kitchen clean-up."

"Oh."

"What do you want with your fish?"

"Beans are always good."

"Beans it is. Let's see, the fish is frozen, so it will take awhile to cook and it says here in the cookbook to cook the beans for three hours after you soak them overnight. Well, since they are already in a can of water I guess they have been soaking long enough. Sopie usually cooks the fish for about 12 minutes, but hers is thawed. I guess I will just leave it frozen and cook it for three hours as well. That way, both will be ready at the same time. Let's see, it says here to pre-heat the oven to 475 degrees. I think I've got it, and that will give you and me three hours to enjoy our scotch and cigars without driving anywhere tonight. In the oven you go little fishies."

Mark sat down after pouring them a drink and lit up one of his panetellas.

"You know, I am so glad you took the time to come see me. I was afraid that your trip to Carolina would be the last time we would ever get together."

"I am always around when I am needed."

"Well, it's nice to know you can just come and visit without being needed once in awhile."

"You needed me or I would not be here."

"What do you mean, I needed you. We have it all right here. A peaceful life with the woman I love. Who could ask for more?"

"Ah Tommysan, it won't always be that way. It's just not your path. You have one more huge trial coming, one that you will not be able to overcome by yourself. This is why Amyra has taken Sopie with her; helping her to realize her full potential as I taught you so many years ago."

"But she is only going to be away a few days. It took you years to teach me."

"You were very hard-headed student. She will learn fast because she already has the power. She just needed someone to help her to realize her gifts."

"Then why are you here for me?"

"To keep your ass out of trouble."

"And you have been doing a mighty fine job of it," Mark said as he inhaled his scotch and choked. "It's been a couple of hours, I guess I had better check and see how dinner is coming. You need anything?"

"Just neglect."

Mark scratched his head and went toward the kitchen just as the smoke alarm sounded.

Smoke was billowing out of the oven. He quickly opened the door to find flames shooting forth. Grabbing a fire extinguisher, he sprayed foam all over the baking dish. When the smoke started to dissipate he saw two black forms where the fish had been.

"Shit! I wonder how that happened?"

As he was admiring the main course, his attention was drawn to the pot of beans, or I should say, pot of molten lava.

"That's gonna be hard to clean." Shouting out to the porch he said, "Bennie grab your coat, looks like it's taco wraps again tonight."

---

THE THIRD MORNING, Sopie again arose at four to meditate on the previous two day's revelations. After a light breakfast she was introduced to her third and final power.

"Today, I will put you in touch with your psychic abilities."

"But I am already aware of my psychic abilities."

"You are in touch with your intuition. You have not discovered the powers that you have beyond this. You have the ability to alter a person's thought process so you can change their course of action. All you need do is be close enough to lay your hand on their forehead, receive their thoughts and make them believe that your thoughts are theirs. Unfortunately, there is no way to practice this unless you need to use it. You will just have to take my word for it that you can do it. Remember, all you need to do is visualize what you want the person to do and they will do it, but you have to have your hand on their forehead."

"I think I understand."

"There is one more thing that you need to know. There is an evil, dark force coming toward you. I do not know where or when, or what form it may take, but you and only you can trick it and defeat it. And only you and Mark together will be able to keep it at bay forever."

Sopie had been expecting a talk like this since they arrived at the reserve. She knew instinctively that her visions and night-mares weren't just tricks of her subconscious. "It's William, isn't it? He's coming for me…"

Amyra shook her head. "This evil is no more William than you are Sopie and your twin is Mark."

Sopie turned her head to the side. "I don't understand."

"William was a human. He was born and has died. But he was home to a darkness you know all too well…his spiritual life was…complicated."

Sopie looked down at the ground.

"But," Amyra continued, "your spirit is strong. And so is your husband's. Whatever evil was manipulating William's soul has been released, but it can be stopped once more."

Revealing a crystal dagger, Amyra continued. "You will have to kill whatever form this evil spirit takes, but if you kill it in any other way except with this dagger, the evil spirit will escape from the shell that holds it and come back again. You and Mark must both have your hands upon this dagger when you strike so that the entity will be trapped inside the crystal. It is only through your combined powers that you will succeed. It is at this time that you must risk your ultimate power once more for time and space travel to carry the dagger to the glaciers up North, so that the spirit will remain forever frozen and not escape again."

Sopie was totally mystified, however, she knew that Amyra spoke the truth. " Okay," she said. "I am going to have a very difficult time trying to kill something or someone…even something that you're saying is pure evil…but I will do as you say."

"I know my child, but you will find the courage when the time comes. You must. This is your mission here. If you fail, more will be lost than just your lives."

"Amyra, I have been having nightmares recently. That's how I knew William was involved somehow… I was shown him being burned alive." Sopie trembled at the image her mind conjured. "And then this dark form appeared from the flames and spoke to me…its voice was so horrible."

"That was the evil spirit inside your ex-husband. Keep in mind, it will try to take the form of William to exploit any vulnerability you may have. It will try to use any mind game it can to trick you, but remember, your mind is stronger, especially now that you and Mark have been reunited; you two are invincible."

"Thank you Amyra, we will do our best."

"I know you will, my dear. I know you will."

"We had better head back to the cabin and check on our boys. Mark is not a very good cook and they are probably starving."

<hr>

MARK AND BENNIE were laying on the couch watching another exciting episode of Mr. Wizard when the girls drove up.

"Hi Sweetheart, I'm home. Why is the SUV caked in mud?"

"Hi! Sorry, I didn't expect you home so soon. We haven't had a chance to straighten up yet and..."

"Mark! What the hell happened? It looks like an H bomb went off in here."

"Zachary correct," chimed in Bennie.

"Honey, I can explain."

"Explain later, clean now."

"Sure, right after we finish this episode."

"Now!" as she reached for Mark's forehead.

"You know," said Mark, "I believe I've had enough TV for one day. Let's clean this mess up, Bennie."

"You clean; I'll finish show."

Amyra drew near with her hand.

"Get away from me you evil twin! Mark, I am on my way."

"Here, you will need these," Sopie said. A mop and broom miraculously flew through the air from the closet.

"Life never be same now," Bennie moaned as he started to mop the floor.

"If you two do a really good job, maybe I will take us all into town for taco wraps tonight!"

"Oh god!" both Bennie and Mark said.

---

BENNIE AND AMYRA stayed another couple of days. It was during this time that Amyra revealed to Mark what she had told Sopie.

"So, you're telling me that we will have to kill this thing using this magic sword, and we both have to hold it or it won't work?"

"Mark, not time to be plick again. Listen to Amyra's words or you both could lose your true souls."

"Alright, let me get this straight. Whatever or whoever this is, it has been possessed by an evil spirit. We have to confront it, but not kill it with anything other than this crystal dagger. We both have to hold onto it as we drive it through its heart and then Sopie has to take it to the North Pole and give it to Santa."

Bennie sighed and shook his head. "You be plick again."

"Sorry, I couldn't resist. But basically, that's it. Piece of cake."

"I seen your cake...everyone seen cake," said Bennie.

"Okay, Okay," said Mark.

Bennie and Amyra packed, loaded the car and hugged their hosts. As they said their goodbyes, Bennie turned, "This is not going to be a cakewalk, but I have faith in you two. There is more love here between the two of you than I have ever seen in my life. You can do this. This is why you were chosen for this mission. It's not impossible."

Bennie then started laughing uncontrollably. Looking at Mark he said, "You even look like old fat Tom Cruise! Bennie make funny." As he continued to laugh, he and Amyra got in the car and drove away.

Chapter Twenty
__________________

The school year had finally begun again the last week of January, and it wasn't long before everyone got back in their daily routines. Mark was busy teaching his elementary music classes and preparing for the spring concert to be held in May. He was also busy after school, assisting Coach Rhodes with the Karate Club.

Sopie returned to her duties, helping the resource teacher with the one-on-one basic student instruction to help keep the students on pace with their grade level.

Then, one morning toward the end of February a special meeting was called before classes began. An eerie hush filled the room as Ms. Hogan began.

"I am very sad to have to tell you..." tears began to stream down her face as she continued, "that our friend and colleague, Mrs. Sky Roma, was found last evening..." Ms. Hogan was choking again on the words.

The teachers in the room all shifted in their seats, fearing the worst. But none could ever in their wildest dreams guess at what she would say next.

"Sky was found in the woods near her home…dead. Her husband and children, as you can imagine, are devastated."

Murmurs echoed through the room. Some fell silent and detached while other burst out with "Oh my God!" and "What happened?"

"All we know right now…" Ms. Hogan clearly hadn't had enough time to digest the situation either. "…is that her body was…it was all torn up. The police are investigating it as a murder."

*Murder*…that was a word that left an impression on the room. No one quite could fathom what exactly it really meant, so no one said anything at all.

"I ask that you keep the family in your daily prayers. Mrs. Banos, I am going to ask you to help me cover third grade in her absence."

"Of course, Ms. Hogan."

An icy chill ran up Sopie's spine as she reflected on the morning's events. Things like this just didn't happen in Meadow Lake. What would she tell the children? Was this the dreaded event that Amyra had warned her about?

<hr>

AT RCMP HEADQUARTERS later that day, the coroner examined the body. It was mutilated beyond comprehension, like a wild animal had attacked and partially devoured the body. The coroner determined that the victim had to have been attacked by a wolf. The problem, of course, was there hadn't been any reported wolf attacks, or even sightings, in Meadow Lake for generations. However, as a precaution, and because he couldn't come up with any other alternative analysis, he decided to have the local RCMP put out a bulletin warning residents to be mindful of wolves in the area.

*THE RCMP HAS POSTED a wolf warning for Meadow Lake and the surrounding vicinity. The warning also covers campgrounds and day-use areas. This warning follows last night's brutal attack on a local citizen. The public is reminded not to approach, entice or feed wildlife and to make sure food, pet food and garbage are stored inside buildings or vehicles.*

---

"THIS IS JUST HORRIBLE, MARK." Sopie was physically and emotionally exhausted from her day at school. So much so that the normal peace she felt when resting at home with Mark wasn't enough to transport her into a state of calm. "We had better watch how we handle our garbage at home for awhile," she said practically melting into the couch.

"I agree, on both counts. Why don't we just eat in town tonight? I don't think either of us have the concentration to work a stove right now."

"Maybe, that would be a good idea." She took a long, slow sip of wine and slowly shook her head. "Although I'm not sure I can eat."

"Yeah," he said sighing, "I can understand that. How 'bout we just go by the Fidrock and get some pizza?"

"Okay by me."

After a few more relaxing moments in their tranquil sanctum, Mark and Sopie headed out to the Fidrock and placed their order. While sipping their beers, they overheard some men talking at a table behind them.

"Sounds like a Loup-garou to me," said a man with a French Canadian accent. "No wolf sightings around here for awhile. It's certainement a Loup-garou. I have heard tales of them before."

Sopie and Mark finished their pizza without a word. They were too tired to talk so eavesdropping was just easier. On the drive home Sopie said, "Mark, do you really think it could be a Loup-garou?"

"I am not really sure what that is, Hon."

Sopie said, "In New Orleans, there are stories of the Rou-garous, a person who turns into a type of werewolf at will. They search out their victims and attack them. If the intended victim is lucky enough to kill the wolf, he in turn becomes a Rou-garou for 101 days and then returns as a normal human again, unless he speaks of it. Then, he becomes a Rou-garou forever. They are not like werewolves that only turn into a wolf during a full moon, and a silver bullet will not kill them, or so I have been told."

"So what is a Loup-garou?"

"Same thing. The French were exiled from Nova Scotia and believed to have settled in New Orleans. That is why the Cajuns speak a sort of broken French dialect."

"Well, I don't want to meet up with either one. Probably old myths and legends is all."

"Maybe so, but we both know that fairy tales and monsters had to come from somewhere. And I know you of all people should be willing to accept that there are things in this world beyond our understanding."

"Touché."

Sopie sighed and rubbed her eyes. "I just wonder if this might be what Bennie and Amyra were warning us about."

"It could be. I guess we had better keep a close eye on the upcoming day's events as they unfold and more information becomes available. We certainly want to be prepared, but we don't want to overreact either."

"Sometimes I just wish they wouldn't have told us anything. I feel like every day I'm looking over my shoulder, or waiting for a building to crumble, or one of the children to…"

"Sopie…" Mark slowed the car and pulled to the side of the quiet road and reached for her hand. "I love you." He leaned over and kissed her. "Whatever is coming, whatever fate Bennie and Amyra warned us against is something we can handle together when the time comes. Trust in us."

As the car moved back onto the road, she felt a truth

blossom inside her heart and a smile grow on her face. "Let's just go home and get some rest," said Sopie. "Today has been an incredibly long day and tomorrow doesn't appear to be shaping up any better." She leaned back in her seat and said, "Thank you."

While neither had a very restful night, Sopie, once again, had a horrible nightmare.

This time it started with the formation of a dark cloud swirling through the air and materializing like a stormy ghost. She saw it hunting, creeping behind a small boy, tracking him like an animal. The smoky figure sprung forward and attacked the helpless boy with teeth like lightning, devouring him instantly. Sopie lurched forward in a sweat.

"Wha...What is it, Honey? Another nightmare?" asked Mark.

Almost too terrified to speak, she muttered, "It was too horrible to describe. I don't want to talk about it."

She got up and fixed herself a cup of tea, settling into the recliner to wait for dawn. She knew there was no more sleep for her tonight. Yet, finally she dozed off around daybreak, but of course, the alarm began to sound. Mark joined her downstairs and poured a cup of coffee.

"Rough night, huh?"

"Yeah, rough night."

"You shouldn't let old men's folklore get into your mind. It was probably just a lone wolf."

"Maybe, but you know what Master Bennie and Amyra told us. I have a bad feeling that this is just the beginning. A real bad feeling."

Mark gulped his coffee and poured another. "Look," he said gently, "I know Bennie and Amyra are very important." He put a hand on Sopie's knee. "Heck, I know that you and I are important if what Amyra explained is true. But, well, I guess what I'm trying to say is…"

Sopie looked at him patiently, but she wore a face which blended ragged anxiety and sleeplessness.

"Those two just operate on such a different timeline from us. From anyone, you know." He reached for her hand now. "So, I know you're worried, but you can't live your life up here worrying about when the next bad thing is going to happen. When you and I are supposed to be useful, we will be. Until then, we just have to wait." He sat in silent reflection while sipping on the steamy beverage.

Sopie wasn't satisfied. In fact, this answer only intensified her curiosity and anxiety. "Well, let's say it is a Loup-garou. We have the ability to kill it and prevent it from killing others, but how do we find it?"

"I don't think that is going to be the problem. I think it will find us."

"Oh." Sopie thought again of the smoky specter that stalked her nightmares. Then and there she knew that what Mark had said was right. The darkness would only reveal itself by its own cruel machinations.

When Mark and Sopie arrived at the school that morning, they soon learned that there was to be a wake for the next two days in honor of Mrs. Roma. This was a time where everyone could come and pay respects to the deceased teacher and share stories, laughter and tears with the family members, much like a traditional viewing in the U.S.

After school, they both headed for the reserve. The crowd was great. Everyone in the area was there to honor Mrs. Roma. Mr. Roma was holding up well, but the children looked so lost and didn't really understand what was going on.

Two days later, she was buried, with the marriage blanket on top of her wooden casket.

There was great sadness, but great celebration at the feast, prepared by the Roma family.

Mark, recognizing the chief, greeted him saying, "Tānisi!"

Chief Manck responded, "Tānisi kiya ? You're Cree is very good, but sounds funny."

"It's probably my Carolina accent."

"Maybe so. Tānisi Atayohkan. It is nice to see you once more. I wish it was under better circumstances. Later, after this day of mourning, you must come and talk. Both of you. I am afraid we have a great problem."

"I sense that, too," said Sopie.

"As I knew you would," said the chief.

Upon turning in for the night, Sopie began to enter an alpha state as a vision came to her.

A smoke cloud appeared, but this time it was white and Chief Machk appeared. His face grimaced as he pointed to a decaying human boneyard. A single tear ran down his cheek as he reached out his arms in quiet desperation. Suddenly, a dark cloud appeared and surrounded the chief and his village. A giant emerged and consumed the village and the chief. Then, there was nothing except a chilling voice saying, *"Beware the Wintigo."*

Again awakened, Sopie stumbled downstairs and fixed herself a cup of tea. This time Mark got up to join her, pouring himself some scotch.

She said, "We've got big trouble." Her hands were shaking so violently that the mug slipped from her grasp and crashed onto the floor. "Shit!" she screamed with more anxiety and fear than frustration. Mark rushed to her side to try and hold her or clean the mess but Sopie pushed away, pressed her back against the fridge and slid down to the floor, steeping herself in the spilled tea and porcelain shards.

Mark hadn't been this afraid since New Orleans. For the first time in a long time, he saw that look of death on his wife's face…the bags under her eyes, the color leeching out of her face, her body shaking like a kettle about to steam.

"Just stop…" she sobbed.

Mark squatted down next to her and let her lean into his shoulder.

"Real trouble," she said. "I'm not sure we can…" She screamed into his chest, "can handle this, but we…"

"We have to," Mark said calmly. "We have to, because no one else can."

Sopie looked up and wiped her eyes. She had a crazy glare on her face of one part admiration and one part *who the hell do you think you are?*

"Look, I know it's not what either of us signed up for, but how bad can it be?"

She rolled her eyes. How could he still not be listening to her? "Bad Mark, real bad. I am afraid, really afraid. Not for my life, but for those around us. We need to stop this thing and we don't even know what it is. By the time it finds us, I am afraid it will be too late for many others. Promise to make me call Vinnie tomorrow and tell him not to come home under any circumstances. I can't do this if I have to worry about his family's safety too."

"I will be beside you dealing with whatever we have to deal with. I ain't no Firkin Percy woman!"

Laughing she said, "I know that. Let's try to get some rest. We will just take it as it comes." And they headed back upstairs, leaving the mess for the morning.

## Chapter Twenty-One

The next afternoon, little Clark Medina, a fourth grader, walked from school through the woods toward home as was his custom.

He would take turns skipping, running, walking and balancing like a high wire performer on tree trunks that had fallen. He decided this day to go down to the lake and skip a few rocks before proceeding on his journey home. Finding some really smooth flat rocks, he began to skip them across the lake.

"One, two, three, four, five, six, seven, eight, nine, ten, ELEVEN!" he yelled like he had just won the Olympics. "Yeah!" Clark shouted.

"That's really good!" a voice came from behind.

"Thanks." Turning to see who had spoken, he saw no one.

Clark shrugged it off and went on his way, venturing farther into the woods.

Approaching the old logging road, he again began to skip and sing one of the silly songs he'd learned in school.

*Wintigo, where did you go?*
*I want to see your whiteness and your sourdough*

*Wintigo, Canadian Albino*
*He always dances a jig*
*Before he strikes his death blow...*

Suddenly, the branches in the woods began to sway and creak. An eerie fog replaced the sky above him as a chilling breeze blew through and carried Clark's cap off his head. As the little boy chased after the hat, he lost sight of all the bends in the road. Before he knew it, he was turned around and not sure of his surroundings. As he tried to find his way back to the logging road, Clark came face to face with a growling wolf. He could feel his chest tighten and his heart race as he tried to think of what to do next. Nervously backing away, he reached down slowly to pick up a stick to use as a club to fight off the wolf, if necessary. Cold sweat beaded down the little boy's neck as fear consumed him. There was a sudden calm in the forest, as time stood still. The two adversaries stared at one another uncertain as to who would make the first move. Frozen in his tracks, Clark waited for the wolf to strike. But the wolf didn't move. Instead, it suddenly turned and took off back into the forest. Confused, Clark breathed a sigh of relief and his heartbeat started to calm.

*"Nice job scaring that wolf off."*

Clark heard the voice in his head congratulating him on his bravery. Or did he? Didn't matter...his heart started to race as fear took control once more. He then began to run in the opposite direction toward home when he crashed right into something giant and solid. "Ouch—ahh jeez!" His glasses went flying from his face and Clark felt around on the ground for them. He felt what must have been the gnarled and bulging roots of the tree he collided with. Patting around further, still humming his Wintigo song to calm his nerves, Clark finally regained his glasses. As he did, he noticed that the roots seemed to wriggle and writhe. Putting the glasses back on his face, he saw that these were not roots at all...but hideous and huge claws that stretched out in front of his kneeling body. Looking up, Clark saw a towering, snarling monster. It looked like some mangled mixture of wolf and man covered in smoldering, snowy ash.

"Am I white enough for you, son?" The voice was like a chorus. There was one horrible body, but many sounds echoed from within it. All were horrible.

Clark tried to scream, but his lungs were frozen solid. He crawled backwards slowly, but the monster took one slow step and towered over him once more. Clark could see its terrible twisted jaws, how they drooled a combination of spit and blood.

In that moment, Clark found his feet. He jumped up and ran with all of his might.

And in that moment, the Wintigo leapt. With its sharp nails, it pinned little Clark to the forest floor, piercing through his baby fat just for the pleasure of making him scream.

"Arrrgh...Noooo! Help!"

But the cries only lasted for a moment. The sound that rang out loudest in the woods wouldn't be the boy's screams or his fearful tears, but the *snap* of his tiny neck.

The Wintigo grumbled and growled. "Still hungry. Gotta find more food. But I like the song."

*Wintigo, where do I go?*
*I want to eat your white meat on some sourdough*
*Wintigo, I'm not white but high yellow*
*I always dances me a jig*
*Before I strike my final death blow...*

"And down the road me go," as he proceeded toward the Flying Dust First Nation Reserve.

---

WHEN CLARK DID NOT arrive home from school that evening, his parents were extremely concerned. He was always home by now and was very dependable. The tribe gathered the men of the village together to set out on a search for the boy while there was still light. They retraced what should have been his path on the way home from school. When they got to the lake, they discovered his tracks in the mud by the banks of the lake as well as an old ball cap that he wore.

There was no sign of Clark though. A few feet later, they found some rather large animal tracks that appeared to be from a wolf, and yet diffferent. The tracks were in pairs, like a man's, but not a man. A hush consumed the men as one dared whisper, "Wintigo."

Later that evening, the Elders of the tribe met to discuss the missing boy and the discovery by the lake. The chief addressed the Elders and shared a vision his daughter had seen concerning this.

"While Amyra was visiting us, she told me she had seen an evil spirit come upon a man, who had been lost in the forest while trapping with his friend. Winter had set in and their food was gone. He killed his friend and ate his flesh in order to survive. This evil spirit then took control of this man, who turned into a Wintigo. I believe this Wintigo is now in our presence. We must hunt and kill him before he kills us."

The Elders agreed that this was the only possible explanation, so they devised a plan to send a hunting party out at first light.

"This is a very powerful being," said the chief, "we have to warn the men that he could stand as high as 15 feet tall, and moves so fast as is able to transport himself through time and space. He is very dangerous and his hunger will never be satisfied." After preparing the men, they set out to hunt for the Wintigo.

However, the Wintigo is also a very intelligent creature and very evasive. Peering down at the village, the Wintigo thought, *"Hmm,...time to find a snack."* He headed toward the nearby stream.

About that same time, two Aboriginal women were drawing

water from the stream to prepare for that day's washing of clothes.

Rosa turned to Sue and remarked, "It is very chilly this morning. My hands are frozen."

"It is especially so with this wind whipping through the trees. And it is very cloudy. I expect we may see more snow later today," said Sue looking up toward the clouds.

Spying the two women, the Wintigo thought, *"They will do nicely if they just move a little closer."*

As they finished gathering the water, they turned to head back to the building that was used to launder the clothes in the village. A dense black fog blanketed the stream as a sudden gust of wind caught the two by surprise.

"Lord, what is that stench?" said Rosa. "It smells like a rotting carcass."

*"Closer…just a few more feet."*

Sue turned to address Rosa, suddenly transforming her native dark skin into an ashen hue, as she dropped her bucket, unable to speak.

"What is it?" said Rosa turning to look back over a shoulder that suddenly disappeared into the creature's mouth.

"Oh my God. Help me!" screamed Rosa. But it was much too late for help to arrive as the Wintigo quickly devoured his prey.

Turning his attention toward Sue, the Wintigo crept forward as she took off running. Sue caught the toe of her shoe on a root and went crashing headlong down the ravine and into the stream. As she struggled to regain her footing, the swift razor of the Wintigo's claw severed her head, leaving her body flapping wildly in the stream until it became limp and lifeless.

The Wintigo sat down watching with amusement.

*"River Dance! I had no idea she was Irish,"* he thought as he savored his second victim.

THE SCENE WAS HORRIFYING. Parts of their bodies were discovered downstream later that morning as some of the children were walking the banks on their way to school.

The Elders then decided that it was too dangerous for the children to go to school any longer and contacted Ms. Hogan to explain their absence.

The RCMP arrived a short time later to retrieve the bodies, or what was left of them, and to take statements from the hysterical children who found them. They were also told of Clark's disappearance the night before.

"It's still looks like the work of a lone wolf," said one officer, "a hellish animal. I've never seen anything like it."

The Elders in the tribe just kept silent, knowing this was one part of their world that the white men could never hope to comprehend.

WHEN MARK and Sopie arrived at school that morning, there was an eerie silence. None of the usual laughter or children running. In fact, there were no children at all.

"Did we miss something on our schedule? Is this a special celebration day or a teacher's workday?" asked Sopie.

"I don't have a clue. Let's go inside and see."

Walking down the usually crowded hallways, they saw the other teachers gathering in the library for a meeting.

"Come on in you two," said Miss Martsey. "Ms. Hogan has a special announcement to share with us."

The three of them ambled into the library to join the others. The room was filled with the same voicelessness that had greeted them at the door. Then Ms. Hogan began to speak. "Last night one of Mrs. Sinclair's students, Clark, disappeared while walking home from school. After a diligent search, all that was found was his ball cap and tracks of what appeared to be a wolf."

A gasp filled the library.

"Oh God," Sopie whispered as she headed for the bathroom. She returned a few moments later and apologized and composed herself.

"It's okay, Mrs. Banos. We are all very upset by this and understand your reaction. You were quite close to Clark, working with him each afternoon. That is also why Mrs. Sinclair is not here."

Continuing, Ms. Hogan said, "For the immediate future, we will be closing school as there is imminent danger on the reserve at this time. Two other women were discovered this morning near a stream. I will spare you the details, but let me forewarn all of you, that this is a very dangerous situation. Be very careful when out of doors and do not leave food outside your homes. Lock up your classrooms before you leave. I will be in touch with you to keep you posted. Please stay safe and pray for those families in the village."

---

MEANWHILE, in town the rumors were flying about a great wolf.

"Yeah, I seen him the other night when it was a full moon."

"Sounds like a Loup-garou."

A gasp fell across the room.

"Do you really think it so?" said one of the patrons at the tavern.

"Me think it so," said the French Canadian, "I have heard men tell of this before in the timberlands to the north, but not here. It must be so..."

"What are we going to do about it?"

"I do not know what you are to do, but me, I will hunt it and kill it," said the French Canadian.

"Bullshit," said the man a few seats down at the bar.

"You calling me a coward?"

"Non, but Whiskey Jack you ain't."

"Maybe not, but with these I can even the odds, no?"he said holding some silver bullets in his hand. "These will do the job, if it is a Loup-garou, or not. I will set out tomorrow at first light. Who is with me?"

Two brave or drunk souls, or fools, said, "Yeah, I will go with you."

"Tomorrow morning it is," he said finishing his shot in a gulp and heading out the door.

As morning broke, the old French Canadian gathered up the other two men in the jeep and headed out on the old timber trail.

Stopping in the ravine near the lake, he said, "Time to get out. We will head out in three separate directions. That way if we see anything, we can shoot knowing where the other two are."

They started walking slowly in the woods, careful to listen for any change in the sounds around them. About 11:30, one of the two other men came across the walkie-talkie.

*I think I have located the wolf's lair and her pups.*

The other men approached the direction in which the other had ventured. As they approached, they heard him screaming and the wolf growling.

"Hold on, we're coming!" shouted the French Canadian as he ran to the sound of the screams. When he arrived, he saw the wolf tearing and shredding at the man withering on the ground. The French Canadian raised his rifle and took aim. "Boom!" He killed the wolf with one shot. Then he yelled, "Quick! Let's get this guy to the hospital before he bleeds to death."

"What about the wolf?"

"We will come back for him. He's not going anywhere."

They rushed to town to get help for the other man, but to no avail. He bled out before they could reach the hospital.

Dropping his body off at the morgue, they returned to pick up the wolf's carcass. They then noticed that this was a huge, female wolf, not a Loup-garou at all. She was merely trying to protect her pups.

"Looks like all of this folklore just got everyone all stirred up. Seems as if people were just at the wrong place at the wrong time. Much to do about nothing," the old French Canadian said.

"Well, let's take it back into town. It may settle some nerves."

When they arrived in town carrying the wolf, there were cheers along the side of the road. The great fear and destruction the people of Meadow Lake had experienced had finally come to an end and life could get back to normal. Maybe.

---

SCHOOL REOPENED and the children soon forgot the tragedies of the winter months. Spring lay ahead as did Mark's spring concert.

Sopie joined him for lunch one day when he had duty.

"How is the production going?"

"Perfect, as expected. I think it will be even better than last year's."

"I'm sure it will be stupendous!" she grinned.

"Thanks. I'm just glad there is going to be a concert. For awhile I wasn't sure if we were even going to have school."

"I still feel uneasy about it. And I miss little Clark so much."

"I know, but at least they caught and killed the wolf that caused all of this and thankfully it was not a Loup-garou, but just a big wolf. So much for Indian superstition and lore."

"I'm still not so sure. It was not a wolf I saw in my vision. I only hope I am wrong."

"Maybe your vision was clouded."

"Maybe...anyway, we should stay on our toes for awhile to come. We might ought to carry that dagger with us in the car as well. Amyra said to keep it close."

"I hope we don't have to use it."

"Me too."

EVERYTHING WENT PRETTY WELL over the next two months. The town had settled back into its normal activities and the folks who lived there had all but forgotten the consuming fears that had plagued the winter months.

Mark's spring concert was a rousing success and the school's closing ceremonies were about to commence. Parents were arriving to share in the celebration that unusually foggy morning in June. The sky was dark with an eerie hue that threatened the day with storms.

"I hope this weather holds and doesn't spoil our celebration," said Ms. Hogan to Rocky Rhodes as they greeted the parents.

"I hope so too, but the sky does have an ominous hue to it. It looks as if we might get a really bad storm before too long."

Just then, Mark joined them, pinching his jacket collar around his neck.

"Whew, this is some chill for June. It looks like we may have to cut the celebration a little short today if this weather doesn't hold."

"We'll see," said Ms. Hogan.

As Rocky and Ms. Hogan approached a couple of parents, Mark caught a glimpse of movement through the fog. Turning, he saw nothing and dismissed it. He then rejoined the duo to greet more parents as they entered the school.

The children were all in their respective classrooms along with their teachers and Sopie was still filling in for third grade. They were getting ready for a final assembly in which they would receive their academic achievement awards for the year and then share in the cake and ice cream that would follow.

The parents were filling the auditorium just as the rain began to start.

"Oh dear," said Ms. Hogan, "Let's hurry the parents in

before this storm gets any worse. I will go in and get prepared to begin if you two will finish escorting our parents."

"Sure thing, Ms. Hogan," said Rocky.

As they approached the facade of the school, Mark began to smell an odor that at first smelled like a gas leak. But as he proceeded out of the front of the school, it started to permeate the area as the stench grew stronger. Something about it reminded him of a dream he once had, or thought he had. It smelled like the anesthetic stench of floating between two worlds, the smell of seeing himself on an operating table all those years ago.

"What the hell is that?" asked Rocky holding his nose.

"Smells like a skunk. I can't see anything in this fog and rain."

Suddenly, the blunt force of a fist struck Mark in the back of the head. It felt like a sledge hammer. Dazed and looking up, he saw the figure of a giant of a man saying, "Out of my way, Banos. I will be back to deal with you later."

The Wintigo moved quickly inside and down the hall to look for Sopie. He used his inter-dimensional abilities to escape detection once inside the school.

"I know you're here!" he shrieked moving down the hallway. "I have been waiting to see you for so long, Sweetie. Don't make me wait too long." The legion of voices demanded and growled all at once.

Locking the classroom door, Sopie instructed her students, "Remain calm and quiet and listen to me very carefully. Everyone get under your desks and cover your heads with your arms."

Then an eerie fog started to come underneath the door sill. It continued until it completely engulfed the room. Then, there was that stench...the smell of death.

*BOOM!* The door flew open and the Wintigo leapt inside. *"Say Kids! Do you know what time it is? It's Howdy Doody Time! How...dy Doody!"*

The terrified children screamed and cried from beneath their desks trembling at the sight of the Wintigo.

Sopie knew what she needed to do. She trusted her immense powers, her honed abilities, her training. She could see a stronger version of herself reach out immediately and put her hand on the creature's forehead to use her psychic mind control.

But this Sopie, the one in the moment she had been dreading for months, could do nothing. She felt the same heaviness in her legs, the same concrete quicksand in her joints, as she did that day on the boat. The smoke in the room hid the real her—it only let her fear show through. Paralyzed, she could only imagine a younger version of herself, as if she were swirling through a wormhole, devolving into a weaker person, slowly becoming unborn.

"What's the matter, hmm? You don't like my jokes anymore?" The Wintigo clutched Sopie's hips with his rotting claws and burrowed his eyes into hers.

She felt that helplessness again, that powerlessness of being taken over. She was reliving every painful touch, every hot breath on her neck, every bit of blood that oozed from tender spots when she was trapped in her first violent marriage. But suddenly, her body moved. It remembered who she had become even if her mind was locked in a state of fear. She thrust her palm to the creature's forehead, intent on ending this.

He laughed at her and said, "This idiot is no longer in control of his body…I am!" He snarled and licked his lips. "Just like I'm in control of *yours* again." He dug his nails into the top of her thighs and raised her up high, drooling from his awful mouth. Holding her with one hand, the Wintigo struck Sopie with the back of his hand, knocking her unconscious.

Sopie awoke to find herself tied to a chair. "Now you can watch as I devour each child before seeking my revenge upon you. Maybe this will teach you a lesson, Sweetie."

Oh that voice. One of the voices…Sopie, too, heard a cacophonous chorus of sinister voices echo from the creature.

But this one, it was all too familiar. It was William's voice, her ex-husband.

"You sound like William, but you can't be William. William's dead."

"You didn't think death could hold me did you?" The creature taunted her relentlessly, just like William did in life.

The children were terrified. They cowered under their desks, crying hysterically at what they were witnessing.

Laughing hideously, the Wintigo jeered, "Now let me see...who will be the first? Let me use my magic mirror to see if I can find just the right one." And then he chanted, "*Romper Bomper, Stomper Do, Show Me Who? Well now...I see David and Charles...and Theresa and... oh yes...little Brooke. Come closer Brooke. This is your lucky day...you get to go FIRST!*

CONFUSED AND DAZED, Mark thought of the dagger in the car. Rocky saw his friend lying on the ground and rushed to help him.

"What the hell happened?" he asked.

Mark stumbled trying to get up, "No time to explain. Just help me up and get me to my car. I've got to save the children..."

"From what? What do you mean?"

"Please, just help me."

Rocky did as he was asked and Mark started the SUV, gunned it and tore into the front of the school, scattering everyone inside. Turning the vehicle down the hall toward Sopie's room, he grabbed the dagger and jumped out heading down to the third grade classroom.

Mark arrived at Sopie's room to find her door had been locked. He laid down the dagger and used his Chi power to separate himself from his body to smash through the door. It ripped from its hinges in an explosion that startled the Wintigo forcing him to drop Brooke on the classroom floor.

Mark then sent a horde of psychic yellow jackets toward the creature.

"No Mark! Don't kill him. It will release the evil spirit within. You know what we have to do."

Mark bent down to grab the crystal dagger as the Wintigo disappeared and reappeared behind him throwing him to the ground.

Diverting the Winitgo's attention from Mark, Sopie yelled, "Okay, William, you can't hold me either." Using her kinetic powers, she worked feverishly to untie the ropes binding her.

The Wintigo flew into a rage. The jaundice skinned creature with its terrifying red eyes, burst toward her, his stench permeating the classroom. She once again used her psychokinetic energy to lift a school desk and launch it into him.

"Quick Mark, bring the dagger to me!" she yelled.

Just as she placed her hand on the dagger with Mark still holding it, the creature made one last lunge and impaled himself through the heart. The evil spirit inside the man was quickly consumed inside of the crystal dagger by a fiery, white light.

"Mark, stand back," Sopie said, "I must finish this."

Mark did as instructed and Sopie and the dagger disappeared through a portal. She journeyed through to the other side of the portal and found herself in the northern glaciers, where she buried the crystal dagger as she had been instructed to do. Once she had done this, she went back though the portal, which again opened in the school. There, she collapsed on the floor next to the frozen corpse of the old trapper that had been inside the Wintigo.

"Sopie, no!"

Ms. Hogan had already alerted the Medevac, which transported Sopie and Mark to St. Paul's Hospital in Saskatoon.

At the hospital, Sopie was rushed to ICU. She was still comatose. A battery of tests were run.

Mark was checked out and released in the ER, with a mild

concussion, one broken bone in his wrist, which had already started healing, and a number of cuts and abrasions. He raced toward the ICU to see Sopie. The doctors were just returning with the blood results. Looking solemn one said, "I am afraid her white blood cell count is through the roof." The doctor paused as if that was enough.

Mark looked puzzled. "White blood cells? What does…"

"Mr. Banos," the doctor said, "I'm afraid your wife has leukemia. I won't know how bad it is, or what type it is until we run further tests."

"Leukemia! How can this be? She has never had any signs."

"Sometimes it just comes on later in life. We'll know how severe it is in a few days. In the meantime, it looks like you could use some rest yourself, eh?"

"I'm not leaving her side. I will be here when she wakes up."

"Suit yourself."

While in the coma, Amyra appeared to Sopie and said, "Rest, my child. You will be fine. You did what I knew you could. Now rest, just rest."

Two days later, Sopie woke up. Mark jumped to her side, "Sweetheart! I knew you would be back."

"Back from where?"

"You are in the hospital. You have been in a coma for the last three days."

"Three days! Well, I guess I needed a little rest."

"Yes, that's all you needed, a little rest," he said, gripping her hand tightly.

"May I have some tea? And...I'm starving."

"You betcha'. Let me get a nurse."

The nurses came in astounded by her recovery, checking vitals, drawing more blood...but no tea.

One of the nurse's finally brought in some hot water and a bag.

"Lipton?" Sopie said.

"Sorry Miss, this is not a five-star restaurant," said the nurse.

"I'm sorry, too. I get a little cranky when I don't have my tea and it seems as if I may not have had a cup in awhile," said Sopie.

As she was sipping on her tea, a doctor appeared and asked the nurse to draw Sopie's blood again.

A little while later, a CNA came in with some yogurt and fruit.

"Oh, goody, just what the doctor ordered. Oops. There I go again. Sorry."

Devouring the yogurt, she turned to Mark and said, "See, I knew we could do it. Hope we didn't make too much of a mess."

"No, just the usual carnage and destruction." Mark choked on his own laughter. "Only you would worry about cleaning up our mess."

"Well, if not us, then who?"

"I don't know, but I hope it is not poor old Earnest. If it is, they won't be able to open the school back up for the next ten years."

Now Sopie was laughing and slowly singing, "Dah ump dah ump pa domp pa omp pa ompf," to the tune of *Bringing Home a Baby Bumblebee.*

They were both rolling with laughter when the doctor again came in.

"Good to see you doing so well, Mrs. Banos, especially after I diagnosed you with leukemia two days ago. However, as strange as this is, there is no sign of the disease now. I have had the tests run twice to be sure. Only thing I can figure is that the trauma must have caused the white bloods cells to elevate temporarily. Never seen anything like it. Everything else says you have the body of a twenty-year-old."

"I'll vouch for that," said Mark grinning and still holding Sopie's hand tightly.

"I mean, I can't stress how unusual this is. In fact," the doctor said, "I would love it if you wouldn't mind granting me your consent to write your case as an article for the Journal of

Oncology. Your recovery is something just simply…." he paused searching for the right word.

"Miraculous," Mark filled in, looking into the eyes of his twin flame.

The doctor, feeling a bit embarrassed at his over-exuberance, muttered a bit and said, "Erm, uh, yes, so, get some rest and I will have you released and ready to go home this afternoon."

"Wonderful. Thank you, Doctor."

Meanwhile the tribal Elders were having a meeting concerning the past few day's events.

Old superstitions had taken hold of the people of the village and of the town as well.

"These two are not normal human beings. They have got to be powerful spirit beings, good or evil, I do not know. All I do know is that they possess supernatural powers and our people are more afraid of them than they were the Wintigo."

"But they saved us from the Wintigo, at great peril to themselves. Mrs. Banos is still in the hospital."

"I know, but the children will be traumatized for the rest of their lives seeing what they saw."

"But is that their fault? If they had not done what they had done, the children surely would have perished!"

"But how did the Wintigo come to our reserve to begin with? Mr. Rhodes, who was following Mr. Banos, said he overheard Mrs. Banos call the monster William. Did she know the evil spirit within him? Did he follow them here to Meadow Lake?"

"Yes, and how did Mr. Banos knock down that steel door to the classroom? Mr. Rhodes said it was like he used plastic explosives, but where did he get those or why would he have them?"

"True, but he also said Mr. Banos just stood there as the

door exploded as if in a trance. This was after he appeared to run down the hallway. I thought Mr. Banos was crippled and walked with a cane. How can this be?"

"I don't know. The children reported that as soon as Mrs. Banos untied herself, desks started to fly around the room until one struck the Wintigo. How is this even possible? Did she not think this was dangerous and could have hurt the children?"

"And what about Mr. Banos plowing his car through a crowd of parents? What purpose could that have served if he had hit one of them?"

"And what happened to the mysterious, crystal dagger that Mr. Banos, according to Mr. Rhodes, wielded against the creature. How did he just happen to have that in his car? And how did they know this would be the way to kill the Wintigo?"

"I just think there has been enough fear and sadness in our little town. I think it is time for the Banos' to leave and go *help* someone else."

The council of Elders decided that this is what would be best for the village. They decided also that if the Banos' were to agree to leave peacefully, they would offer them a fair price for their property as they needed a new council meeting hall.

The old chief, Machk, although knowing what had really transpired and the truth about the Banos', remorsefully agreed to do as the council had requested. He then, contacted Ms. Hogan at the school to tell her of the council's decision.

"I don't know what to think," said Ms. Hogan. "They always seemed so nice and gave so much of their time to work with the children. But in the aftermath of the last few days, I can see your point. They would be a constant reminder of what happened here. We have got to move forward and get beyond this. I will meet with them once Mrs. Banos returns from the hospital."

WHEN THE BANOS' returned from Saskatoon, they passed the school to find a tarp covering the entrance that Mark had plowed their SUV through.

"I have a feeling someone is going to be pretty mad about that. I wonder if our insurance will pay for any of the damage. Didn't really consider that at the time."

Sopie said, "I can't imagine why," and then breathed a sigh of relief. "At least everyone is safe and we can start getting our lives somewhat back to normal."

As they approached the cabin, there was a car in the driveway that she didn't recognize. Once they got out of their car, they saw Ms. Hogan exit the vehicle in the drive along with Chief Machk.

Sopie greeting them saying, "Thank you so much for coming to see how we are. This is certainly an unexpected pleasure. Won't you come in?"

"Thank you, Mrs. Banos."

After everyone was seated in the living room, Sopie offered drinks to her guests.

"No, thank you," said Ms. Hogan, "We won't be staying long. I guess I need to get right to the point. No sense in beating around the bush. The council of Elders is afraid that you two represent a danger to their children. At the very least, they feel you would be a daily reminder of the events at the school. That is something we just must push past."

"So, what are you saying?" asked Mark.

"We just feel that, even though you have done so very much for everyone here, it might be better if the two of you resigned your positions at the school. I don't think we would ever want a repeat of this past month's events."

"I see and I understand the council's fears," said Sopie sadly.

"And I am here, also at the council's request," said the old chief reluctantly. "They want me to offer you a fair price for your property, in hopes that you will decide to leave."

"You want us to move away? We love it here!" said Mark.

"It might be for the best," interjected Sopie.

"What?" Mark replied.

"You two talk about it and decide. I know the truth of what you did, and it was quite heroic and this is a sorry way for us to treat you. We should be having a victory celebration and yet we try to run you out of town because of superstition. It's not right, but if you stay, it will never be the same for you here," said the chief getting up to leave. "I will be back in touch in a few days to hear of your decision. Goodbye, Atayohkan."

"Alright. Goodbye Chief. Goodbye, Ms. Hogan," said Sopie.

After they left, Sopie turned to Mark and said, "Well, this is certainly not what I expected to come home to." She couldn't help but let hot tears flood her eyes. "I guess my psychic channel must be down."

"Well, we are getting older and we have talked about retiring back to Carolina one day. It might be time," said Mark, putting his arms around his beloved.

"Maybe. I just hate leaving Vinnie, Angel and my soon to be grandson in Toronto, but when you get down to it, it's really no farther away than we are now," said Sopie.

"Right! We've been over this before. It's over 2,000 miles from here and only a little more than 800 miles from Atlantic Beach. That's less than half as far," said Mark. "We would probably get to see them more often, plus, we're both getting too old for this cold weather up here anyway. If the council is willing to buy us out, that makes it all the easier on us. I say let's do it!"

"Wither thou goest, my ardent traveler, I will go. I'm in."

"Ok, it's settled. Let's start packing up!"

"Whoa, Zebediah. How about a glass of wine first?"

"Okay, sure, sure. What was I thinking?"

## Chapter Twenty-Two

$\mathcal{B}$ecause of the whiplash from their emotional roller coaster ride over the last several months, Mark and Sopie had all but forgotten that their lives would change dramatically in yet another way—they'd be grandparents shortly.

"Call Vinnie and find out what's going on," Mark said as they set out on their new journey.

Sopie squinted through her reading glasses at her phone while Mark piloted them across the great Canadian highway. "Hi, Honey. What's the news? Wait, wait…I want to put you on speaker phone so Mark can hear too." She fumbled with the screen a bit more.

"Hi, Vinnie!" Mark said overly cheerfully.

"Say 'Hi' Honey."

"Hi, Honey," Vinnie said with a giggle. "No news yet, Mom. Angel is two weeks overdue and they are going to put her in the hospital tomorrow to try and induce labor. If that doesn't work, they will have to do a C section. We're both really worried. I wish you and Mark were here."

"Good news," Mark shouted with one finger pointed towards the sky—not that Vinnie could see the gesture.

"We are actually on our way," Sopie said reassuringly. "I promise, Honey, everything is going to be fine. You'll see."

"Really, Mom? That's great, thank you both. I will see you when you get here."

"Love you, Honey. Goodbye."

"Wow."

Sopie sighed. "We couldn't have timed this trip any better."

"Always right on schedule," said Mark. "Banos' to the rescue!"

Three days later, they arrived at the hospital in Toronto to find Angel nursing her newborn son.

Unable to contain his excitement at the thought of a young new whipper-snapper to corrupt, Mark burst in the door with a celebratory, "Hi ya, Sonny Boy!"

"Hi Angel," said Sopie with a bit more tranquility. "How are you doing?"

"I'm a little tired, but no worse for the wear. They didn't have to do a C section." She smiled a pitiful pale smile. "I was able to have him a couple of hours after they induced labor. Isn't he beautiful?"

"Yes he is." Sopie felt a warmth flood through her skin followed by a twinge of timidity. Can I...I mean, do you mind if...?"

Angel smiled and lifted Sonny just enough for Sopie to grab ahold of him. "Of course you can hold him, Nan."

"Come here, big boy," said Sopie to the giggling and cooing baby. "Oh, you're so happy aren't you? You should be with having such wonderful parents and grandparents."

"Speaking of parents," Mark said, "where's Vinnie?"

"He went down to the cafeteria to get me a cup of tea. Should I call him and get him to bring you one, Sopie?"

"No, thank you. Between Mark's driving and my nerves I've

had enough tea today to where I could just explode. I am definitely ready for some wine and shut-eye, though."

Mark poked around the room a little bit and noticed a styro-
foam tray. He nosed out the door a bit and peaked down the
hallway."The hospital cafeteria sure brings back memories for
me. If it wasn't for withstanding the bad coffee there, I might
never had found Sopie again."

"Really? I thought you two met at the beach?"

Mark laughed. "Sometimes love is meeting the same person
over and over again. But, that's another story for another day."
He put his arm around Sopie's shoulders. "You look like you
could use a little rest yourself. We'll come back a little later after
we've had the chance to shower and rest some."

"Tell Vinnie we'll see him later when we get back," said
Sopie handing Sonny back to Angel.

"I will. See you later." They were nearly out the door before
Angel said, "And guys, thanks for coming. It really means a lot.
To both of us."

Mark and Sopie checked into a hotel near the apartment so
that they wouldn't crowd the new parents. After showering and
having a cocktail, they rested for the remainder of the
afternoon.

Upon waking, they decided to catch a quick bite for dinner
downstairs at the hotel restaurant and then head back over to
the hospital. Once in the maternity ward, they looked through
the glass at all of the babies and quickly spotted Sonny just
grinning.

"Babies are so cool. No problems, just happy to be alive,"
said Mark.

Sopie stared through the glass at all the little lives waiting to
blossom. She watched as proud fathers came by, admiring the
features of themselves and their spouse they could see in the
newborns. Suddenly, a wave of emotion came over
Sopie. "Yeah…"

"Hey," Mark said, taking his wife's hand in his own. "What's the matter?"

"Nothing," Sopie said, feeling a pressure behind her eyes. "It's stupid but, I was just thinking how nice it would have been to have had children with you."

Mark looked confused. "Well, we have Vinnie," he said. "And now Angel and a new baby. I don't think we could have done any better."

Sopie smiled. "You're right. I can't imagine it nicer if they were of my own flesh and blood."

Mark kissed her on the forehead. "Family's not about flesh and blood. It's about love."

As they headed back to Angel's room, they bumped into Vinnie coming out of the door.

"There he is," Sopie exclaimed. "Come here my beautiful boy!" Sopie ran to him and threw her arms around Vinnie's neck. "We are so proud of you."

Vinnie laughed and thanked her with a kiss on the cheek.

"Your mother's right," Mark said. "Congratulations. Now get out the way so I can see my grandchap!"

Vinnie clapped a hand onto Mark's shoulder. "You'll have to wait a little bit. Nurses are taking vitals and all the jazz that they do."

"That's fine. How are you, Honey?"

"Me? I'm on cloud nine! I'm a Dad." Vinnie's face lit up like a Christmas tree. "Can you believe it? Me, I'm a Dad."

"Well," Mark said sternly, "you're a father now. That's nothing really special. Anybody can be a father."

Vinnie's face was all twisted up. He was equally confused and hurt.

Mark put his arm around him and said, "You'll become a Dad when you teach your kid to fish and help him with his homework and go to baseball games and *all that jazz*," imitating Vinnie and giving him a wink.

Then with the air cleared, they both had a laugh.

"So how is business? Have we made any money yet?"

"Close," Vinnie said.  "We just sealed the deal in Saskatoon."

"Man, that's great.  I knew this would catch fire."

"That's wonderful, Honey.  I am so proud of you."

Vinnie said, "Let me go in and see if Angel can see us."

A few minutes later, Vinnie came back and said, "I hate this, but it's time for her to nurse the baby.  Can you guys come back tomorrow?"

"Sure Honey, it's no problem. We understand."

"We'll see you tomorrow," said Mark.

"Goodnight Mom." Vinnie gave her a hug and a kiss.

"See ya later, Vinnie," Mark said with an outstretched hand. "Congratulations again."

Vinnie shook hands with Mark but then stepped closer for a hug. "Thanks…Dad. For everything."

The word sank into his heart like a rock in a lake. Tears welled up in Mark's eyes as he hugged the boy he'd watch become a man. No one had ever called him that before.  It was the highest honor that was ever bestowed upon him. What meant even more was that it came from a man he was eternally proud to call *son*.

THEY STAYED in Toronto for awhile, giving Angel a break with the baby's care. It was quite an experience into the world of the mundane for our duo, since neither had any previous experience with babies.

"Mark, can you make some formula? It's time to feed Sonny."

"Man, that kid can eat...and poop."

Measuring the formula, Mark added the water per the directions and shook the bottle.

"Here we go, big guy," Mark said as he held the baby and began feeding him. "Oh, he's got to burp."

Placing him over his shoulder, Mark patted him gently on the back...and then he burped, then he spit up...then he farted, then he grunted, then he pooped.

"Shit!" said Mark, "Again? Really?"

"Would you please be a dear and change him this time?  I have been changing him all morning."

"No problem," said Mark, "I've seen the Three Stooges do it a thousand times."

Sopie said, "Maybe I should help."

"Well, if you insist," said Mark wryly.

Mark and Sopie had seen some true evil unleashed upon the world, but nothing quite like the odor that permeated the room upon removing the lad's diaper.

"Holy shit, that smells like..."

"Shit?"

"Yes! God," said Mark making heaving sounds.

"Oh, stop it Percy and get a baby wipe and clean his bottom."

With a wipe in one hand and pinching his nose with the other, Mark somehow managed to clean him off.

"Well, that wasn't so bad, if I do say so my...Oh damn, shit! He just pissed in my eye!"

Sonny just laid there and grinned.

"Damn monkey," Mark muttered as he cleaned up the unexpected mess. Taking some baby powder, he sprinkled him like he was salting a steak. "Sopie, hand me a clean diaper please."

"Here you go, Big Guy."

Giving her one of the looks that she usually gives him, he proceeded to put on the diaper. "There, that oughta hold him."

Mark, much more tuckered out than he expected, lay down on the sofa and put the baby on his stomach. The two boys, now all clean and tidy, napped on the couch. A short time later, Mark awoke to some more grunting. "Oh no, not again."

Then it happened…Sonny pooped…and pooped and it went everywhere. It was all over the baby. It was all over Mark. It was all over the couch, the floor, throughout the hall like there was a shit trail leading to Sonny's room.

"Goddamnit!" yelled Mark.

Sopie rushed in to see what was the matter.  It didn't take her long to figure out what had happened.

"Oh Mark, you put the diaper on backwards! That's why it didn't hold."

"Wish you had noticed that a little earlier. How can you tell?"

"The front goes in the front and the back in the back."

"Oh, that makes perfect sense. Why didn't I see that?"

"Here, let me help you clean him up. See what you can do about cleaning yourself up, then we'll clean the rest of the house."

Putting Sonny down for a nap, the exhausted couple just plopped down to catch their breath.

"Riggs, I'm just getting to old for this shit!"

"Amen," said Sopie.

Angel finally woke up and asked, "Where's Sonny?"

"Oh, he's just taking a little nap."

"I think it's time to feed him."

"We just did a little while ago."

"Oh, well he probably needs changing."

 "We just changed him."

"Well, what am I supposed to do?"

"For right now, anything you like. Take advantage of it. 'Me time' won't last long, especially after we hit the trail."

"So, you decided to retire in Carolina where you met. How romantic. I believe you said it is a lot closer to Toronto than Meadow Lake, so maybe we will see more of each other."

"Oh, I'm sure we will. Gotta see me grandson," said Mark.

"Well, you might have seen him enough for one day," Sopie laughed.

"No, just gotta rest up for round three. This baby shit is hard work."

"You can say that again..." sighed Sopie.

"Say, I know what I'll do. I can make you all a red velvet cake like the one Angel made for us on your birthday," said Mark.

"Like hell you will," said Sopie.

"What happened in Meadow Lake was just a little accident. Bennie and I cleaned it up, didn't we?"

"After some encouragement. The answer is NO."

"Who's Bennie? What happened?" asked Angel.

Sopie cleared her throat and relished in the thought of re-telling a classic tale of dumb-assery. "To make a long story short..."

"Ah, you're not going to tell this tired tale again, jeez..."

"As I started to say, Bennie is Mark's mentor from years ago. Mark was trying to make the cake; Bennie was watching Mr. Wizard make an H-bomb."

"An H-bomb?" exclaimed Angel.

"Yes, an H-bomb. Well, Mark decided it would be good to try it at home and got some things out of Vinnie's chemistry set. They blew up a coffee can, hit the wall switch that turned on the mixer and..."

"Oh, crap. I can see it coming," said Angel.

"Yep, red velvet kitchen...that they didn't bother to clean up for three days."

Without a moment's hesitation in her voice, Angel said, "No Mark. Step back, no cake for you!" with her best Soup Nazi impression.

"What?"

After another two weeks of diaper duty boot camp, they were once again on the road to Carolina. They had decided not to share the events leading up to their leaving Meadow Lake. They just told Vinnie and Angel that they had decided to retire and move back to the beach in Carolina where they had first met. It was just time for a change, since neither could stand the cold anymore and they longed for *Carolina Barbecue with hot slaw*...of course they did.

---

<h1 style="text-align:center">Chapter Twenty-Three</h1>

When Sopie and Mark arrived at their new home in New Bern, they were surprised to be greeted by two familiar faces.

"You folks need a hand?" shouted Marty with F.P. grinning behind him.

After exchanging hugs, Mark said, "How in the world did you two find us? We hadn't told anyone we were moving back here yet."

"Did you forget I used to work for the FBI?" F.P. laughed, "Besides, I always keep track of my business investments."

"Well, we only carried personal items," Sopie said as she stretched her legs, "so there's not much to carry in.  The movers are coming behind us with everything else, so let's go in, pull up a floor and chat."

"That won't be necessary. The movers brought the furniture yesterday.  It might take some rearranging and tweaking, but Marty and I got it pretty much squared away." F.P. was speaking in his all-business, just-the-facts tone as if he were reviewing a meeting agenda.

"Wait...how did you get in?"

At this question, however, F.P. remembered that he was among friends. "If I told you that, I would have to kill you," he said laughing.

"Come on," Marty interjected, "let's go inside and see what you think."

"I can't speak for her," Mark said, "but right now I think any place with a beer is a place I'd be happy to call home." He reached out and hugged his long-time friend. They didn't need to say much to each other in the way of catching up—some folks are friends for a reason, some for a season, and some for a lifetime. Mark and Marty were definitely the latter, fully content with picking up their palling around right where they left off.

"Wow," Sopie said in awe after walking through the front door. "This is a lot nicer than it looked in the pictures the realtor sent us." She hurried over to the giant windows in the den. "Look at this view overlooking the Neuse River!" She beamed with nostalgia. "Carolina is as beautiful as I remember.  But we have got to go back to the beach."

"Oh yes, we do," said Mark as he caught up with her and locked his arms around her waist.

She craned her neck to look in his eyes. "What do you think, Hon?"

"I think it's beautiful! I also think it's high-time we fixed our guests a drink."

Marty cracked his knuckles before regaling the happy couple with the happy news. "Blue Moons and Sopie's Seeker wine are in the fridge, scotch is on the bar, and I believe some panetellas are not very far." He was always trying to be the poet that didn't know it.

As they settled in on the back patio, F.P. said, "I hear the Injuns run you out of town. Lucky they didn't scalp you. Something to do with carnage, death and destruction?"

"My goodness," Sopie said in jest, "I knew you were old, F.P, but I had no idea you were a frontier man! Did you ever meet Buffalo Bill? Lucky Luke?"

Mark laughed. "You know, after living up there for so long I had kind of forgotten all the wacky traditions white folks associate with our Native friends—when you're up there on the reserve you stop seeing them as any different from regular jerks like you two."

"What's that?" Marty said in a burp.

Sopie rolled her eyes playfully and leaned back into her chair, happy to be out of the car and back in warmer weather with warmer friends. "To answer your question," she said, "it was pretty messy."

"That doesn't surprise me, you being with this old man.  I've seen him in action before, and he's not a very good driver," Marty said.

"You can say that again.  You should see the school!" Sopie blushed when she thought about the gaping hole Mark had left in their wake.

"Well, I'm not sure what went on," F.P. said, "but if you two were involved in it, I'm certain it couldn't be helped; and I'm glad I can call you friend." He raised his glass for a toast. "But," he continued, "you guys sure do have a knack with attracting trouble."

"I am hoping that we will just be able to put this behind us. It's a shame. We really liked it up in Meadow Lake and loved the people there. I guess we shouldn't get so involved is all," said Mark.

Sopie looked over at her wistful husband and put her hand on his. "I'm not sure that's the answer. We can't help but care… it's who we are."

Mark smiled. Then he remembered it might be time to catch up his friends on recent events. "You know Vinnie married Angel and they had a baby, didn't you?"

"Yes, I spoke to Vinnie just last week before you got there." F.P. lit up at the thought of a new kid to spoil. "They said they were going to name their son after your suggestion and call him Sonny. I can't wait to get back up there and see him. By the way, did you know that he has contracts extending from Saskatoon to Winnipeg? He also picked up Moose Jaw and the area surrounding Thunder Bay. We, my friend, are going to make millions on his idea, so here's to Vinnie, Angel and Sonny," said F.P. raising his glass.

"Cheers!" resounded everyone.

"So, Marty what are you doing these days?" asked Sopie.

"Same old, same old. Teaching and drinking," he said laughing.

"Still got that old S-10?" asked Mark.

"Oh yeah. Couldn't part with that."

"Maybe we should all go beach cruising in it sometime soon. You know, for old times sake."

"Sounds good to me!"

"Well, it's time we shoved off and let you two get settled. Come on Marty," said F.P. "Maybe tomorrow we can do a little pier fishing down in Atlantic."

"Yeah, and then head to the Beach Tavern," said Marty.

"I am afraid Mr. Banos is going to be very busy over the next few days. If he does a really good job, I might let him come out and play with you boys," said Sopie.

"Right. See you all later. That is what you say down here isn't it?"

"Close enough for Rock 'n Roll," said Mark as he headed to the car to grab a few more things before disappearing inside with Sopie.

Mark jumped right on his honey-do list over the next few days and, true to her word, Sopie let Mark go play with the boys. They headed down to the coast to the Oceana Pier, as this was the only pier left standing after the last hurricane. The days of eating hot dogs on the Iron Streamer Pier had come and gone twice since Mark's last visit. It was rebuilt once more, but succumbed to the winds of the last hurricane.

Jumping out of the truck, they headed down on the pier to try their luck. The afternoon was filled with Blues and Sand

Sharks.  The Blue's weren't really keepers either, so the trio headed for the Beach Tavern: the happiest place on earth.

It had changed as well. Not the place that Becky and Roy had run so well all those years. It still had the beach elegance, but no arcade games or pool tables like in the old days.  And, believe it or not, there was no smoking allowed. Sacrilege!

"I thought I noticed a funny odor in here," said Mark.

"Yeah," Marty said, "clean air!"

"It just ain't right," Mark sighed.

"Sign of the times, boys, sign of the times," said F.P.

"What'll you have?" asked the bartender.

"Blue Moons?" Marty offered.

"That's fine with me," said Mark.

"For me as well," said F.P.

"A lot has changed down here," Mark said as he settled on his stool. "This used to be a real night life beach for adults, but if you noticed the circle, there are no Beach Clubs left.  The Pavilion is gone too."

"Sad," Marty said shaking his head. "They have been trying to turn this place into a more family-oriented venue."

"Sign of the times," said F.P.

"I wonder if the old resort is still standing?" Mark wondered. "Why don't we make a trip down the road and see?"

"Okay by me," said Marty. "As soon as I finish me beer."

What he actually meant by "finish me beer" is that if Mark took off to the bathroom, he would come back to find Marty having another. So Mark went, and Marty gulped another one down, as expected.

They soon left the tavern and headed down Salterpath toward the Ramada. What used to be a road filled with reeds and sea oats was now lined with shopping centers, restaurants and condos.

"Amazing," said Mark. "Nothing looks the same."

"Everything changes, my friend, like it or not, life evolves," said F.P.

"I'm not sure this is such a good thing."

"It doesn't matter, it will change and there's not a whole lot you can do about it. But, one thing I keep reminding myself of, is that nobody can take your memories."

"That's true." Mark smiled. He wanted to believe that, he really did. But something inside him told him that one day, not even the memories he cherished so much would withstand the test of time. That one day, his most beloved thoughts would be replaced or obscured, that his mind would eventually become just some beach he used to know.

Seven miles out they saw the old inn rise out of the sand.

"Thar she blows," shouted Mark, "I wonder, I just wonder..."

"Wonder what?" said Marty.

"Come on. I want to inquire about an old friend," Mark said.

Going in, he asked if Melvin still owned the hotel.

"Sure does," said the clerk.

"He wouldn't happen to be around, would he?"

"It's five, he's on the beach..."

"Taking down the umbrellas?"

"Yeah, how did you know?"

"And Doran's in the bar?"

"No, I'm afraid he passed a few years ago."

"Oh, sorry to hear that. Let me go say hey to Melvin."

Heading out the back door, he beamed. "Finally something is the way it's supposed to be!" He darted up the deck to the beach, where sure enough, there was Melvin doing Melvin duty.

"Hey, old man," he yelled. "You got any room at the inn?"

Looking up in disbelief he said, "Mark?"

"Yep, it's me, always turning up like a bad penny."

"Well, I'll be. How have you been all these years?" said Melvin as both old men embraced.

"Pretty fine. I'd like to introduce you to a couple of good friends of mine. This is Marty and F.P."

"Nice to meet you. F.P. Hmm....what does that stand for?"

Mark yelled, "Don't ask!" followed by raucous laughter.

F.P. just stuck out his hand and ignored him.

When he calmed back down, Mark looked to Melvin and said, "Sorry to hear about Doran."

He sighed. "Yeah, it's kinda hard to run this place without him. You know he quit drinking years ago and really cleaned himself up. You remember my wife? She died last year from breast cancer."

"Sorry to hear that Melvin."

"Yeah, I really miss her too, especially now that the girls are grown. But I have my work to keep me occupied. How 'bout you? Ever marry?"

"As a matter of fact, yes I did. Believe it or not, I met her here at the inn the first summer I performed here. We ran into each other again in New Orleans, the year Katrina hit."

"Yeah, you always had to have a little drama in your backdrop."

"You might say that. Anyway, I just became a grandfather this past month."

"Are they all down with you as well?"

"No, they live in Toronto. It's just Sopie and me, living over in New Bern. I will be sure to bring her down to see you next time I am down this way."

"You do that, son. Now let me get back to work before the sun goes down."

"Need some help?"

"No," the old man laughed, "you never were much help before and I wouldn't expect you to be now," he said turning back to his work.

As the trio headed toward home, Mark said, "Let's turn here and go home by way of Matthews Point. I want to take a look at the marina."

As they veered off the main road and approached the marina, something caught Mark's eye.

"Stop here for a minute."

Marty pulled in and Mark jumped out to inspect a sailboat with a "For Sale" sign on it.

"Two great days in a boat owner's life," said F.P. "One is the day he buys it and the other is the day he sells it."

Ignoring his comment, Mark looked the vessel over stem to stern.

"She's beautiful!" Mark said in awe. "I have got to show this to Sopie. Can't live in Coastal Carolina without a boat."

"Do you know how to sail?" asked Marty.

"Certainly. I was raised here," said Mark indignantly. "Look, they're only asking $35,000 for this Catalina. It would be perfect for traveling the Pamlico Sound and the Intracoastal Water-way. I have got to tell Sopie."

Upon arriving home, Mark was so excited he couldn't stand himself.

"You won't believe this. I found us a boat. Not just a boat, but a Catalina sailboat. It's perfect for around here. We can make some short excursions and have the time of our lives."

"Slow down, Mr. Adventure. How much is the time of our lives gonna cost?"

"The owner has an asking price of $35,000, but I'm sure we could do a little dickering and get a better price."

"Well, that's not a bad price for a sailboat, but do you know how to sail?"

"Of course I do! Remember I was raised here. It's been awhile, but I am sure I can get the hang of it again. Do you want to go see her?"

"Well, yeah."

"We'll head down to the marina tomorrow then."

"By the way, you'll never guess who I ran into down at the beach."

"Who?"

"Melvin, at the old inn."

"Really, how is he?"

"Fine, just taking down the umbrellas like usual."

"Good…some things don't change," said Sopie grinning.

---

EARLY THE NEXT MORNING, the couple headed down to the marina to look at the vessel.

After Sopie examined the boat, she said, "Well, I don't know anything about boats, but this one really looks good. Almost new. I wonder why the owner wants to sell it?"

"I don't know. Why don't we call and ask him?"

"Well, you're right. If we are going to live here, we would be foolish not to own a boat. Go ahead and call him."

A few minutes later they reached Sam Piner, the boat's owner.

"Sure, I'd be glad to talk to you about the boat. I can be there in about 45 minutes.  Will that be alright?"

"Yes, we are here waiting."

After he hung up, Mark said, "Mr. Piner said he would meet us here in about 45 minutes."

"That's fine with me, can we get something to eat over there at Bojangles while we wait?"

"Sure, let's hurry."

Upon entering, Mark saw something that brought back home. Bojangles now served Cheddar Bo biscuits.

"I can't believe this. You have got to try one of these, Sopie. They used to make these after we got through playing shows down in Little Washington. They were wonderful. I'm sure these aren't as good, but even if they are half as good it will be great."

They ordered the cheese biscuits and sat down to eat.

Sopie said, "These are good, but it is just cheddar cheese and biscuits."

"But baked together in an oven! Mmm."

"You have some funny tastes as to what you think is so special," laughed Sopie.

"Better watch out calling yourself funny like that—because I think you're pretty special." Mark laughed and looked at the simple cheese biscuit in his hands. "I guess it's just the memories that are so good." Looking over to see a pickup pull in at the marina, Mark said, "We'd better go. I think Mr. Piner just arrived."

The two made their way back over to the boat.

"Hi, Mr. Piner?"

"Yes, Mr. Banos. Is this your lovely wife?"

"Yes, this is Sopie.

"Pleased to meet you. She's a fine craft isn't she? I meant the boat, not you ma'am. Sorry."

"She certainly is, on both counts," grinned Mark.

"Why do you want to sell her? Did you buy a bigger boat?"

"No, no…" Mr. Piner trailed off for a moment. "I'm afraid my sailing days are over." A tear formed in the old man's eye as he said, "My wife had a heart attack while we were sailing out on the intracoastal waterway and I couldn't…" he had to stop to catch his breath. "I couldn't get her to the hospital in time. Died right in my arms," he said coughing a bit. "Excuse me," he said, "it's just tough to relive."

"I'm so sorry," said Sopie. She put a hand on Mr. Piner's shoulder to comfort him.

"Yeah… Her name was Darlene, and as you see on the back of the boat, this is the Darlene II. The two great loves of my life. Couldn't bear sailing anymore after that, so I thought selling her would be the right thing to do."

"I see," said Sopie.

"So you're asking $35,000 for her?" asked Mark.

"Yes, I know I could get more, but I just have to sell her."

"Will you take $40,000 for her?" asked Sopie.

"What?" said Mark.

"That's mighty generous of you ma'am."

"Well, I don't want to see you get hoo-dooed. We'll take it for forty," said Sopie.

Mark said, "She's right, it is worth that."

Mr. Piner smiled wide and thanked them gratuitously. "It's a deal."

He signed over the title and they wrote a check, and Sopie and Mark now owned a Catalina sailboat.

Later that afternoon, they checked around as to where the best marina might be to rent a slip for their new boat. They settled on Matthew Point Marina since it was close to the house. This would ensure they would be able to get a lot of use out of their new investment.

Mark had Marty help him with pulling the boat to the marina, since Mark didn't have a hitch on the SUV yet. The three hopped out and approached the office to fill out the information for renting a slip.

"That's a beauty of a boat. Is that old Sam Piner's?"

"Why yes, did he used to keep it here?"

"Yeah, he had it for a few years, but it's still a very sea worthy vessel for the river and sounds. I guess Sam and his wife can finally move to Florida, now that he has sold it."

"Wife?" asked Sopie. "I thought she died?"

"Oh God," said the marina owner. "Did he tell you the tale about his wife dying in his arms aboard the Darlene? He is so full of crap. He just told you that so you wouldn't dicker the price down too low."

Sopie's face turned ashy grey, then beet red. "That ol' sum bitch!" she said without thinking and then began to blush with embarrassment.

"Oh, don't be too hard on yourself. At least you didn't pay him extra."

Sopie started to tear up.

"Did you? Oh my. Well, if it makes you feel better, the blue book on this boat is around $46,000, so maybe you didn't take too bad of a beating."

Sopie's normal coloring returned to her face as she said, "Well, we gotta nice boat, didn't we, Sweetheart?"

"Yes, we did, honey. That we did. One of the best two days in a boat owner's life.  Sam got his two, we got our first one. It was a good day."

---

A COUPLE OF AFTERNOONS LATER, Mark kept his promise to Sopie as they headed back to Atlantic Beach together for the first time since 1975. He told her, on the way, that there was a lot of changes, but the Ramada stood as it always had, tall and proud.

Upon arriving at the old hotel, they immediately hopped out and ran…well, *ambled* to the beach, to once again walk along its shore and breathe in those sights and sounds from long ago.

"Oh Mark, it's just like I remember it," she said, locking arms as they walked.

"Am I?"

"What? As I remember you? Of course you are. A little more battle-trodden maybe, but still the man I said I would marry, so long ago."

"And that you did…and I held you to it, too."

"I just got a bit side-tracked."

"Yeah, thirty some years of side-tracking, but I finally caught you!" said Mark picking up Sopie and swirling her around.

"Stop it you big bully or I'll…tell Melvin."

"Oh God no! He might shove an umbrella up me arse!"

"And then I would open it, so watch it Mister."

"Aye, Aye Dragon Lady." He saluted her.

"Dragon Lady…why you…" and Sopie took off chasing him down the beach, which would have been pretty easy if Mark didn't switch dimensions as she got nearer.

"No fair!" yelled Sopie.

"A man's got to do what a man's got to do," he said plopping down on a sand dune.

She quietly sat down beside him as they both sat and watched the sun begin to disappear.

"This beach holds a lot of our secrets," said Mark.

"And our dreams," added Sopie.

He put one hand around her waist and placed the other gently on her cheek, staring deeply into the ocean of her eyes. "And what dreams do we now share, my Sopie?" asked Mark in the stillness of the twilight.

Sopie placed her lips on Mark's, lingering there for a moment before whispering into his ear, "What dreams may come, Sweetheart, what dreams may come."

## Chapter Twenty-Four

Summers come and summers go.  Before they knew
it, Mark and Anna had spent five years on the
coast. Vinnie and his family decided to pay the now elderly
couple a visit for the summer.  Sonny, who had just turned five,
was every bit a boy, ready to go wherever *the guys* wanted to take
him.  Naturally, there was fishing and sailing involved. And no,
there was not any drinking involved...yet...he's five, for God
sakes. What were you thinking?

"Show that boy how to bait his hook, Vinnie." Mark grinned
from his seat in the sun.

"Sure, Dad" as he took a minnow from the pail. "See Sonny,
you take the snout off of the clam and bait your hook, being
sure to hide the hook."

Sonny nodded intently, quite sure of himself. "Got it, Dad."

In a few minutes, his rod began to bob.

"I got one! I got one!"

"Easy does it. Reel it in slowly so you don't lose him."

As he reeled it in, he discovered he had caught his very
first Spot.

"There, that will be your dinner tonight, Champ."

"Yeah! Let's try again."

They ended up catching a total of eighteen nice Spot. A fine dinner it would be.

The ladies, exhausted from a day of shopping in Morehead, were so glad to be greeted with the prospect of cleaning fish.

"Oh no, no, no," said Angel. "If you catch 'em, you clean 'em!"

"And cook 'em!" said Sopie.

"Oh no!" said Vinnie, "I've had Dad's cooking before. Jeez!"

"Now wait a minute," said Mark as he tied an apron around his waist, "Sopie has been teaching me for about three years now, and if I do say so myself, I'm getting pretty good at it."

"Yeah, he's way beyond the fiasco that happened when Master Bennie came to visit us in Meadow Lake," said Sopie. She nudged him with her elbow and scooted past to fetch the wine from the fridge before things got too fishy.

"Wait...who's Master Bennie?" asked Vinnie.

"That's another, rather long, story." Sopie kissed her handsome son on the cheek, careful to avoid his hands, which smelled of fish. "Maybe later, but Angel can enlighten you as to the Red Velvet Kitchen episode of the Mr. Wizard show," she said.

"Why am I just now hearing about this?"

"Well, it's not one of those days that great culinary chefs like myself would brag about," said Mark.

"Thank God Vinnie, you managed to do away with the Mr. Wizard reruns on your new Wifi network before somebody got killed," laughed Sopie. She poured a glass of sauvignon blanc for Angel and then herself.

"All episodes tucked safely away in my vault, Mom. No chance of them ever being seen again," winking at Mark. "Okay, let's do this. I can't wait for the Master of Disaster Chef to begin."

Mark prepared a remarkable dinner, with grilled Spot, asparagus, corn on the cob, and red potatoes.

"Man, I can't get over how good those potatoes were,

wrapped in aluminum foil, laced with garlic and covered with Italian dressing. Hat's off to the chef!" said Vinnie.

"The corn in the husk was amazing!" said Angel.

"What about my fish?" asked Sonny.

"It was just fabulous!" echoed everyone.

"Hey Mark," said Vinnie, "you know I just had a great idea for a syndicated show on our Wifi network. Why don't we feature you on a cooking show? We could call it Beachin' in the Keetchin' and feature your low life, I mean low country recipes and maybe some of Mom's recipes from New Orleans." He chuckled a bit and waggled his eyebrows towards the ladies for some encouragement for the new idea.

"Hmm. Sounds like a possibility, but maybe call it "Beachin' in the Keetchin' with Scotch." Everybody pairs wine with meals, but nobody knows anything about whiskey. This would be a chance for me to show off my expertise and try some new and interesting scotches."

"Cool Beans, as Mom used to say. We could try to film a short segment while I'm down here."

"Okay, I'll go get some crabs and we can do a dry run on steamed crabs."

"That sounds good!"

The next day, Mark called the local seafood market and ordered some #1 Jimmies.  For you foreigners out there, that's the biggest male blue crabs you got. When Mark arrived at the market, the owner's grandson and his wife were there.

"You got my Jimmies?"

"Sure do, let me get 'em."

Out he came grinning, "Here you go Mr. Banos, that will be $75.42."

Mark paid the bill and headed home saying, "We want to make sure we get home and cook these rascals while they are still alive." Rushing inside he prepared the pot.  He put a cheap beer, a Natty Bo, in the bottom and then added water and vinegar. When it came to a boil, he placed the steamer on top and said, "Ok Sopie, roll 'em!"

She said, as the narrator, "This is the infamous blue crabs. Dad hasn't named them yet, but look inside this bag."

"Ooooo," said Mark, "they're alive."

"Yes, but not for long."

"Alright Charlie, Darryl and Wally..."

"You throwing them in?"

"Yep, throwin' them in...in the pot."

"Okay guys, we have a bunch of crabs going in the pot."

"Those are females! Those are females!"

"Are they?"

"Yes, those are not Jimmies."

"Uh, oh."

"I am pissed. Oh man."

"You couldn't tell that when you picked them up?"

"I didn't look."

"Let's hope they're good."

"I don't eat those...turn the water off...I'm takin' 'em back."

After calling the store, they realized that they had mixed them up with the old man at the store's dinner.

Mark said, "There already half dead. Do you want me to go ahead and cook 'em?"

They said, "Go ahead." So he did.

About 20 minutes later, the old man himself showed up grinning with Mark's Jimmies. He apologized and then said, "By the way, thanks for cooking my dinner," as he left down the hall.

Then the episode continued: "Take two. #1 Jimmies in the pot. This is the apron, which the other one was not."

"They look like little mini penises."

"Yes, little mini penises."

"Well, now I know what a Jimmy and a Sook look like."

"See this one, still kicking around, they ain't happy."

"But, Dad's happy!"

"Yeah, I'm happy. Do my little happy dance. Okay...film over."

"That was great!" said Vinnie.

"The shit I go through just to fix dinner. We need to throw in the potatoes and corn when the crabs come out. How are the hushpuppies doing, Sopie?"

"Almost done."

"Good! Cut!...Bless and eat!"

---

BEFORE THE HAPPY family knew it, summer vacation had ended. Vinnie and his crew had headed back up to Toronto. Sonny was getting ready to start school. It seemed like he just started to walk. Somehow, the calmness of their oceanic life seemed to make the years feel like weeks. It's as if they were rolling down a flowery hill, softly tumbling to the end of time without a care in the world.

F.P. came down again in October to do some fishing. Fishing is always great down there then. He and Mark took the Karli Anna, (that was the name they christened the sailboat…of course it was) out on the Pamlico Sound and dropped anchor. After about fifteen minutes, they started to get results.

"Oh, lord," Mark yelled, "I got one."

F.P. echoed, "Me too!"

For the next twenty minutes or so they were pulling them in as fast as they could get their hooks in the water. Striped bass and flounder alike.

"What a haul!" Mark said.

"You got that right. There must be thirty in the boat."

When they got back to the marina, they counted twenty-eight, twenty-two striped bass and six flounders.

"Man, this was quite a day!"

"You betcha. I really enjoy it when I come down here. So

much excitement. Well, maybe not as much as in the old days, but it will certainly do now."

Funny. They didn't hear from F.P. over the Christmas holidays. Sopie and Mark went to Toronto to spend Christmas with the rest of the family. When they returned a few weeks later, an attorney greeted them.

"Hi, Mr. Banos, Mrs. Banos. I'm Martin Bridgeforth, F.P Kroner's attorney. Mr. Kroner asked me to personally stop by and talk to you."

"Well, certainly. Won't you come in?"

As the man came in and sat down, he began, "Mr. Kroner has had some health issues as of late and he chose not to disclose them to anyone. Anyway, he developed pneumonia in early December and passed away."

"Oh my God, no!" said Sopie.

"I'm afraid so, ma'am."

"Bottom line is he had no family or heirs. So, after dispersing his estate to various charities that he had endowed, the remainder of his estate is bequeathed to you and Mr. Banos. He said in his will that he was sure that you would do things as he had intended, had he continued to live.

"That is a great responsibility. I only hope we can live up to his expectations."

"He told me that he knew you would say that, and to tell you that you already had. From this day forward, you will receive all of his monthly royalties from IKEA and all of his other investments will be signed over to you for you to handle as you see fit. His private jet, property and other holdings have already been liquidated and will be placed in your account as soon as you instruct me as to which bank you wish it deposited."

"I'm sorry. This is quite a lot to digest. Can I call you tomorrow, once we have had a chance to wrap our heads around all of this?"

"Sure, take your time. I know this must be quite a shock. No way to come off a holiday. F.P. was a close friend of mine as well. He just didn't want a big to do when it came time for him to go. That's just the way he was. Not much for pomp and circumstance. He was cremated and his ashes were scattered over Pamlico Sound. He said that was where he had the best times of his life, and wanted to remain there."

"He also said that his share in the Wifi company belongs to Vinnie and Angel. He willed his fishing tackle to Sonny."

After the attorney left, Mark and Sopie were just in a state of shock. They had no idea that F.P. was ill, nor did they have any thoughts as to receiving an inheritance from him.

"I just had no idea," started Mark, "He always looked the picture of health."

"I guess he was just good at concealing his private affairs," said Sopie. "It's good to know that the greatest pleasure he received in life was hanging out with us."

"That's kinda sad, too," said Mark.

"Let's call Marty and give him the news and maybe tomorrow or the next day we can take the Karli Anna out on the sound and show our respects in some way," said Sopie.

"That's a good idea. It would give us some form of finality to his passing," said Mark. We had better call Vinnie, too. I doubt that he and Angel have been informed."

The next day, the three of them gathered on the Karli Anna and headed out in Pamlico Sound. When they got to the center most area, they stopped and placed a wreath of flowers at the spot and recited the twenty-third Psalm. Mark, then, pulled out what remained of the Macallan M that F.P. had purchased for him. He poured four drinks, one for each of them and one for his departed friend.

Raising his glass, Mark said, "You saved our lives, you took us under your wings and gave us more than hope, you gave us your friendship and your love. We can never repay the kindness that you showed us throughout the years. We will never know why you did what you did, but I swear, that for the rest of our lives we will honor your name and finish those things that you have started, touching and blessing other lives as you have."

Taking a sip of the whiskey, the others did the same.

"Here's to you, Firkin Percy. May you rest in peace."

"Mark! That was just wrong," said Marty. "Why did you have to go and call him that?"

"That was his name, my friend. Now you know why everybody just called him F.P."

Mark and Sopie just started to laugh, an uncontrollable laugh that people usually do at the most inappropriate times.

"Do you remember when he first told us his name," laughed Sopie.

"Yes I literally was laughing my ass off, rolling on the floor."

"How come I never knew his real name? How come nobody told me?" asked Marty.

"Because, if we told you, then we would have to kill you!" said Sopie almost falling overboard with laughter.

Marty just scratched his head and downed his shot, "He will be missed."

"Here, here!" echoed Mark and Sopie, lifting their glasses and finishing the scotch. Then they headed back to shore.

## Chapter Twenty-Five

"You know Mark, I've been thinking" said Sopie, "This is a lot of money that we are responsible in handling. I'm not even sure how much there is, but it is certainly more than I've ever had to deal with. I'm not even sure where to start."

"I agree," said Mark, "I'm afraid to touch it for fear of making a huge mistake and losing it all. I think we need some professional help. Do you suppose Mr. Bridgeforth would be willing to help us? You know, he had to have had a pulse on all of F.P.'s affairs for all of those years.  Let's call him."

"Yes, good idea."

They set up an appointment the following week and met Mr. Bridgeforth at his office in Silver Spring, Maryland.

"Hello, Mr. Bridgeforth, it's good to see you again," said Sopie.

"Nice to see you both, and it's Martin. How can I help you?"

"We were wondering, since you had handled the financial affairs for F.P., if you would be willing to continue to do so for us," said Sopie. "This is a large amount of money and we just don't need much at our ages. We are afraid we might mishandle it. We would like to ensure that it will do a lot of good, now and in the future and we're just not sure where to start."

"Well, you sound just like F.P. did, once he bought a jet and a limo and got a handle on his spending spree. He had me do pretty much the same thing for him as you are now asking me to do for you."

Laughing Mark said, "Really, I always thought of F.P. as more of a spendthrift."

"Not at first. Initially, he was quite the playboy. But he got bored quickly and settled down. Why don't you consider setting up a foundation or maybe a charitable trust?"

"I like the sound of that," said Sopie, "We could put it in the name of F.P."

"Right the Firkin Percy Trust," smirked Mark.

"Yeah...maybe the Kroner Foundation would be better," said Martin.

"I like the sound of that," said Sopie, "What do you think, Mark?"

"I think it's a great idea and then we can contribute to causes we believe in with total anonymity. Sounds good. I think we should do it."

"I will set everything up and have the funds transferred to the foundation. I will then have an investment advisor manage the funds so that you don't have to worry about that. You will receive monthly statements as to the foundation's investment activity and quarterly and annual reports as to the charitable grants that are dispersed. You two will have the final say so, as to any grants that are made and you, of course, will be allowed to make suggestions for grants to projects that you deem favorable."

"Exactly what we wanted. Thank you so much. I feel like a burden has just been lifted from our shoulders," said Sopie. "Goodbye."

"Goodbye and I will be in touch."

SONNY, now seven, got to spend his summers in Carolina with his grandparents. Mark, of course, took him fishing and sailing as well as making sure he got frequent trips down to the beach. Vinnie and Angel would come down to retrieve him in August, a great excuse for a beach vacation. The business had grown to mammoth proportions and Mark's cooking show was a hit across Canada.

Bidding their adieus with the promise of seeing them at Christmas, they turned and went back in their home, now filled with wonderful memories of the warm summer days.

The next morning, as Mark was looking at the online newspapers, he ran across an article concerning Charity Hospital in New Orleans. It had never reopened since Katrina hit and the city had decided to tear it down, displace 189 residents and build a new hospital on their properties.

"Sopie, come look at this."

As she read, he continued, "I think I have an idea for our first Firkin grant."

After she punched him, she said, "Yes, I think I know what you are thinking. Let's call Martin."

They reached Martin and asked him to look into the possibility of saving the hospital. He then arranged a meeting with the board at the hospital. He inquired as to whether or not they had a continuation plan, if they were to receive funding to restore the hospital.

"We do," they said handing Martin a packet. "As you can see, though, the plan to restore this hospital and make it the modern facility that we foresee it to be, requires a great deal of money. The city has decided that it would be much less expensive to just buy out the residents and build a new facility. That is not what we want, but it may be what we get as we have no other source of funding other than what the city will give us and that is not enough to renovate this existing property. FEMA will only allow us the 10 million dollars to remove the equipment inside for salvage. There is no money coming from them to rebuild."

"I see. How much do you need?"

"387 million dollars."

"And that will provide all of your needs?"

"Yes, and then some. All of the plans and health care models to be established once the building is restored are in the packet."

"Let me look this over and discuss it with my board and I will be back in touch next week."

"Thank you so much for coming down, Mr. Bridgeforth."

"My pleasure."

Mark and Sopie got a call three days later from Martin.

"Their plans look sound, but why would you want to invest this kind of money in an old hospital in New Orleans, if you don't mind me asking?"

"Well, sir, we were there with the children during Katrina and saw first hand how the hospital staff reacted and stayed with the patients during a time when their lives were in great jeopardy. Mark and I had lost everything during that flood and we both know what those folks in the surrounding neighborhood must have gone through to restore their homes. And to think, it was just to have the city come in after and make them move out. Will our plan work? Can we get that much money?"

There was a deafening silence on the line.

"Are you still here?" asked Martin.

"I'm still here. Well, do we have that much?"

"You have five times that much."

"Oh! Well, let's do it."

"I'll let them know tomorrow and the funds will be transferred to a special account that will disperse the money at each stage of construction and renovation as the need arises."

"Thank you, Martin."

"No, thank you. Goodnight."

"We just built our first hospital!" exclaimed Sopie.

"Not bad for a couple of stiffs, eh?" said Mark.

"Oh, I had forgotten about us being declared dead down there. Well, they won't know it's us. It's coming from the Firkin Percy Trust."

This would, of course, not be the end of their benevolence. This would simply be the match that lit the fire. Like any other compulsion, giving begets giving and before they realized it, they had helped build a children's hospital in New Bern as well as the Bayside Nursing Home. The feather in Sopie's cap, though, was the six million dollar donation to build a new Animal Rescue facility for the SPCA. She adored dogs and kept several of the rescue animals at her home until the new building was complete as well as constantly visiting the new shelter to play with the animals.

---

SONNY HAD NOW REACHED the age of 15, when he arrived that summer. He was the same age as Vinnie was the year that Mark had finally reunited with Sopie. Mark was ready to take Sonny out fishing and sailing, but something had changed. It didn't appear that Sonny was all that interested in those things now. He spent most of his days either on his iPhone or the laptop. He was constantly chatting with friends online and on SnapChat.

"What's with Sonny?" asked Mark. "He doesn't seem to want to do anything except stare at his phone all day."

"I'm afraid he's hit the terrible teens," said Sopie.

"Come on, Sonny. Ride with me down to the marina. I've got to do some work on the boat and you can keep me company."

"Alright..." Sonny said dragging his heels.

When they got to the boat, Mark started to do some minor repair work on it while Sonny sat on the dock cross-legged listening to his iPod through the headphones. A little while later, a teenage girl walked by and sat down next to him, swinging her feet off the dock. As he glanced toward her, a big grinned filled his face.

"Hey," he said removing his headphones.

"Hi. Whatcha listenin' to?" she asked.

"Some old jam that my grandfather introduced me to. I think the band is called, *The Band of Oz*."

"Oh, beach music. I love that stuff."

"Yeah? My grandfather used to play. From what I hear, he was pretty good. Played a lot of the clubs around here."

"Really? What's his name?"

"Mark Banos, but he went by the stage name of Tom Marks."

"No kidding, I think my Mom has an old cassette of his. It's called Tom Marks Live."

"Small world. Hey, I'm Sonny Banos from Toronto. I usually come down here and stay with my grandparents in the summer. Are you from here?"

"Yes, I'm Amy...Amy Miller. My dad owns this marina."

"Oh, I met him. Mr. Miller, right?"

"Yes, that's him," she said laughing.

"So Amy, what do you all do down here for fun, besides fish and sail?"

"Well, that can be a lot of fun, but I guess we do the same things here as you would in the big city, have parties and dances and go to the movies."

"You're right, we just kinda hang out and try not to get into too much trouble."

Amy giggled, "Say, how about coming with me to the pool party this Friday night. They'll have food, a live band and dancing."

"Sounds like fun. You got yourself a deal."

"No, I've got myself a date," she said before landing a kiss on his cheek and running off toward the office.

"Hey!" Sonny yelled, "Where and what time?"

"Pool at the marina, 7 o'clock. See you there."

When Mark looked up from doing some patchwork on the boat, he saw Sonny grinning like a cat that had just swallowed a canary. Then he caught sight of the image of a young girl disappearing into the office.

"What is this? You haven't smiled since you got here. Was it this beautiful sunshine out today or maybe the smell of fresh fish chum?"

"It was the fish chum...definitely the fish chum," he smiled in the direction of the office. "Big Guy, I have been asked to go to a pool party Friday night, here at the marina.  Would it be alright if I went?"

"It wouldn't be right if you didn't," laughed Mark. "My Sonny Boy is growing up."

"Can I help you with the boat?"

"Sure can, come aboard."

---

Friday night dragged it's feet, like Christmas used to when you're a kid. Sonny was a little nervous and not sure what to wear. Nan, should I wear the blue shirt or the yellow print one?"

"Blue will look nice with your eyes."

"Yeah, but the print is way cooler."

"Okay, that will look good too."

"But you think the blue will look better?"

"You will look just great, no matter what you wear. The young lady is not interested in your wardrobe."

Arriving at the pool, Sonny was greeted by Amy.

"Hi," said Amy grabbing Sonny's hand. "I want you to meet some of my friends. Come on. Hi guys, I want you to meet Sonny. He is from Toronto."

"Man, you are a long way from home. Good to meet you, Bro," said Duncan.

"Same," said Sonny.

"I'm George and this is Annette."

"Good to see you."

"So what brings you down from the big chill?" asked Duncan.

"My grandparents live here in New Bern and I usually come down in the summer and stay with them."

"Cool," said George, "how did you come to meet Amy?"

"Well, she kinda met me. I was sitting on the dock listening to some jam and she came up and started talking. We ended up talking for quite a while and then she asked me to come here to the party."

"Hey, they're bringing out the food. Let's go!" shouted George.

Amy and Sonny ate snacks together and tried to talk over the band. Then the band played an old tune, "If" by Bread, and Sonny asked Amy to dance.

"Oh, you are a good dancer," exclaimed Amy, as Sonny pulled her closer.

The song finished and they started to play a fast song, so they kept on dancing.

"Twirl me around," said Amy.

And he did, and as he did he lost his balance and...yeah, you guessed it, he fell into the pool. Before he had time to recover and get embarrassed, Amy yelled, "Hey, Sonny is doing the Swim! Everybody into the water!"

They all jumped in with their clothes on flailing about like they were dancing, having a fantastic time. Upon exiting the pool, everyone was dripping wet and roaring with laughter.

"Man, you know how to get a party started," said Duncan. "Never seen that before. Is that what they do up in Canada?"

"All the time, Bro...all the time."

The party ended around eleven, and everyone's parents came to pick up the wet, motley crew.

"See you tomorrow?" asked Amy.

"Sure, see you tomorrow."

"What in the world happened to you?" asked Sopie as Sonny climbed in.

"Long story, Nan...long story."

The next day Sonny had Mark drop him off at the marina and found Amy waiting on the dock.

"Ahoy there!" he yelled.

"Ahoy!" Amy echoed.

"That was some party last night, huh?" said Amy.

"Yeah, some party. Thanks for saving me from what could have been life ending embarrassment."

"Not a problem. It turned out to be the best part of the evening."

"Well, thanks. It meant a lot to me."

"Well, you kinda mean a lot to me, I mean, you not being from here and all. Someone's got to take you under their wing."

"Let's go down on the shore and walk awhile," said Sonny.

"Okay."

The two walked down the shore near the marina, watching the boats enter the channel to the sound.  After a few rounds of throwing stones in the water, they sat down on the beach and rested.

"Kinda nice and peaceful out here."

"Yeah, I will hate it when I have to go back to Toronto."

"When do you have to leave?"

"My parents usually come back in August to pick me up."

"But you'll be back, eh?" she noted, making fun of his Canadian dialect.

"I certainly hope so. It will be a lot harder to leave this year."

"Why this year?"

"Well, I just met this beautiful girl and..."

Amy leaned over slowly and asked, "And who might that be?"

"Well..." he leaned in and kissed her.

She put her arms around him and returned the kiss. Then,

they sort of turned away, somewhat embarrassed and not knowing what to say next.

After a minute or two of silence, Amy said, "That was nice. Yeah, it's definitely going to be harder when you leave."

The two joined hands as they stood up, looking out to the water, watching it break against the shore.

"Come on," Amy said, "I'm getting hungry. Let's go to the snack bar."

"Sounds good. Race ya!" And off they went.

---

THE NEXT DAY MARK SAID, "How about riding with me over to Beaufort? I've got to pick up a few things over there."

"Alright" said Sonny curiously. Mark usually didn't go down east.

When Mark got to Beaufort, he didn't stop. Instead, he turned left and headed out toward Cedar Point.

"Where are we going?" asked Sonny.

"For a ride...well, I'm going for a ride. You're going to drive."

Drive! Me? I don't know how to drive."

"Today, you learn," laughed Mark.

They switched places and Mark instructed, "Put on your seat belt first. Then adjust the mirrors so you can see what's behind you. Now turn the ignition switch. The car is in park. When I tell you, pull this lever toward you and pull it down in "D". The car will then move forward. This pedal is to accelerate and this is your brake. Don't get them mixed up. When you push the acceleration pedal, do so slowly as not to jerk our heads off."

"What about the blinker signals, where are they?"

"They're on the left of the steering column, but you won't need them. This road only goes up and back."

Sonny put the car in gear and inched forward.

"Give it a little gas."

Sonny did as he was instructed and the car lurched forward.

"Keep your foot steady on the gas and stay on the right side of the road, but don't run us in the ditch."

"Aye, aye, Big Guy."

"Nice job. Keep her straight."

"I'm meeting a car. What do I do?"

"Just keep to the right and raise your finger on the wheel."

"What? Why?"

"It's just polite. That's how we say howdy down south," grinned Mark.

The car passed and the driver raised his finger back.

"Cool beans!"

They drove about ten miles toward Cedar Point and Mark said, "Turn around and I'll drive back."

"How? Where?"

"You'll have to do a three point turn. Turn to the left. Stop. Back up. Go forward. Proceed."

Sonny followed the directions and handled the maneuver with ease.

"I did it!"

"Yes, you did. Great job. Now give it a rest. Pull over and let me drive back."

When they got back home, Sonny raced into the house and yelled, "Nan, Mark taught me how to drive!"

"He did, did he? And who taught him?" she joked.

"Yeah, just a few more hours to build his confidence he will be all set and ready to get his learner's permit when he gets back to Toronto," Mark confirmed.

"Wow! I can't wait!" Sonny ran off to his room to call Amy and tell her.

"Seems like he finally got himself interested in something other than that computer," said Mark.

"See...nothing that a pretty girl can't fix," noted Sopie.

"Right! Smooth sailing from here on," teased Mark, which as usual got him punched in the arm.

VINNIE AND ANGEL arrived on schedule to pick up Sonny, although it was a lot sooner than Sonny had anticipated. He really enjoyed living in New Bern this summer. Of course, Amy had helped the summer fly by. It was almost time for him to go back when he asked Mark to take him down to the marina one last time.

Spotting Amy, he yelled, "Ahoy there!"

"Ahoy!"

Running toward each other they quickly embraced as she gave in to a long kiss.

"My," she said, "you know how to knock a girl off her feet."

Grinning Sonny said, "I'm afraid this is my last day here. I have got to go back to Canada in the morning, but we can Face-Time, if you like, while I'm gone. I will be back next summer."

"I'd like that," she said. "I wish you would just move down here. Then we could have fun and go sailing together."

"Well, maybe someday I will, but we could go sailing now."

"Really, how?"

"I'll take you out on my grandfather's boat."

"I didn't know you knew how to sail."

"Well sure, I've been out with him hundreds of times. Let's go."

They walked down to the boat slip and jumped on board. After untying the ropes, Sonny started the engine and pulled out of the slip and headed toward the sound.

"Oh, this is so cool. Why haven't we done this before?"

"I guess we never thunk it," said Sonny.

And perhaps they shouldn't have thunk it this time either. As the two headed out into the sound, Sonny cranked the sail. There was a nice downwind that carried them out. Unfortunately, there was a sudden gust that caught Sonny off guard, and the boat rounded up, capsizing the craft.

"Holy shit!" he yelled, "Are you alright?"

"Yes, I'm okay."

"Grab onto the boat and hang on. Don't let go of the boat."

Thank God, they had their life vests on. It made it much easier to stay afloat. As there was not another boat in sight, it looked like they would be out there for quite awhile.

"Now what do we do, Captain Marvelous?" asked Amy with no humor left in her voice.

"Err...we hold on and wait," said Sonny sheepishly.

A few minutes later, a small cruiser came into sight on the sound. As it got closer, they started waving their hands. The next sound that Sonny heard was Amy's voice.

"Oh shit, it's my Dad."

Looking up, Sonny recognized another couple of familiar figures on the boat besides Mr. Miller.

"Oh shit, it's my Dad and Big Guy. Storm clouds are a brewin'. Crap."

"Havin' a little engine trouble?" Mark jeered. "Come on. I'll put the ladder down for you."

As they climbed aboard Vinnie said, "What in the hell were you thinking, taking the sailboat out by yourself?"

"I guess it was kinda stupid. I was just trying to show Amy a good time before I left."

"I imagine she's had better times," said Mark.

"Actually, I was having a great time, until he tried to kill me," she said, glaring at Sonny.

"That'll be enough young lady. We'll talk when we get home," said Mr. Miller.

As they disembarked and headed home, Vinnie said, "What would you all have done if no one had showed up? You would have drowned, that's what. I thought you were more responsible than this. Sonny. I am very disappointed. Do you have any idea how much towing a sailboat in and cleaning it costs? Thank goodness, Mark had the foresight to unload most of the elec-tronic navigational system as he was preparing to dry dock for the winter. That would have been a pretty penny, if he hadn't."

"I'm sorry, Dad. Big Guy, I will work and pay you back for the losses."

"You betcha!" said Mark. And so I can make sure you will, beginning next summer you will stay down here with me, for good, so I can keep an eye on you and you learn how to properly sail a sailboat."

"What? You mean live with you and Nan? Dad, is that okay with you and Mom?"

"Yes, we realized, after talking to your Big Guy, how much you love it down here, and I guess I don't blame you."

"Really?"

"Not only that, but with your love for mathematics, we have an idea that might appeal to you," said Vinnie.

"Yes," Mark continued, "The county is always in desperate need of statisticians. Being that this place is so far from the big cities, though, it's hard for them to hire someone that would have a tie to the community and live here long term. If you finish up this year in high school and do well in statistics, as you have in your other math classes, the county commissioners said they would allow you an internship as long as you stay here to finish your senior year. When you finish your degree, if you return here, they will guarantee you a permanent job with the county.  How does that sound?"

"Let me put it this way, it sounds a whole lot better than anything else I've heard in the last fifteen minutes."

"Oh, you ain't outta that boat yet!" said Mark.

After the salvage company brought the boat back in to shore, Mark and Vinnie assessed the damage.

"Well, I guess the Karli Anna has seen better days, but with a little elbow grease, she'll be as good as new."

"I will get right on it, Big Guy" said Sonny.

"It will wait until tomorrow. You able to take a couple of extra days, Vinnie?"

"Oh, I think so. The least he can do is clean up this mess."

"Aye, Skipper," said Sonny to Mark.

As they arrived back at Sopie and Mark's, they all went in to a surprise. Angel and Sopie had fixed a down east clam pot for supper.

"Now, you talk about sumpin' fittin' to eat!" said Sonny, using his finest Carolinian accent.

Everybody laughed and enjoyed their dinner.  Afterwards, Sonny called Amy to see how she was doing and if she was still mad at him.

"Mad? No, why should I be mad? You just tried to drown me and I got grounded for the next two weeks," said Amy.

"I'm sorry. I didn't mean to..."

Amy couldn't contain herself any longer, "Stop. I was just trying to string you along."

"Really?"

"Yeah, actually, it was the best day of my life. You are a hoot."

"You think so?"

"Yes, dummy. So, are you leaving me tomorrow?"

"No, I have to stay a couple of days to clean the boat, then I'm leaving. But I'm coming back."

"Next summer?"

"Yes, but then"...the was a pause on the line, "I'm staying...for good!"

"What? Are you kidding me. Now that makes this the best day of my life. Say, will you take me to the senior prom?"

"I might. If I'm not busy that night."

"Oh," said Amy with disappointment in her voice.

"I won't be busy...I promise."

"Awww."

"I really like you, Amy."

"I really like you, too, see you soon."

---

## Chapter Twenty-Six

And they did see each other soon. As expected, Sonny did incredibly well in the subject of statistics. He came to Carteret County in the summer and got the internship with the county.

He graduated from West Carteret High School with a 4.5 GPA and immediately enrolled at the University of North Carolina in the fall to finish his math degree.

He also did take Amy to the prom, but their lives started to fork on two separate paths, as young love does. While he went to UNC, she went to Duke, but both were so busy with their studies that they rarely contacted one another.

She was in the field of marine biology, and upon graduation, accepted a job in Galveston, working in conjunction with A&M while furthering her education there.

Sonny, on the other hand, accepted the job offered by Carteret County as their statistician. Careers were paramount to both of them, so neither had time for any kind of social life, although occasionally, they kept in touch with an email or text.

As time marched on, Sopie and Mark were somehow heading down the road approaching ninety. Mark was now 89 and Sopie almost 87, mere reflections of the superheroes that used to exist in their fragile shells.

Vinnie and Angel came down twice a year, once for an extended stay in the summer, and of course, at Christmas. They both knew that the trip to Toronto was way too much of a journey for Mark and Sopie now.

As summer ended that year, Vinnie said, "Dad, don't you think it's time you got rid of the sailboat. Sonny really has no interest in it and you certainly have no business on it."

Maybe you're right. There is a lot of upkeep on her and we really don't spend the time on her like we used to."

"It's probably a good idea...surely, something to consider."

So Mark and Sopie discussed it and decided that it was time to let her go.

"Maybe, we should go out on her one more time," said Mark, "For Auld Lang Syne, eh?"

"It would be nice, but are you sure you have the sea legs for it?" asked Sopie.

"Sure, steady as a rock," he bounced around, almost falling.

"Yes, I see," said Sopie laughing.

Mark had always carried a cane since his accident in L.A. all those years ago, but, as of late, he'd actually been needing it for more than a fashion accessory. The exertion of constant inter-dimensional balancing and stabilization was just beginning to be too much for his aging body.

"Oh, what the hell," Sopie said. "We can do this. *Boat Driver, once more 'round the sound,"* she sang.

They grabbed their wraps and went down to the marina and hopped, or nearly hopped, on board. Once they were underway, they set sails and headed out into the sound.

As they leaned back, the gentle breezes blew through their hair as a sweet smile pursed from Sopie's lips.

"That smile is just as bright as the first day I met you," said Mark.

"Do you still see me the way you used to?" said Sopie.

"Of course I do, Sopie. Look in my eyes. Can't you see that I've loved you every day since the first day you ran into me on the beach. No amount of time can alter that. Nothing's changed."

"Oh, but we've changed."

"Only in appearance. Do you love me as much as you once did?"

"More, oh, so much more. You are the light of my life and my afterlife. There is not, nor will there ever be another." She sighed and leaned over onto his shoulder. "Mark, do you remember that first date, when after diner, we walked on the beach and bared our souls to each other as if we had know each other all of our lives. It was a very special moment for me. I knew then that there was but one man for me."

"Yeah, the next day when you were leaving, you gave me a picture to throw darts at and I gave you the necklace...the necklace that you still wear."

"I have worn it everyday since. Funny, it may have saved my life."

"Yeah."

"And after fifty eleven phone conversations, I asked you to marry me."

"Oh Mark, you have no idea what an emotional day that was for me. I was dancing on the ceiling."

"I would have loved to have seen that."

"Stop! And then you came to my house in Ohio and we went out and danced. It was a magical evening for me."

"So magical that you made me leave."

"Now Mark, you know I didn't have any choice."

"I know, I'm sorry. It was just very hard for me, not knowing, not understanding, for years."

"It was hard on me, too. Married to a man I didn't love to keep the man I did love from being killed."

"Yeah, but even through all that, I, by chance, placed that call to you in Chicago. Of course, I had no idea it was you."

"But I did, once you sent your cassette tape to me. My heart was so filled with a mix of joy, sadness and responsibility I could hardly bare it. And then, you asked me to marry you again...and I couldn't stop myself from saying anything but yes."

"And again, you left me."

"I'm so sorry. You know I had to, especially since Vinnie was with me."

"I know," Mark sighed looking off in the water. But that day, at the hospital, when you just happened to walk by and I caught a glimpse of the necklace...it was a chance meeting that I will never forget."

"Do you really think it was just a coincidence?"

"Fate. Just like when we met. Like Bennie and Amyra kept telling us, Twin Flames."

"I think so. Well, we did finally get married."

"You betcha." He placed his arms around Sopie, and gave her butt a little squeeze.

"Watch it old man! We're getting a little too old for PDAs."

"Oh, I don't think so," he leaned over to give her a kiss.

She leaned back again, "Have we got anything to drink?"

"Yes, of course we do," he said, opening a bottle of white wine. "Here you go, Sweetheart."

"Thank you. Well, it was a beautiful wedding. I could not have planned better."

"Man, that F.P. was something else. He put together a wedding and honeymoon package that no one else could have ever pulled off. It was an incredible time and you have never looked lovelier."

"Awww. Thank you, Handsome," she relished the memories.

"And F.P., could you believe that guy? Taking us on his jet to Canada, buying us a home and car, just to have a place to come to and fish."

"Yeah, unFirkinbelievable! Here's to F.P."

"Yeah, and here's to us!"

Sopie said, "Mark, we have really been blessed. Great

friends like Marty and F.P., a son, a daughter-in-law, and a grandchild, who are all very loving and successful. It's been a tough road, but I wouldn't have traveled any other path."

"And let's not forget Amy. I have a feeling, even though I'm not the resident psychic, that she will someday return to Sonny's life. They both are just wrapped up in themselves and their careers. I think that they, much like us, are destined to be together."

"We'll see...just maybe."

Mark looked at her quizzically. "Say...you know the answer, don't you?"

Sopie just grinned.

Mark looked up and said, "I need to check the jib. It's not acting right."

"Be careful, you old fool."

Climbing on the bow of the boat, he looked back and grinned at Sopie. "I may be a fool but I'm...."

And he was gone. The words from his lips dropped off as suddenly as someone startled from a dream. Mark's foot slipped and he tumbled into the water. The jib, that he had a hold of, ripped as he fell and he was helplessly wrapped up in the sail.

Every bit of tranquility, every happy memory the loving couple shared, all of it plummeted into the depths of the sea in that moment.

"Mark!" Sopie yelled as she saw what was happening.

No sound bubbled up from the waters, and in that moment, Sopie started to panic. The only thing she could hear was the pounding blood in her ears. "Hurry! Grab this!" She scrambled to grab an oar, but Mark's arms were wrapped up in the sail. He was tangled like a fish in a net, unable to swim or climb or...or breathe. He was going to drown.

Sopie, having no other alternative, jumped in the water to save him, but she too, quickly got caught up in the sail. Her body felt so unreasonably helpless, so inferior to what it used to be, and this filled her with something unexpected. She wasn't afraid or anxious...instead, her every vessel throbbed with an undeniable rage. As both of them were bobbing up and down in the water, it would only be minutes before they both drowned, and Sopie was the only one that could do something to stop it. Without hesitation, she opened up a portal that engulfed them both.

"No, Sopie! You can't!" These were the words lost in the ocean's depths, the words Mark's heart was screaming, the words that drowned in his salty lungs before they could ever be put to use. It was too late.

A few seconds later, they had reached the shore. Mark coughing up brackish water, breathing heavily, looked down at Sopie. He could only say one thing. "Why? Why in the world would you do such a thing, old woman?"

She shook her head. "You already know the answer to that, Old Man. So tell me something sweet instead before I go."

Mark was wild-eyed and at a loss for words. They had just sailed down memory lane together and he wasn't ready for their love to be a ghost or a photograph or something written on a stone. Mark held the hands of his beloved and felt that old anger creeping into his blood, that hatred that crippled him all those years ago was trying to take hold once more. He shut his eyes tight and felt the lids burn with hot tears. Nothing sweet was coming, nothing beautiful.

"Mark," Sopie whispered.

He opened his eyes and saw the most beautiful person in the universe through a film of tears. And, as if nothing terrible had ever happened in the world, as if there were no death or pain, Mark felt his mind relax and his heart soften. Then he heard a voice singing, a melodious voice that once belonged to him cascading in with the tide.

"*IF a man could be two places at one time I'd be with you, tomorrow and today...*" He started to choke, not wanting to finish the line, not wanting Sopie to ever leave him. But in that moment he looked into her eyes and he understood...this was just another door, another day, another lifetime. *"Beside you all the way…"*

Looking up deeply into Mark's eyes, Sopie grinned and said, "Riggs, I'm just getting too old for this shit." The two shared a smile, and Sopie's spirit separated from her body.

The words "I love you" floated in the seaside breeze.

———

# Epilogue

"Hello, Mom?" said Sonny in a whispered tone.
"Hi Sonny! How are you?"
"Not so good, Mom."
"What's wrong, Honey?"
"Is Dad there?"
"Well, yes."
"Can you put him on the phone as well?"
"I'll get him, give me a minute."
"Sonny, are you there?" asked Vinnie.
"Yes, I'm here."
"So what's going on?"
"Well..." Sonny said, now in tears, "there's been a horrible accident on the boat. Nan is…" Sonny cleared his throat, unsure of what to say. "Mark is in the hospital and Nan is...gone."

There was a long silence on the other end of the line, then the sound of something like crumpling wax paper.

Angel finally spoke. "Your dad…he...Sonny are you still there?"

"Yeah I'm here. Is Dad?"

"He had to step out a moment honey...what exactly happened?"

"I don't really know. As far as anyone can tell, Nan and Mark took the sailboat out."

"What in the world were they thinking?"

"I don't know, Mom. Anyway, it looks like they fell into the water when the jib sail tore. I'm not even sure how it's possible, but they both managed to get to shore...but...Nan died. Mark is in the hospital. They said he had a mild stroke that has left him very unsteady on his feet. Mom, he really can't walk. He is having to use a transport chair. The doctors think he will have to use it from now on."

"What hospital is Mark in?"

"Carteret General."

Sonny took a deep breath, still trying to wrap his head around what he was saying. "They have to do an autopsy on Nan due to the circumstances. I guess we will have the funeral sometime after that. I just don't know."

"I know this is hard on you, Honey. We will be out on the first flight tomorrow. Do you have anyone to keep you company?"

"Marty has been by a couple of times to check on me. He's stayed at the hospital with Mark the whole time since he heard."

"Marty has always been a good friend."

"Mom, I've got to go...someone's at the door. Text me your itinerary when you have it."

"Okay baby, I will. Goodbye."

"Bye, Mom."

"Just a minute," Sonny shouted at the door.

---

MARTY CREPT into the hospital room quietly as he saw Mark sleeping.

"What the hell are you doing sneaking around my room? asked Mark.

"Whoa, Jackson! I just saw you sleeping and..."

"Well, try not to scare the piss out of an old man. If you want to do something, help me to the turdlet."

"Sure, old friend."

As he rolled Mark into the bathroom and waited, Marty couldn't help but feel a little annoyed by his friend's behavior.

"Well, I can still wipe me own ass...good."

Wheeling him back out and helping him into the chair, Marty said, "Is there anything else I can get for you?"

"Neglect, just neglect."

"What?"

"You fucking heard me. Do you always have to be such a buffoon."

That was it. Mark had never talked to him this way before.

"Look, I understand what you're feeling..."

"How in the fuck could you?"

"You know, everybody that knew Sopie loved her. We are all suffering right now."

"Suffering? You gotta be kidding me. You don't know a damned thing about suffering until you kill the woman you love."

"Mark," Marty sat down beside him "you didn't kill her. It was an accident."

Marty put a hand on Mark's shoulder, but it was quickly slapped away. "Accident my ass! It was goddamn suicide...assisted suicide."

"What the hell are you talking about?"

"I fell the fuck overboard and got trapped in the jib sail. She saw me, jumped in and tried to rescue me, but she got wrapped up in the sail as well. We were both about to drown when she opened up a portal..."

"A what?"

"A fuckin' portal, Moron."

"Hey," Marty stood up suddenly, "I'm the best friend you got, okay pal? You don't need to talk to me like that when all I'm trying to do is help."

"I'm sorry, but this is more than I can take." He clasped his hands around his skull and stifled a scream. "A portal, Marty, is an inter-dimensional gateway...kind of like a time warp. Sopie used one to bring us back to shore. Only problem was, she was old, Marty, she'd put too much stress on her body over the years and she…" Mark slammed his wrinkled fist against his wheelchair. "Goddamnit, Marty...she did it because she said she loved me more than life itself. So, I killed her. It's my fault."

Marty took a moment and shook his head to clear his mind. "Now Mark, I don't quite get the sci-fi stuff you do, but I know that if you say it was a time warp, it was a time warp. All I can say, my friend, is you didn't kill her. It wasn't your fault."

Mark said nothing but his eyebrows furrowed and his head tilted lower. He felt that same anger seething in his blood. He tried to hold on to the peace and love that Sopie left him with, but it was so much harder with her gone.

"She gave her life freely. It was hers to give. Not yours to keep." And then Marty went a little too far. "Quit being so selfish," he said.

Mark's eyes went cold and his voice was low. "Get the fuck out of here, Marty. You don't know shit. You weren't there. Just shut the fuck up and get out."

---

SONNY WENT to the door and opened it. A young lady stood at the screen and said, "Well, are you going to let me in?"

Startled Sonny said, "Of course, come in, Amy."

"I came as soon as I heard." She dropped her bag and threw her arms around Sonny. "How is your grandfather?"

"He's still in the hospital." Sonny motioned toward the living room and showed Amy to the couch. "He is having a really rough time of it."

"I'm sure he is."

"Can I get you anything? Something to drink?"

"No, no, I'm quite all right, I just wanted to see how you were holding up."

"How did you find out? Did you fly all of the way from Galveston just to see me?"

"Daddy, called me and told me what happened. And yes, I jumped the first flight out...of course I did."

"Well, you are a sight for sore eyes. It's funny, when I really need someone to talk to, you always show up."

"Like a bad penny?"Amy laughed.

"Oh, I don't think so. More like a rainbow after the storm."

"Awww, that's sweet."

"It's the truth. You have always been there. When I was at my peak of stupidity, you bailed me out. You didn't even get mad at me for nearly drowning you..."

Amy started to laugh at the foolish memory of when they were teens, but she noticed Sonny's face change.

Sonny broke down. "I wonder if Nan suffered."

Amy put a hand on his back and leaned in closer to comfort him. "I think that your Nan was a strong woman that always seemed to take life as it came. I'm pretty sure she handled dying in the same way."

"Yeah, she was a gem." He wiped the tears from his eyes. "I'm beginning to see what Big Guy saw in her."

Amy didn't have much to say, so she just kept rubbing Sonny's back, trying to give him the breathing room he needed.

"Are you staying long?"

"Until the funeral is over, then I need to fly back to Galveston to finish up my stent there for the next few years. Then it's on to my new adventure."

"And what might that be?"

"I have been granted a position at the University of North

Carolina Institute of Marine Sciences in Morehead City. I guess you can take the girl out of Carteret County, but you can't take Carteret County out of the girl."

"Are you shitting me? That's fantastic! Will you go to the prom with me?"

"Hell no, but I will go out and have a drink with you. Is it a deal?"

"It's a date!"

VINNIE AND ANGEL arrived a couple of days later. They along with Marty, Sonny and Amy gathered at the Banos' residence for Mark to be brought home.

Wheeling Mark in, Vinnie said, "How are you feeling, Dad? Anything I can get you?"

"I'm fine." He wouldn't look up at any of them. He just let his head hang down, eyes cast towards the lifeless legs dangling below. "Just find me some scotch...a lot of scotch."

The old man retired to the back deck and sipped...no, he gulped about a half of a fifth of scotch before he uttered a word.

"Guess I have been a horse's ass to most of you; the people who are here to help me the most. *You always hurt the ones you love...*" he sang as he downed another shot. I'm really sorry. This has been the worst of the worst for me. Sopie was my steering wheel. She would keep me on the road when I veered off the highway. She was my life, my love, my partner in crime...and now she's gone. What do I do now? Just what the fuck do I do now?"

"Marty, I'm sorry for talking to you the way I did in the hospital."

"It's okay, Mr. B" said Marty saluting.

"No hell, it's not okay. Sopie was as big a part of your life as she was to everyone that's here. I had no right. It was grief. And

I know that she would never condone me acting that way...to anyone, especially you. I hope you can forgive me."

"It's forgiven and forgotten, old friend," said Marty.

"Well, let's toast to the finest woman that ever lived. She had to be if she put up with my sorry ass for all of these years, but I loved her dearly and always will."

"Here, here," said everyone as they lifted their glasses.

***

THE COUNTY CORONER WAS BUMFUZZLED. He had gone over and over the results of his findings. There was no signs of abuse, yet every bone in Sopie's body was broken, except for the bones in her face. She appeared to have died from a blunt force trauma, like someone that had been beat to death with a sledge hammer, but there were no marks on her skin. There were no red blood cells in her system either. There was no way that Mr. Banos had beat her to death and even if he did, there was no way to account for the non-existent red blood cells. As unusual as it was, the coroner had no choice but to rule it a death by accident. The body was released to the mortuary.

***

BY THIS TIME, the entire community had learned of Mrs. Banos' death. Mark received an outpouring of sympathy from the county that they had supported with their philanthropy. It didn't take long for the anonymous board of trustees of the Kroner Foundation to become known in the community. There had never been a larger crowd for a funeral in Carteret County history.

With Vinnie, Angel, Sonny, Amy and Marty by his side, Mark was wheeled to the graveside where the interment was to take place.

There was a lot of inaudible words spoken as Mark just

stared off into space. He thought he could see a blonde haired, brown-eyed Greek girl running down a beach. He saw the woman he loved in her wedding gown, greeting him at the altar. He saw her vision of loveliness as they cruised the sound. Then he heard these final words from the priest's lips just as a butterfly circled the family and landed on the old man's hand.

"And if I go and make ready a place for you, I will come again and take you to be with me, so that where I am, you may be too."

"Of course, she will," he whispered tearfully. Of course she will..."

---

___________

"Spencer Michaels" is the pen name of the father-son writing team comprised of Michael and Spencer Bennington. When friends ask how the collaboration began, son Spencer is quick to joke that his dad, Michael, guilted him into becoming a writing partner. That wry sense of humor smacks of modesty as Spencer is also an Adjunct Professor of English and a doctoral student at the University of South Florida and works as a free-lance writer.

One might say that entertaining is in Michael Bennington's blood. Prior to becoming a novelist, he worked as a professional musician for over 50 years playing varied venues from night clubs to coliseums and even recorded CDs and served as back up to nationally known recording artists. He shared his love of music as a teacher at Sacred Heart Catholic School for 13 years before retiring in 2012. He says that these days his music is limited to playing at his church where he serves as choir director.

Spencer's first book was inspired by what he believes is an inspiration to many a writer...the love of a beautiful woman. He also credits the stories his dad told about his early days as a nightclub entertainer with sparking his imagination.

Michael notes that his love of writing began rather acciden-tally when he suffered a stroke. Not being one to rest on his laurels, Michael launched into writing and convinced Spencer to jump on board as his partner. Michael lists The Baltimore

Orioles as his other passion, along with single malt scotch. He jokes that those wondering what to get him for Christmas might consider Yamazaki, an 18-year-old Japanese Whisky Sherry Cask he has his eye on.

Originally from Denton, Maryland, Michael and his wife, Susie, have called Danville, Virginia their home for the past 40 years. Spencer describes his birthplace as being a small southern town community with big city dreams. Although Michael remains in Danville, Spencer has relocated to Tampa, Florida where, in addition to his studies and teaching, he is an accomplished Tae Kwon Do instructor.

Besides their son Spencer, Michael and Susie, have one other son, Miki, two grandchildren, Tyler and Kayla and a Sheltie named Luci, who the family considers their only daughter.

*Stay in touch with Spencer Michaels here…*

https://spencermichaelsbooks.com

9 781630 991203